EULOGY

THE EAGLE ELITE SERIES #9

by

RACHEL VAN DYKEN

Eulogy
Eagle Elite Book 9
by Rachel Van Dyken

EULOGY
Copyright © 2018 RACHEL VAN DYKEN
ISBN-13: 978-0-9971451-8-2
Cover Art by Jena Brignola
Formatting by Jill Sava, Love Affair With Fiction

To all the readers who hated me after Enrage — it's time for our revenge.
Enjoy!

EAGLE ELITE FAMILY

AUTHOR NOTE: I'm adding this in here just in case you guys need a refresher on who belongs to each family and which couple belongs to each book.

Nixon Abandonato married to Trace Alfero (Granddaughter to Frank Alfero). Nixon is the boss to the Abandonato family. (Elite/Elect)

Frank Alfero married to Joyce Alfero (deceased). Boss to the Alfero Family (for now). (Elite & Enchant)

Chase Abandonato married to Mil De Lange (Phoenix De Lange's sister, deceased, RAT). Mil was the new mob boss to the De Lange Family, one of the most hated in The Cosa Nostra.
(Entice)

Tex Campisi married to Mo Abandonato (Nixon's twin sister). Tex is the capo dei capi, which basically means he's their version of the godfather. (Elicit)

Luca Nicolasi (deceased). Never married, but had a small affair with the love of his life Joyce Alfero, this produced two children. Dante and Valentina Nicolasi. (Enchant & Enrapture in the Hurt anthology)

Phoenix De Lange married to Bee Campisi (Tex's sister). He is the new boss to the Nicolasi dynasty. He knows everyone's secrets and keeps black folders on every individual close to them, himself included. (Ember)

Sergio Abandonato married to Andi Petrov (Russian mafia, deceased). Sergio was forced to marry her for protection, and later marries his soul mate Valentina Nicolasi. (Elude, Empire)

Dante Nicolasi married to El De Lange. Dante is the new boss to the Alfero Family. (Enrage)

Ax Abandonato married to Amy De Lange. He's a made man for the Abandonato Family. (Bang, Bang)

Nikolai Blazik married to Maya Petrov (both Russian Mafia). He makes a brief appearance in many EE books, and is known as The Doctor. (Rip — EE spinoff)

The Petrov Family is the Russian dynasty out to destroy all five Sicilian families. They have now spread from Chicago, to New York, and even Seattle.

EULOGY

Noun, plural: a speech or writing in praise of a person or thing — especially a set oration in honor of a deceased person — high praise and or commendation. i.e.: the man refused to praise the dead — after all she was still haunting the living — and for that very reason, there would be no words, for they would be filled with empty lies and angry threats. A Eulogy — she did not deserve.

PROLOGUE

BLOOD. BLOOD. BLOOD.

It covered my hands.

It surged through my heart.

It dripped from my fingertips onto the concrete floor.

Trapped.

Broken.

Finished.

Hungry.

Insanity scratched its way into my psyche as I eyed the door and waited. One heartbeat, two heartbeats, three...

It opened.

I fired two rounds, and acrid smoke filled the air.

I thought I knew what love was. I was a fucking idiot. Every single bone in my body shuddered with rage, with the need to rip something apart, someone, anyone — all of them. My friends. My brothers. I brought the war to our house, and they would finish me because of it.

I'd thought I loved her.

Our love had been a lie.

Her betrayal my only truth.

And now?

Now, I finally knew what love was. I'd seen it, smelled it, tasted it.

And lost it.

I'd fucking lost it.

They would pay. They would all pay.

For taking her.

For turning her against me.

For making me believe that blood was everything, only after mine was spilled.

"I'm not worth dying for," she'd whispered. *"But you, Chase Abandonato… you're worth living for, breathing for, existing for. The only way to break — is from being already broken."*

"I am broken."

"But…" She'd placed a hand on my chest, my heart surging to life. *"You don't have to be…."*

Two more steps, three. I kicked the door open and fired as bullets whizzed by my ear, and when one struck true, and I collapsed to the ground; I swore up at the barrel of the gun.

I'd live.

For her.

I'd choose life.

I wanted life.

Not this.

They surrounded me.

I wasn't afraid.

I'd cheat death.

With a bloody smile, I crawled to my knees and yelled, firing rounds into the ceiling surrounding me as my screams of pain filled the room.

As the broken…

By finally shattering…

Became whole.

"You've made your choice," he whispered, closing his eyes and turning his gun to my head. "And this was it."

"I don't choose me." Blood trickled down my chin. "I choose her."

CHAPTER ONE

"Chase Abandonato should have been boss. It was his birthright, but he gave it up for his best friend. He'd never been groomed for that position and claimed he didn't want the responsibility. It wasn't much later that he'd married Mil De Lange in order to align the De Lange family back into the fold. The problem with that sordid situation was that he thought he'd finally found his purpose in protecting her — and that woman didn't want what he had to offer." I tapped my thumb against the metal desk. "Can I go now?"
— *Notes from interview with Agent P, FBI*

Chase

Empty.

The sound of someone choking, gasping for air, filled the empty space in the large foyer.

My blurry eyes darted around in a frenzied attempt to find the source, only to realize a few seconds later.

It was me.

I was the one choking.

I was the one sobbing.

I was the one making that bloodcurdling noise as I fell to my knees, then very slowly, pulled out my gun and started shooting.

I took out the walls first. They were her favorite; she'd said she wanted something modern, chic.

"Make it impressive, Chase," she'd said in that sultry temptress voice before sashaying off in her tall red heels.

So I'd done it.

I'd painted the entry walls a blood red.

I'd had no idea at the time that it would be my future, being dipped in that blood, her blood, the blood we shared.

Gone. Gone. Gone.

I fired at the wall, again and again, until a picture, our wedding picture, the only picture in the house, crashed to the floor, shattering glass across the hardwood.

And then I was angry again.

So fucking angry.

She'd wanted those floors, too.

God, was there anything in this house that was me? For her. I'd done it all for her.

And…

She'd.

Betrayed.

Me.

I would have cut out my own heart and handed it to her on a silver platter while I watched the last two thumps give way.

I would have killed hundreds, thousands, millions.

And it would have still never been enough, would it?

Not enough.

Not me.

Not the house.

Not my money.

Not my love.

I moved to my feet and slowly walked over to the fallen picture, as glass crunched beneath my boots.

She was grinning up at me, even though our wedding day hadn't been a happy day. And the sick part?

I was looking down at her the way I'd always looked at her, with barely restrained awe at her strength, her beauty, the way she took situations and molded them to her will.

I just never once imagined — I'd end up her victim.

Instead of a partner.

Slowly, I picked up the picture and then dropped it again onto the floor, only to lean over and slam my fist into it until I couldn't see her face, until blood ran down my knuckles, until I felt slices of pain pierce my skin.

The doorbell buzzed.

I jerked my head toward the sound and slowly rose to my feet as it opened, and seven De Lange associates walked in, their eyes cold, their movements sluggish as if they knew no matter how slow, how fast, how strong, I would end them. All of them.

Which was a pity, since in all my rage I wanted to hunt each one of them down until they felt such intense pain that their ancestors cringed in their graves.

"Didn't think you guys would show," I said in a gravelly voice that sounded half-possessive, half-sad, like I'd stayed up all night alternating between crying and cursing her name to the fiery depths of hell.

Which, I was ashamed to admit, had happened more often than not these past few weeks.

"Didn't think we had a choice," one of them piped up. "When the Capo calls—"

I'd asked Tex for a favor, and since my wife's betrayal, he was more than happy to give me whatever I wanted.

And I wanted them.

All to myself.

I nodded toward the living room.

They followed.

I even gave them my back, something I'd never done to an enemy before. I was way past the point of caring — because they knew just as much as I did, that since Mil betrayed the Families — we were untouchable.

Royalty.

We were gods among men.

And I would exercise my iron fist over their pathetic lives.

Adrenaline pulsed through my system as I took a seat on the white leather recliner, one of the only pieces of furniture that had been delivered before her untimely death.

I sat and placed my hands on the armrests as fresh blood slowly dripped down the front and onto the pristine floor.

The gun in my hand became almost a living extension of me as I pointed it at the men and placed my other palm over it, as though I was resting.

"Defend yourselves," I barked.

One man stepped forward. "We can't."

I leaned back in the chair as I eyed each and every one of them. They had wives, families, friends who would miss them.

And for the first time in my life...

The guilt at what I was about to do.

Was nonexistent.

"A life for a life," I whispered before opening fire on the first.

And drilling bullets, one by one, into each of their skulls until I had seven bodies littering my floor.

I dropped my gun and picked up my phone. "Seven dead. I need cleanup."

Nixon sighed heavily on the other line. "Ours?"

"Theirs." The word dripped with hate.

He hung up on a curse.

And ten minutes later, Dante was opening the door to my house and shouting orders at his associates.

"Is it my training that has you acting like a badass, or have you always been a badass?" I wondered aloud.

He rolled his eyes. "Looking like shit, as always. Have you even showered today?"

I leveled my gun on him.

He hung his head and pointed toward the kitchen. "Whiskey?"

"Where it's been for the past week." *Where it's always been.*

"Two glasses?"

I stared down at the dead bodies, my vision blurring with hatred as the stench of blood filled the air. "Bring the bottle."

CHAPTER TWO

"Phoenix." I laughed, even though there was nothing funny about that sick prick. "How to explain..." I sighed. "He has fucking black folders on every single human being on this planet that poses a threat to the Italian scum. Luca Nicolasi made sure that when he left this earth, he left it in the hands of the devil himself. Phoenix De Lange should be your worst nightmare. He would kill his own wife in cold blood, and not even blink if it meant he saved the legacy of the five families. I almost... respect him." I chuckled. "Almost."
— *Notes from interview with Agent P, FBI*

Phoenix

My cell buzzed on the nightstand. I glanced over at Bee and felt *something*; that meant I was still alive.

Not rotting in hell.

Not yet.

I felt.

I wasn't numb.

Not yet. Not yet.

I clenched my eyes shut and tried to focus on the good things in this miserable existence: my son's cries, the way he clutched my hand, his tiny fingers wrapping around my thumb.

Inhale.

Exhale.

Breathe, damn it, just breathe!

I finally looked down at my phone and saw blood. It wasn't real. It was never real. My phone wasn't covered with it, slathered in its wet metallic stickiness, but every time I looked down, that was what I saw.

No amount of showering could wash away my sins.

The sins of the dynasty I'd helped build.

And the one I was going to help destroy.

I owed him that, at least.

More than I ever owed her.

Bitterness threatened to take over the rage as I finally read the text from Nixon.

Nixon: Seven dead bodies—we need to rein him in before he takes out the entire bloodline.

My bloodline.

But not my family.

I might be De Lange by blood — but I wanted nothing to fucking do with that blood. I was Nicolasi now, through and through. My son... Nicolasi. My wife... Nicolasi.

And it was time I made the exchange.

Time I died to my birthright.

And took what was given to me by Luca, officially ending the blood that ran through my veins, officially shutting out any part of that existence, and making them fugitives.

I closed my eyes against the numbness that took over. It always took over when I needed to make a choice.

And all of my choices were hard.

Life was hard.

Bee's hand snaked up my chest and wrapped around my neck as she snuggled closer. I kissed the top of her head and shook away the memories of my sister's face.

The blood.

The calmness that had claimed my soul when I fired the shots.

And the look on my brother's face when she glanced at him one last time.

It was possible to lose love.

To replace it with so much hate you couldn't see straight.

I knew that kind of hate.

I didn't wish it on anyone.

Especially someone who had been the glue that held the five Families together.

There was something worse than the numbness.

Something worse than the monster inside me.

It was the one inside him.

Eating away at his soul while he watched, while he fed it.

There would be no peace.

Not for a while.

I sent a text back to Nixon.

Me: Let him.

Nixon tried calling.

And for the first time since becoming boss, I turned off my phone. I turned a blind eye, pulled my wife close, and ducked my face against her neck. I breathed in her strength.

I breathed in her goodness.

And prayed to God that I wasn't just a rotting corpse with a face.

No soul.

No heart.

Just lungs.

A body.

Just existing.

I'd killed her.

And I would do it again.

I'd killed her.

I'd killed her.

I'd killed her.

Blood, so much blood.

I squeezed my eyes shut and forced myself to sleep,

even as the images of her crashing against the concrete filled my mind.

My lullaby.

My addiction.

Blood.

CHAPTER THREE

"Nixon Abandonato hasn't gone soft. Anyone who says that hasn't seen his recent body count. He's the head of the Abandonato Family and scary as hell. He knows everyone and will manipulate whoever he needs to for his own purpose. He's too rich. Too intelligent. And one day, someone's going to piss him off bad enough that he's going to lose his shit. I hope like hell I'm there to see it. Better yet, I hope I'm the one to cause it."
— *Notes from interview with Agent P, FBI*

Nixon

CHASE WAS SITTING in a white leather chair, blood still dripping from his fingers. Ax, one of my most trusted made men, was piling bodies into black bags while Chase drank straight from the bottle as if he hadn't just ended seven lives for no reason other than the blood that ran through their veins was *hers*.

Ax was trying not to react. I'd never seen the man scared.

He was terrified.

It was evident in every jerky movement, every threatening glance he sent Chase's way.

His wife was pregnant.

She was a De Lange.

And not five minutes ago, Chase had sworn to take out the entire bloodline for simply existing.

Phoenix, the one person I thought could talk some sense into Chase, had turned off his fucking phone.

And Dante had just enabled him by giving him more alcohol.

This would not end well. Not for my family. Not for his. Not for anyone. And I couldn't blame him. The sick part was that I knew if I was in his situation, I wouldn't be acting with any sort of sane logic; I would use my gun, and I would silence anyone who dared to try to stop me.

And that was the problem, wasn't it?

None of us could blame him for taking retribution.

And yet, he couldn't do it.

I couldn't allow it.

We all had children, families to protect — everyone but Chase.

Damn it!

I slammed my hands against the leather couch; the plastic still covering it clung to my blood-caked palms. At least we didn't have much to clean up.

Chase didn't even look up at me. Didn't acknowledge my anger or my position as his boss.

My heart jackhammered against my chest in rage, in confusion, in hurt, in anger. We all dealt with pain in different ways. His was wrong.

But the Chase I used to know...

My best friend...

Closer than a brother?

He was lost to me.

And I hated him for it.

"Chase," I tried again. "There are rules for this sort of thing."

"We break rules all the time..." He took another swig and shrugged. His eyes were glassy; dark circles rimmed beneath the blue irises. He looked straight through me as if he didn't recognize me.

As if he was choosing not to.

I leaned forward and held out my hand. He handed me the bottle. I took a swig of Jack, wiped my mouth, and handed it back. "Let's talk about this."

"Nothing to talk about," he said quickly, smoothly. "I'm handling it."

"Yeah." I looked around the empty, haunted house

he refused to leave, said it fueled his anger. Dante had found him on several occasions just breaking shit, screaming. "Looks like it."

"Fu—"

"All done, boss." Ax never dropped "boss" to me; we were related. He'd been second in command since Chase left to help Mil with the family and now... now Chase wasn't anywhere, was he? Or anything? His identity had been killed right along with his life.

And a man without an identity...

Without a conscience.

And armed man?

Was a danger I couldn't afford.

"Boss," Chase repeated the word and laughed. "You always talk to him like that?" He stood and walked casually toward Ax until they were chest to chest. "Tell me, *Ax*." He spat his name. "Being married to a De Lange, does she spread her legs like the whore she is? Like all De Langes? I bet she doesn't even feel you—"

"Enough." I stood, ready to do battle as Ax clenched his hands into fists, apparently ready to beat the shit out of Chase.

He loved Chase like a brother.

But the trust.

The trust between all of us was fragile and, little by little, Chase was pounding the glass walls, until one day, I was afraid things would shatter beyond repair.

It was my job to keep them safe.

To keep us together.

I'd never been so resentful of being boss in my entire existence.

"Better listen to your boss," Ax said through clenched teeth. "Before I hand you your ass, Abandonato."

18

"I'd like to see that." Chase gave him a smug grin. "Or at least see you try."

"Enough!" I yelled.

Chase didn't back off.

"Ax, wait outside."

Chase lifted his chin into the air. "Run along, Ax."

Ax muttered, "Asshole," under his breath, but the door slammed behind him, leaving us alone.

"What's with all the yelling?" Dante rounded the corner.

Chase lowered his head. I saw it then. The guilt. The guilt over the fact that Dante was his protégé, Chase, his mentor, and that he wasn't himself.

I saw the flicker of guilt.

I saw the grief.

And then... I saw the *rage*.

I backed away and shook my head. "I don't even know you anymore, man."

"Maybe you never did," Chase whispered.

I left it at that and went to the door.

I could feel the tension in the house; the walls wailed with sadness, with a heaviness that wasn't healthy for a man insane, a man like Chase.

"If you were smart, you'd move." I didn't turn around.

Chase answered immediately. "If I was smart, I'd stay and kill her ghost in the process. It haunts me, and I'm sending her to hell."

"I think you've got that wrong, man." I hung my head and pulled open the door. "You're the one living in hell. Not her."

I shut the door.

Leaned against it and eyed my Range Rover.

Trace was waiting inside it.

Our one-year-old was with her. My daughter. My very soul existed outside of my body the day she was brought into this world.

Tears filled Trace's eyes as I approached.

She rolled down the window. "So?"

"It's bad."

"Let me try—"

"Hell no," I snapped. "I'm not letting you walk in there. He just shot seven people in less than ten seconds without blinking. You're not walking into his house and trying to calm him down."

She looked straight ahead. "Someone has to. And it's not going to be you, or Dante, or Phoenix. That just fuels his madness."

I didn't want to tell her that there was nothing different about her or me; Chase was angry at the world, and she was living in the world he was angry at.

It didn't matter.

But I knew Trace.

Stubborn as hell.

I wiped my face with my hands. "I'll take Serena home, but promise me you'll keep Dante by you at all times."

I opened her car door. She stood up on tiptoes and kissed my mouth with the hunger that always made my chest ache. "I promise."

"I love you," I whispered against her mouth, angry at my own desperation to make her stay instead of walking into his house.

Into his grieving arms.

It felt wrong.

Like I was lending the one woman he'd always loved in order to soothe the hurt of the replacement who'd broken him beyond all measure.

"Trust me." Trace's eyes flickered between my mouth and eyes before locking on my gaze. "Trust us."

I nodded, having no confidence in my voice, as I slowly walked around to the other side and got in.

The engine started.

The Disney station started playing *The Descendants'* soundtrack, "Ways to be Wicked."

And I had to shake my head and look up at the cliché.

Wicked.

Disney?

Sorry guys. The mafia has that covered.

And the bodies to prove it.

Serena started to sing along as best she could, then, "Daaaada!"

I clutched the steering wheel so tight my fingers lost all feeling. This, this was why I would do anything, I would stop at nothing.

And maybe I already had my answer.

Why Phoenix was turning a blind eye.

We had so much more to lose now.

So damn much.

"Love you, baby girl." I forced a smile in the rearview mirror then reached back and grabbed her chubby leg and gave it a shake.

She giggled.

Sticky hands gripped my finger.

I'd burn down the entire fucking world for my girls.

"Damn it, Chase," I whispered to myself. "Don't make me kill you."

CHAPTER FOUR

"The harsh reality of this life is that you aren't afforded the luxury of love, and if you think you have it — you're an idiot. She was lost to him the minute she walked in that door. Do I have any regrets? Does it look like it?" I spread my arms wide. "I own his mind right now, and soon, I'm going to own yours. Just wait... You can't keep all your animals caged. Why not let loose your only weapon?"
—*Notes from interview with Agent P, FBI*

Chase

6 months earlier
St. John's Cathedral

"WE'RE HERE TO mourn the loss of one of our own," Tex said from his spot at the front of the church. I closed my eyes against the burn of tears and clenched my shaking hands in front of me as his words fell flat on deaf ears.

Trace rubbed small circles on my back.

I wanted to jerk way.

I wanted to yell.

I wanted so many things.

Things Mil never gave me.

Things the world never allowed me.

I jerked away from Trace's touch.

I didn't want her pity.

Her love.

I'd never needed it, had I?

Never deserved it, had I?

I hung my head as Tex's words pounded into my brain: loving wife, loving sister. It was all bullshit; the only person she'd loved... had been herself.

And me? Well, I was collateral fucking damage.

My hands shook as Tex called out my name. "Now, Chase Abandonato will be giving the eulogy."

I stood.

My legs froze in place.

And rather than walk toward the front of the church.

I turned on my heel.

And walked away from us.

From her.

From the fantasy.

I turned my back on her.

Like she had turned her back on me.

Present Day

"Chase?" Dante snapped his fingers in front of me. "Anything I should know about what set you off with the seven dead bodies and broken glass? Or is it just a Tuesday?"

I wanted to smile.

My lips twitched.

Such a smart-assed little shit.

I held the bottle to my mouth and took another gulp as the amber liquid burned down my throat. It didn't help. Nothing helped. Nothing but blood.

Dante sighed and tossed a towel in my direction. "At least get some of the blood off."

"Blood stains," I said hoarsely. "Let it."

Dante's eyes locked with mine. I was hurting him just by existing. But I couldn't bring myself to end my own life, not when I had so many others I needed to take.

What did I even have left?

What legacy?

She'd taken it all.

Even the heart I'd offered her on hands and knees.

I jerked my gaze away from Dante. It was too hard to see the disappointment in his eyes, even worse to see the concern aging him every day.

Welcome to hell.

It aged us all.

The door opened and closed.

"Nixon, I already said—" I stood, ready to go head to head with him if need be, when Trace rounded the corner, arms crossed. "Trace."

She nodded to Dante.

He looked between us, muttered a curse, and walked out with his hands up like he wasn't going to be held responsible for whatever blood might be spilled.

"You shouldn't be here." I took another swig. Already, my vision was blurring. I'd drunk half the bottle. Why the hell hadn't I passed out already?

Trace pried the bottle from my hand.

I let her.

With one swing, she thrust it against the wall. Amber liquid flew everywhere, and brown glass joined the glass on the floor.

"That was wasteful," I muttered.

"You're wasteful," she fired right back, making my lips twitch.

"Come up with that all by yourself?" I rolled my eyes. "Go home, Trace." Home to your husband, to your child, to your fucking life.

"Just because Nixon's my home doesn't mean you aren't." Tears filled her eyes as she glanced at my hands — my cut-up, bloody hands. Without speaking, she grabbed them both in hers and kissed the blood with her innocent lips. I tried to jerk away.

She held fast.

"Stop." I clenched my teeth.

I didn't want it.

I didn't want her love.

I rejected it.

She'd rejected me.

I didn't even want her friendship.

It hurt too much.

She was my best friend's wife.

The last thing she needed to be doing was kissing my hands, kissing my sins, my mistakes, my failures as a husband.

As a human being.

A protector.

I closed my eyes tight against all the voices in my head, voices that screamed my worthlessness, that fueled my rage.

"Come on." She pulled my hand, and for some reason, I followed her. Maybe the Jack was finally hitting me. I swayed a bit on my feet as I trailed her into the master bedroom.

The one I was supposed to share.

I froze at the door. "Not here."

Trace sighed and walked down the hall to the next room. It had a mattress on the floor and a new comforter set in blue.

Why the hell had I picked blue?

The thought made me cringe and then laugh out

loud. Yeah, the Jack was hitting hard.

Trace shoved me in the general direction of the mattress, and I collapsed on top of it. And then she left.

Or I thought she did.

Minutes later, a warm rag was getting dragged across my palms, my fingers, and then the comforter was covering my body. My shoes were tugged off.

She sighed and rubbed my back. "Come back to me, Chase. Come back to us."

"Maybe," I slurred through a drunken haze, "I was never yours to begin with. Theirs. Hers."

I could feel her sadness.

The air was heavy with it.

But my anger won.

It always did.

I jerked away from her. "Go away."

"You'll have to kill me first," she challenged in a voice that sounded too sweet to be threatening.

"Don't tempt me," I dared, feeling instantly guilty at the sharp intake of breath, and then, she kicked me while I was down.

Literally dug the point of her boot into my ribs several times, until I turned around and grabbed her leg and pulled her to the mattress on the floor, hovering over her, angry, so angry.

"Don't ever threaten me again." Her chest heaved, brown eyes lit up with tears. I hung my head, bracing my hands on either side of her.

I'd been this way once with her.

Pushing her against the ground.

Holding her there with my body.

I'd tasted her lips.

I'd been hers.

And then I'd been nothing.

And now, now she was still there.

I wanted her gone.

I leaned down and whispered in her ear, "If you don't want me to threaten you again, I suggest you get out."

"Or what?" The challenge hung between us.

I wasn't relenting.

Neither was she.

But she reminded me of everything I'd lost.

Of every reason why I'd lost it.

"Trace..." My body shook. "...understand this. You're no longer safe with me. Get. Out."

I slowly moved away from her as she got to her feet and said, "I never was, jackass."

I fell asleep to the sound of laughter.

Mil's laughter.

And wondered if she'd always haunt me that way.

Mocking my life.

Even in her death.

CHAPTER FIVE

"Nikolai." I hated that the name chilled me. "We aren't on speaking terms anymore. And the only thing I want to say to that betraying, fucking rat is, 'Meet you in hell.'" I laughed. "He'd probably just say, 'You first.'"
— *Notes from interview with Agent P, FBI*

Luciana

I was going to get fired.

Fired.

My hands shook as I made my way into Nikolai's office. I'd only ever spoken to him three times.

The first time I'd almost blacked out from nerves and forgotten my own name.

He hadn't been amused.

The second time had been at the office Christmas party. I was singing karaoke, and I wasn't necessarily doing a bang-up job. The YouTube video was paired with howling dogs, if that gives any sort of clue to how great of a performance I gave.

And though I'd like to say the third time was a charm... it wasn't. I had toilet paper stuck to the heel of my shoe, and he'd been kind enough to point it out during a staff meeting.

My face was red for a week.

Suffice it to say, I did not have high hopes for this meeting. There were only three reasons Nikolai called people into his office. To fire them, yell at them, or make them disappear.

I knew it was an urban legend, office gossip, something that they tell the new employees in order to put the fear of God in them, but it wasn't necessary. He was terrifying without all the stories about him working for the mafia or, my personal favorite, being a distant relation to Jack the Ripper.

I inwardly rolled my eyes.

People needed to get lives. You'd think that working for one of the richest men in the world, one of the more infamous, would be exhausting, and it was, but my co-workers still found time to spin story after story.

"Miss Smith." His lips curled around the word in amusement as if he knew something I didn't.

I winced at the use of my last name, the only name that had been given to me before I was dropped off at the local orphanage was tucked away on my birth certificate and on old school reports, I'd taken my adoptive parents' last name of Smith the minute I turned sixteen and never looked back. I was a Smith.

My old name held memories of foster care, being passed from home to home, never finding a place or a purpose.

Until a family had finally decided they liked me enough to adopt me.

Mom and Dad were in their seventies and hadn't even spoken English when I'd first moved in with them, but they loved me.

And love didn't really need words, did it?

Just actions.

I took a deep breath and smoothed my hands down my black pencil skirt. My electric blue heels clicked loudly against the marble floor as I walked through the massive glass door and faced my doom.

Maybe it was the caseload? I was a junior assistant to one of the ten lawyers he kept on retainer, and I never complained.

But I did tend to take on too much.

Which meant I could be missing something.

Shoot.

I mentally kicked myself; that was what I got for trying to claw my way to the top.

"Miss Smith." Nikolai didn't even bother to look at me. Maybe he really was a serial killer; the man had no heart! I was getting fired most likely, and he was staring out the window birdwatching! "Have a seat."

I quickly sat in the nearest leather chair and folded my hands in my lap, then unfolded them, only to fold them again. I was losing it. He wasn't going to judge my posture.

Though when he did turn around, I straightened.

Mouth dry, I watched his dark eyes take me in, as if he was taking stock of every damn thing I was doing wrong by simply existing. My hands started to sweat as his perusal continued.

Finally, finally he let out a long sigh as if the world was disappointing him — a if my presence disappointed him — and sat.

It was hard not to notice the tattoos on his fingers.

Had those always been there?

"Tell me, Miss Smith, do you enjoy working for me?"

Was this a trick question?

I waited, weighing my words, and finally just chose honesty. "I love my job. I've been staying late so I can take a bigger caseload. If there's anything more I can do to—"

"No," he interrupted, "that's not why you're here."

"Oh." My heart raced as I waited for him to say

exactly why I was sitting in his office after hours.

In the dark.

"I need you..." He lowered his voice.

Oh no, was he hitting on me? He was a married man. His wife was gorgeous; she was on every magazine in the world for her classic style. They were like American royalty.

"...to do me a favor."

"A favor?" I shot up out of my seat as anger sliced through me. "Look, I don't know what you thought was going to happen, but I don't give those sort of favors, sir."

His lips twitched, and then a laugh escaped between them.

It sounded so foreign.

So gruff that I immediately decided the man had probably laughed twice in his life. It was the only explanation.

"Sit." He full-on grinned.

I didn't sit.

"You'll do better than I thought." He seemed amused at my outburst. "If you let me finish, I'll continue with the job offer, or are you too offended for me to continue? By the way, I love my wife, my very pregnant, very beautiful wife."

Shame washed over me. "I-I'm so sorry. You just said favor and, I know I've reported a few cases of sexual harassment—"

"Come again?" His voice thundered. "Sexual harassment? Who's been harassing you? Name. Now."

I fired off the names of two of my superiors; one had cornered me a few times near the restrooms by my desk; the other tried to grab my breasts from behind then said he'd been joking.

He wrote the names down. "They won't be living very long."

My eyes narrowed.

He just shrugged. "I know people. Consider it done. It's the least I can do since I'm about to owe you a favor and, Miss Smith, I do not like having debt."

"Living?" I was still stuck on that part of the conversation. "You mean they won't be... living, breathing—"

"Let's focus on you." He changed the subject and stood. "You'll need to move. The situation is delicate. And you'll need to sign an NDA. If you break the NDA..." He shrugged.

I half expected him to laugh and say, *"I'll break your legs."*

He didn't.

"What exactly is this... favor?"

"A business associate of mine is in desperate need of a lawyer, a good lawyer, someone young who can stay with the business for life."

"Life?" I repeated. "You're joking."

"I rarely joke."

Shocker.

"Can I think about it?"

"You'll be given a company car, your choice, of course." He ignored my question.

"My choice of the cars they have?"

"Your choice of car. Period. They'll take care of the details. I believe they replace the car every two years. Your housing is taken care of. You have six weeks' vacation every year, and your salary will start at six figures. The particulars are up to them, but their last lawyer, upon retirement, could afford to buy an island and live on it."

My mouth dropped open.

He smiled, or at least his face moved a bit before he opened a leather black portfolio and turned it toward me. "You just need to sign on the dotted line."

"But—" I pressed my fingers against my temples. "—you can't be serious? What if I hate it? What if I'm not good enough? I'm only twenty-five."

"Ninety-day-test period." He shrugged like the entire offer wasn't insane. "If you hate it, or if it doesn't work out, we'll find someone else."

"I'm not..." I hated to ask it, but a car? Housing? "...I'm not doing anything illegal, am I?"

He didn't answer. He locked eyes with me and whispered, "Nothing we do in life is ever truly legal, Miss Smith. And I'm not at liberty to discuss their business deals, but know you won't be burying bodies, no."

He seemed amused at his own joke, while I was ready to puke at the idea. After being beaten in some foster homes, passed off like trash, the last thing I could stomach was violence of any kind.

I was the girl who actually threw up while watching *Die Hard*.

Pathetic.

"Think of the money." The guy just wouldn't stop. "Your parents could retire. You could send them on a nice long vacation. They still work their hands to the bone. Imagine the life you could offer them."

Straight to the point.

My heart clenched.

Dad had a heart condition.

Mom still worked as a bookkeeper, and Dad had done janitorial jobs until he couldn't work anymore.

They'd worked their whole lives, sometimes two jobs to help put me through college. Part of the reason I'd even taken the job with Nikolai had been because I could help support them, but it wasn't enough, it never was, especially with Dad's medical bills.

There really wasn't anything to think about, was there?

It was life-changing money.

It would give them back what they'd given me.

My greatest purpose had always been to repay what they'd given me the day they said they'd always wanted a little girl, in their broken Italian accents.

I bit down on my lip and nodded. "Where do I sign?"

"Good girl." He winked and handed me the pen.

The minute my name slid across the white paper, the minute the black ink stained my thumb, I felt it.

Like the universe was trying to warn me.

Like the air itself was charged around me.

I wasn't just signing for a job.

My hand shook as I finished writing the date, and when I looked up into Nikolai's black-as-death eyes, he whispered, "Raise hell."

CHAPTER SIX

"Look, I did my job. I answered your questions. Talking about Chase isn't going to get you any closer to infiltration... now, is it?"
— *Notes from interview with Agent P, FBI*

Chase

I WOKE UP with a pounding headache between my temples and the all-too-familiar feeling in my chest.

When I sucked in a breath, it felt like my chest cavity was cracking in half; I exhaled and tried to focus on something other than the sharp ache tightening around my body, threatening to tear me apart. The pain of loss was always shocking, severe, and then, suddenly gone.

Followed by complete emptiness.

I slammed my hand down on the mattress and checked my phone. Nixon had called. Frank had called. Even Phoenix had called.

What? Did they think I was dead?

I winced; even the simple movement of turning onto my side had my body ready to heave everything I'd eaten the day before onto the floor.

Had I even eaten?

My blurry vision narrowed in on the massive amount of texts from the guys and then the missed calls.

The only thing that mildly intrigued me was a voicemail from Nikolai, probably checking in to see if I wanted him to kill me.

I'd texted him last week with one thing on my mind.

Death.

Mine.

And he hadn't tried talking me out of it, just calmly listened as I told him my plan to take out the De Langes as painfully as possible. Once every single one of them was dead?

I had nothing left.

He'd agreed on one condition.

The bastard never said what the condition was, but I figured he would tell me when the time was right.

I squeezed my eyes shut and let the silence of the house surround me; it still smelled like new paint.

The smell made me want to puke. It reminded me of painting; it reminded me of her.

And yet I stayed here.

Haunting her, the same way she was haunting me.

I peeled off my shirt and flipped onto my stomach in an attempt to get comfortable and sleep off my hangover. I was just dozing off into another nightmare of her face as she fell in slow motion to the ground, blood dripping from her nose, when the doorbell rang.

I put a pillow over my head and gritted my teeth.

It rang again.

I didn't even know it had been installed.

"Son of a—" I quickly put on my discarded jeans. Whoever was on the other end of that door was going to meet a quick death. I grabbed my gun and shoved it in the back of my pants as the doorbell continued to ring as if it was a competition to see how many rings it would take to make my head explode between my ears.

I stumbled to the door and jerked it open. "What the fuck?"

A woman.

Really?

Had the guys really resorted to prostitution? And what the hell kind of prostitute wore a cheap business suit from the nearest mall?

I pinched the bridge of my nose as I leaned against the doorframe. "Go away."

I couldn't even look at her fully.

But I glanced enough to see honey highlights, a wide smile, and large eyes.

"What the hell are you smiling about?" I groaned. "I said go away. I'm sure they'll still pay you for your..." I waved her off and tried shutting the door.

A black and white heel wedged between the door and the frame.

I sighed down at it and said in a low voice, "Listen very closely. I have absolutely no problem burying a body in my back yard. Yours won't be the only one, and I'm sure the others need some female companionship. If you don't leave, your only choice will be knife or gunshot."

"That's not funny." Her voice was low, a bit husky.

"Wasn't joking." I crossed my arms and finally stared her down. She was pale, her right hand held a portfolio, and she was gripping it so tightly her fingers looked like they were going numb. I frowned and narrowed my eyes. "Why are you still here?"

"You hired me," she said slowly, and then her eyes widened. "Am I at the wrong house?" She quickly grabbed her phone with shaking hands, dropped it onto the ground face down, then mumbled, "Shoot," before picking it up and looking at the severely cracked screen. "This is Bella Sera Way, right?"

Every fiber in my body said to lie. "Yes, it is. Sorry

for the trouble. Have a nice trip back into the city."

I tried shutting the door again.

That damn heel wedged between the door for the second time.

"Look." My control was barely holding on, and I meant every word about burying her body; I just needed to grab a shovel. "I need you to listen to me very carefully. Can you do that?"

She nodded, her smile back.

I hated that smile.

I hated her. Immediately. Immensely.

Hate wasn't a strong enough word for what I felt for the woman who'd interrupted my nightmare, who smiled like there was a reason to.

"I need you…" I spoke slowly. "…to get the hell off my property before I shoot you." I pointed to the driveway. "So walk back to your car—"

She winced.

"Where the hell is your car?"

"I was told you would provide one."

Hands shaking with rage, I managed to at least get out, "Wait here," before I ran back up the stairs, grabbed my phone, and actually checked my text messages.

Nixon: New lawyer for the Families. She's headed your way, Chase.

Phoenix: Don't shoot her, Chase.

Phoenix: I mean it.

Phoenix: Chase? You can't keep burying people in the back yard.

Sergio: She'll need access to everything. I'll be there in a half hour.

Phoenix: Chase. Answer me, damn it!

Tex: Kill her.

Tex: Do it. Phoenix is turning purple.

Tex: Just a flesh wound.

Phoenix: Don't listen to Tex. He's probably as hung over as you are.

Dante: ...Are you awake? Bad news. A woman is headed your way, try to be nice...

Dante: You do remember what that word means, right?

I scrolled through the rest of the texts and finally got to the very first one from Nixon, sent this morning at five a.m.

Nixon: You dropped the ball with the one job I asked you to do. I asked Nikolai for help. He's sending someone for the Families. She's starting with Abandonato finances — and you're in charge. Happy hunting. Oh, and don't kill her. He said you owed him a favor anyway.

Why did everyone assume I was going to kill her? Damn it, Nikolai.

They didn't need to know that I'd told her I would at least three times.

I quickly dialed Nixon's number.

"Shit," he breathed. "She has a family. You can't just go around killing people because you're pissed at the world!"

The old Chase would have laughed.

The new Chase was annoyed as hell.

"I didn't shoot her." Yet. It was still on the table if she kept sticking her damn shoe in the doorway. "And what the hell is she doing here? Now?"

"Nikolai put her on a jet last night, sent over the paperwork early this morning." Serena started crying in the background. "Look, I've got shit to do, deal with it!"

"Nixon—"

He hung up on me.

The bastard actually hung up on me.

I called Phoenix.

"Fuck..." Phoenix threw something. I heard a shatter and then, "Where's the body?"

"I didn't—" I started pacing. "Do you really think it's smart to send the new family lawyer into the lion's den? I already threatened to kill her."

"So you didn't?"

"If I had, I'd be calling Tex, not you. He's the only one capable of burying a body in under fifteen minutes."

Phoenix cursed under his breath. "Stop timing it, Chase. That's a new low, even for you."

"Coming from a rapist?" I snapped, my anger taking over.

"Wow," Phoenix's voice cracked. "You know what? Good luck."

He hung up.

Sergio didn't answer.

Tex's phone was off.

What the hell was I supposed to do?

I tried Nixon again.

He answered amidst Serena's screaming. "Do your job, Chase! This shit ends now! You want to kill people? You want the world to feel your pain? *Fine*. Do it on your own time, but you still work for me. So get your pathetic ass off the phone and into the shower and make it work!"

He hung up.

Again.

I stomped over to the door and jerked it open. The woman nearly fell against my chest in an attempt to stay upright.

I glared so hard my eyes burned. "Don't speak."

She gulped.

"Keep up and lose the heels."

CHAPTER SEVEN

"The number doesn't matter. This guy's going to wipe out an entire family line. It's beyond their control. He's beyond their control. He died right along with her. Send me in, and I'll do what they can't. What they won't."
— *Notes from interview with Agent P, FBI*

Luciana

IF I DIDN'T get my shaking under control, I was going to be worse off than I already was. I hobbled on one foot and pulled one heel off then grabbed the other, leaving me completely barefoot in a stranger's home.

His tanned back was covered in tattoos.

His rock-hard stomach.

Neck.

Arms.

Ink was everywhere, in every different color of the rainbow; some of it looked new, as if he was trying to cover up the maps drawn all over his body.

The only reason I was able to look away from what I'd already decided was the most beautiful and angry man I'd ever met in entire life was because he scared me more than he intrigued me.

His words were harsh.

His tone menacing.

He carried himself like the world owed him everything — and with every fiber of my being, I believed he'd stay alive until he felt as if he'd squeezed every drop of what was owed him into his waiting hands.

The longer the silence stretched between us as he

scrolled through his phone, the more uncomfortable I got.

Nikolai didn't mention a cranky underwear model with too much money.

And yet there I was, standing in a mansion that looked as if it was either in the process of getting remodeled or gutted.

Pieces of furniture were covered in black tarp; some still in plastic as if the store had recently dropped them off. A large dining room set was shoved against one wall in the entry, and a bare marble table with a small black lamp was in the center of it. The walls were red, picture frames lined the floor leading up the stairs, and it was dark, so dark it was like walking into a cave, despite the fact that it had numerous windows and an open floor plan.

I did a slow circle, my heels crunching a piece of glass. "Are you... gutting it?"

"Did I ask you to speak?" He didn't look up from his phone.

I flinched.

I'd never been treated so horribly in my entire life, and I worked with a man people called a sociopath.

So...

I jumped when the guy shoved his phone back in his pocket and put his hands on his hips. Every muscle was hard-earned; you could tell in the way they stretched taut across his stomach like trophies. Dark and red ink swirled near his right hip; a huge eagle spread across his chest with blood dripping down from its feathers. It would be pretty...

On a normal day.

In a normal situation.

Like, if I was sitting at a bar and the guy just spontaneously ripped his shirt and asked me to take a picture for his Instagram.

I highly doubted this guy even knew what Instagram was.

"May I—"

He glared.

Death wish, that was what I had.

I kept talking.

"May I use the restroom?"

"I let you in my home, and now you want something from me? Is that how this works?" I couldn't tell if he was being serious or teasing.

His nostrils flared.

Yeah, he didn't have a teasing bone in his body.

Nothing but anger up in there.

And something else I couldn't quite place and didn't want to even fixate on; the faster we got started, the faster I could leave. According to Nikolai, I'd be working with the heads of each family, except for Nixon, who was too busy to deal with me.

Those were the exact words given to Nikolai.

"Well?" He crossed his bulky arms. "Have an answer for me?"

So. Condescending.

So cruel. And for what purpose? To make me feel bad about myself? Talk about hostile work environment.

"Look." I tried to match his glare. "I'm being paid to be here. I have a job to do. If you could just point me in the right direction, I can get started and get the hell away from you."

His eyes flashed.

Poor life choices just kept getting made, didn't

they?

I jumped when a knock sounded at the door, followed by someone letting himself in.

He had dark hair past his chin, looked a bit older than Mr. I-Can't-Even-Adult-Today, and at least wore a ghost of a smile across his full lips. Hey, at least he was wearing a shirt, unlike some people.

"Miss Smith?" He winked.

Chase snorted. "Smith? The name they give people who have bad last names. Could you be any more generic? Plain? Boring?"

"Enough, Chase," the man snapped. His eyes were lethal as Chase held up his hands and shrugged. "Now..." He turned his attention back to me. "...my name's Sergio. I'll be giving you electronic access to all the files you need. You've already signed the NDA?"

I nodded and finally found my voice beneath all the giant balls I'd swallowed in my throat after being insulted for being plain, boring, basically the stupidest person on the planet. And maybe I was. I took the damn job without asking if I'd be put in the seventh circle of hell with Satan, aka Chase. "All the paperwork has been signed, yes."

Sergio exhaled loudly and glanced between me and Chase. "Is this going to be a problem?"

I frowned. "The job?"

He shook his head slowly. "Nikolai didn't give us any warning. The only person capable of handling you right now..." His voice trailed off. *Please don't say Chase. Please don't say Chase.* "Is Chase... He promised..." He spat the word promise as if it was a blood oath. "...to take care of finding a new lawyer, and since the ball was dropped, it's his new job to show you the ropes.

You'll be working for the Abandonato family first, learning how things were done from the notes your predecessor left…"

I nodded. "I'm capable. I can do it."

"I'm not questioning you." He drew out the word you then glanced behind me to Chase. The air crackled with heat, anger.

I heard something loud get slammed against a wall, and then Chase was storming past us and up the stairs.

I finally exhaled as if I hadn't taken a breath since entering the house. "He always like that?"

Something flickered across Sergio's face before he whispered, "No." And then, "This is… new."

"His shining personality is new?" Yay me.

Sergio locked his green eyes on mine. "Sometimes, life doesn't play fair. I've seen my share of death and destruction. I am not a good man." Why was he telling me this? Dread washed over me. Just who were these people? "But that doesn't change the fact that nothing, nothing in this damn world could ever prepare me to go through what he's lived through."

"He looks too young to have gone through a war." I tried to lighten the mood.

Sergio's head snapped toward mine. "All wars are different. Some are lost with words unsaid."

Heaviness settled across my chest at his pained expression. He grabbed a flash drive from his pocket and handed it over to me. "It's encrypted." He handed me a set of codes. "They change every hour. Be sure to put in the right code or the system starts attacking itself in order to burn all the information."

"Burn," I repeated. "As in a fire?"

"As in, you get burned and lose your identity, your

social security number, your life, and your eye color. Burned. You no longer exist. This file gets burned, and we no longer exist, so try not to kill us."

"Okay." I was scared shitless. I grabbed toward the codes with shaking hands.

He didn't hand them over right away but gripped them tightly. "Nikolai says you're capable."

I gave him my most confident glare. "Trust him. And trust me."

He released his grip and stepped back, just as something else crashed upstairs.

I flinched.

"Do yourself a favor..." He pointed me down the hall. "Lock the door to the office you're in."

My eyes widened. "Lock the door?"

"Keep the monster out." He bit down on his lip as if he was trying to decide if it was smart to leave me and then he held out his hand. "Cell phone?"

I expected him to plug in his number, not grab it, drop it to the ground, and stomp all over it until it was shattered.

He handed me a new iPhone X. "Every number needed is plugged in. Don't dial the number that says God unless you're dying, and don't call Chase on it. He doesn't like anyone right now, especially humans who smile."

I smiled.

He shook his head. "Ill-advised."

My smile fell. "Alright, so do I just call you when I'm done?"

Sergio's mouth twitched. "You're working for the Abandonatos. Chase is your man. Make it work and pick a room."

My stomach fell to my knees. "Pick. A. Room?"

"There are thirty-seven." He shrugged. "Might I suggest grabbing the one farthest away from wherever he's miserably existing?"

"How long?" I croaked. "How long do I have to stay here?"

"Finish the job. Move on to the next family."

Finish the job. Move on to the next family. That was going to be my new mantra.

"And transportation?"

Sergio put on a pair of sunglasses and smirked. "Just don't take his favorite car, and you'll be fine." He turned to leave.

"Wait!" I called. "Which one's his favorite?"

He chuckled. "No clue. Good luck."

CHAPTER EIGHT

"Chase wouldn't try to take back the Family. Not now. He may be crazy, but I don't see him making that move so aggressively. And if he does — he will rip apart the Abandonato dynasty faster than any of us could. On second thought, why not plant the seed?"
— *Notes from interview with Agent P, FBI*

Chase

SHE JUST HAD to be pretty, didn't she?

My gut churned until I ran into the bathroom and puked all the whiskey and then some into the toilet. I grabbed a towel and wiped my face then grabbed some mouthwash and swished it around. I didn't recognize the man in the mirror. The one with haunted eyes and dark circles beneath them.

Anger was like a second skin wrapped tight around my muscles, my bones. It was as much a part of me as my own damn lungs.

I slammed my fist into the mirror, shattering it on contact; pieces of glass stuck in my knuckles.

My expression in the mirror shifted.

More anger.

And sadness.

My blue eyes landed on a few pieces of dark inky hair that fell across my forehead.

I gripped one of the shards of glass from my right hand and inspected the blood as it trickled down my wrists. I don't know how long I watched the blood leave my body and remembered the way it left hers.

Blood had trickled down her chin.

She'd reached for me...

Her hand outstretched as if to both beckon and stop me.

I squeezed my eyes shut.

"Chase!" Her voice screamed my name over and over again in my head, always begging me to forgive her, begging me to understand.

I wouldn't forgive.

I wouldn't understand.

I wasn't that man anymore.

I would never be him.

I held the towel to my bloody hands then tossed it back on the counter and slowly walked into the bare room. I refused to keep anything that reminded me of her — of us — in the house. In a fit of rage, I'd grabbed every piece of clothing, every picture, every single thing she'd touched, tossed it in the back yard, and lit a match.

Half of her things were singed before Phoenix could douse the fire. The only reason I hadn't burned part of my body was because he'd shown up. I'd been ready to take a step into the inferno, needing to prove to her ghost that I would walk through hell in order to punish her.

And when Phoenix left, in a moment of temptation, when the flames called again, I took another step. Dante knocked me on my ass and punched the shit out of me. I rubbed my jaw at the memory.

Six months.

It had been six months since I sat in that church.

Since I refused to look in the casket.

Since my soul died.

And I didn't feel better.

Weren't people supposed to feel better? Time healed. That was what Sergio said.

He'd never been so wrong.

Time? Time was the fuel to my rage, because every day I woke up still smelling her; every night I reached across the bed only to find a cold, empty memory of the lie I'd lived — I felt a little less human.

And a hell of a lot more crazy.

I jerked on a black t-shirt and tried to regain control of my thoughts. I couldn't be weak, not with what I had to do.

Ten more families with cousins, sisters, wives, associates.

And I was going to end them all.

Shut down the De Lange bloodline — the bloodline that should have never existed in the first place. All they'd brought was pain, bad luck, anger, betrayal.

I'd been keeping vigorous notes on locations, aliases.

Sergio thought it would help me heal.

It took me two days to get all the intel I'd ever need.

The social security numbers.

Identities.

Locations.

I'd memorized each one.

And never said a word to my own blood about it.

It was my fucking right.

So why did I feel like death every time I fired the gun, every time I took another life? My death toll was suddenly substantially higher than the rest of my family. I was darkness.

Loneliness.

Pain.

It was all I had.

What I lived for.

I walked down the hall, fully intent on grabbing the

keys and heading out to get drunk off my ass, when I saw an ass.

Not mine.

Just pushed up into the air behind a black pencil skirt.

The annoying girl was on all fours, organizing folders that looked older than Frank.

"You're still here," I said with disdain. "And I thought I scared you away." I leaned against the door to the office.

"Shit," she muttered under her breath.

"Such language." Her ass was still pointed toward me. I walked over to her and bent down, intimidating her on purpose because she represented everything that was so wrong with this world. A pretty girl, in pretty clothes, thinking that she was owed something, some semblance of power or respect just because she looked the part. "You should have locked the door, princess."

She stiffened and then looked over her shoulder. "I thought you were upstairs punching things. Had I known you knew how to carry on an actual conversation that didn't include insults or yelling, I would have sought you out and introduced myself as your new roommate."

She held out her hand.

I stared at it.

Then at her.

Then back at her hand. "The hell you are!"

"Look…" She stood on bare feet and put her hands on her hips. "…do you think I want to stay here? I signed a contract. A contract that would take an act of God to get out of, so yes, I'm staying here until I finish going over all the court cases attached to your name, until I look at all the overseas accounts and business holdings, until I know every inch of Abandonato Dynasty. And then when I'm finished, I'm starting in on a new family. You can either help or be a hindrance. Your choice."

"Hindrance," I snapped. "And you aren't staying here. Find a hotel!"

"Sergio said—"

"Oh, Sergio, huh? On a first name basis with him? What, did you offer to spread your legs for him, too? Is that why you wear such tight skirts?"

She frowned and looked down. "My skirt isn't—"

I held up my hand. "Do yourself a favor. Don't speak."

"But you just—"

I took an aggressive step toward her. "I need you to listen very carefully." I squeezed her chin between my thumb and forefinger, ignoring how soft her skin felt and wondering why my heart suddenly started thudding louder than it had in six months. As if it wanted me to remember its presence loud and clear. "I don't want you here. At all. I don't want you breathing the same air, I don't want you showering with the same water. As far as I'm concerned, you don't exist. If you seek me out, you'll regret it. In the meantime, I'm talking to Sergio about your living situation. Don't fall asleep until I get back." I released her skin and rubbed my hand against my jeans.

Her lips trembled. "Is that a request?"

"It's an order."

"I may work for you, but—"

"What did I say about speaking?" I tilted my head.

God, the nerve of the girl. Didn't she know who I was?

Her body shook.

Shit. Me.

He wouldn't.

Nikolai wouldn't do that.

He wouldn't send...

I narrowed my eyes, briefly opened my mouth, shut it, then opened it again. "Do you know what I do for a living?"

She didn't open her mouth.

"Answer the question."

She bit down on her bottom lip and then shrugged. "Business?"

I burst out laughing; it wasn't a joyful one, more of a mocking, *holy shit you're in for a treat so try to survive* laugh.

"What's so funny?"

"Alright, princess." I pulled the gun from behind my pants and pointed it at her. "I do business, capiche?"

She let out a scream so loud my ears rang and then ducked to the ground as if I'd somehow miss if she was pancaked against the wood floor.

"Like I said, don't fall asleep until I get back. Don't touch anything and try not to burn the house down. It's harder than it looks."

I left her on the ground trembling.

I shoved on my sunglasses and felt zero guilt as I got into my new Maserati and drove like hell to Nixon's.

Answers. He was going to give me answers.

Or I was going to shoot him in the lung.

I smiled.

And my hate grew a little bit more.

CHAPTER NINE

"Tex Campisi, the Italians' version of a Godfather, if there ever was one. Sicily bows to his every order, and the Russians are petrified of pissing him off again. He's royalty. He will crush anyone who stands in his way, but we all have weaknesses. Lucky for you, I know his."

— *Notes from interview with Agent P, FBI*

Tex

"SIXTY PEOPLE TOTAL," I whispered under my breath in disgust as Nixon shook his head at me.

We both knew what was happening.

What *would* happen.

"We either join him, or fight him." Nixon slammed his hands against the table. "We can't justify killing sixty people, including teenagers. Are you kidding me right now? Is this what she did to him? Is this what *we* did to him?"

I was quiet.

We all had a darkness inside us.

Some of us fed it.

While others feared it.

I was safely between both options, wondering if there would come a day when I would watch myself lose my soul to it and embrace the darkness as my friend.

I grabbed my gun and stared it down then put it in the holster strapped to my chest. "Look, Nixon, there is no right answer here."

Nixon started to pace a hole through the wood floor as I sat in silence in his office.

Chase wanted his vengeance.

And while we killed rats.

We didn't take out entire bloodlines.

That was more Russian than Italian.

But Chase wasn't listening to reason.

All he wanted was every memory of her dead.

None of us blamed him to begin with.

But now? Now he needed a fucking leash.

And nobody had a chain big enough to tie him down.

We'd lost complete control because each of us figured he'd snap out of it and start with the jokes again, and easy laughter. That one day he'd wake up, and it wouldn't be all gloom and darkness.

But Chase Abandonato, my brother, my friend... I hadn't seen him since the day she left this world, and a part of me feared she'd taken him with her, leaving only a shell of a man.

With no soul.

"Call a commission," I whispered.

Nixon's head jerked to attention. "The last time we did that—"

"I know. I shot my dad. Good times. All I'm saying is... if we call a commission, we can at least have the Families' vote, bring in the big guns from Sicily to stand with us, and if need be—"

Nixon closed his eyes.

I didn't need to finish the sentence.

If need be... we'd end him.

Was he even human anymore?

How many times had Nixon's little girl walked to Uncle Chase and clung to his leg only to have him walk away from her?

One time she'd even fallen and scraped her hand.

I'd never been so pissed in my entire life.

I'd been surprised Nixon hadn't pulled a gun on

him right then and there.

Nixon stared me down, his eyes filled with so much sadness it gutted me, ruined me. These were the days I hated being the Capo, hated making the tough decisions.

"Make the call," Nixon finally said. "I'll tell the others."

"Tell the others what?" came Chase's voice as he pushed the door open and found a seat in one of the empty chairs.

Blood caked his fingertips.

He was a stranger to me.

A stranger to us.

I eyed him up and down. "You look... great."

He flipped me off.

But there wasn't even any joy in the way he tried to verbally spar with me. Everything was just... dead inside.

My chest tightened. I looked away. I had to.

I'd always given Chase shit.

I would do anything to get that Chase back.

Instead of this haunted stranger sitting in front of me.

"We should talk." Nixon sat.

Chase scowled. "Yes, let's talk about the sexy woman you sent to my house this morning." His eyes flashed with fury. "She can't stay with me."

"Sexy?" This was news. My eyebrows shot up. "What's she look like?"

Nixon gritted his teeth. "Tex, any time but now would be good, literally any time but now for you to be yourself."

Chase didn't even flinch — no smile, no laugh, no

joining in. God, he sucked ass.

"I pulled a gun on her." Chase shrugged. "She has no clue how deep she's in, and she's been at my house for two hours."

"Two hours, and she's already driving you insane?" Nixon pointed out.

"Her presence is irritating." Chase's jaw clenched. "I want her gone."

"The contract states we provide a place to stay during her training, and since you volunteered to house all the records and documents in your several safes, that means it makes sense for her to stay there."

Chase looked ready to explode.

I intervened. "Chase, I looked at your plan."

Chase leaned forward. Blood in his eyes. Killing in his soul. "And?"

"The five families can't sign off on this. Hell, not one of us is willing to sign off on a contract that ends up killing sixty people. You're talking four generations of—"

"Rats," Chase finished. "This is what we do!" He stood and slammed his hands onto the desk.

I stood. "Let me finish."

He crossed his arms. "I'm listening."

My eyes flickered to Nixon; he gave one small nod of encouragement.

I didn't need his blessing, but I was glad to have it anyway. I continued. "We're going to call a commission, explain the situation, if you get a winning vote, you have our support."

God, it hurt to even contemplate it.

"And if I don't get a winning vote?"

The room crackled with a tense silence.

"What happens if I do it anyway?"

Nothing.

I said nothing. Just stood to my full height.

"Unbelievable!" Chase roared. "The one time I need you guys to have my back, and you're plotting my own death against me!"

I rolled my eyes. "You've never been dramatic. Don't start now."

"I need this!" Chase's voice was filled with so much anguish I wanted to pull him in for a hug, but he'd only answer with his gun. He'd refused to let anyone touch him since the funeral. "No!"

He jerked backward from the room.

Nixon reached for him.

Chase just shook his head. "If you won't support me, maybe I'll challenge your position." He eyed Nixon with hatred. "Boss."

Nixon glared. "Fucking. Try."

"Alright, then." I separated the two of them and stood in between. "Let's go have some wine… I'm sure the commission will agree. After all, this isn't crazy, your idea of vengeance, totally normal. I'm sure they'll see it your way."

I rolled my eyes once I left the room.

And nearly puked when Mo walked toward me and winked then rubbed her flat stomach.

Shit.

Sometimes, I hated the mafia.

Today.

These last four months.

I hated it the most.

CHAPTER TEN

"The only way to infiltrate is from within. We've already noticed how fiercely they protect their own. That's the Italians for you. So how do you attack a monster in full body armor? You find the chink. And believe me, there are several."
— *Notes from interview with Agent P, FBI*

Luciana

I DIDN'T MOVE from the spot on the floor.

My stomach growled as I stared at the open door and the empty hall. The house felt haunted, forlorn; there was a heaviness to it that managed to suck the life right out of a person.

Everything about it screamed enough money to buy an island for every friend of the family, but it was half empty, and what furniture I had seen was either covered in plastic, or broken.

What the heck had I gotten myself into?

I contemplated calling the police.

My fingers had hovered over my cell screen for at least ten minutes before I finally put my phone away and continued to wait.

Because what was I going to say? *"My employer, the one paying me an obscene amount of money that I'm now realizing he most likely got illegally, just pulled a gun on me. Send help?"*

Plus, the phone in my hand had just been given to me. I suspected there was a reason I wasn't allowed to use my old phone, mainly because he was going to track every single conversation I had.

I was a logical person.

Rational.

Until I walked in that door and saw my life flash before my eyes.

It was unfortunate he was so gorgeous.

Then again, even his inked skin and blue eyes couldn't cover up the monster lurking beneath. He'd threatened me, yelled at me, made me feel unsafe and unwanted.

Ugly.

Stupid.

All within the span of six minutes.

The sound of a door slamming jolted me out of my pity party long enough for me to start to panic again as footsteps neared. I could feel my heart racing beneath my chest as I counted the steps.

One.

Two.

Three.

Pause.

I lifted my head.

Chase stopped directly in front of the doorway and braced on it with both hands gripping the sides. His middle finger and pinky both had black inky tattoos on them in Italian. I couldn't make out the script, but they stuck out against his tan skin and the white walls he was currently clutching as if he was seconds away from snapping the wood in half, or maybe just the door.

"You." His blue eyes jerked to mine in such a jarring, hateful way that I almost made a run for it; probably would have if I hadn't been trapped in a small room with him blocking the exit. "You didn't move."

Was that a question?

I gulped.

"Why?"

Was he crazy? I licked my lips and answered in a small voice. "Because you said not to." Dumbass. Was this guy for real?

"I had you pegged as a more defiant type." He waved his hand in front of me and then turned around and started walking away. "Keep up."

I stumbled after him and nearly ran into him when he stopped in the middle of the hall and turned around.

I was still barefoot.

"There's glass." He pointed to the floor.

"Okay." I turned to grab my shoes when he suddenly heaved me over his shoulder and stomped down the hall as if it was completely normal to manhandle employees.

My ass was pressed against his right cheek.

Great.

I looked down.

His ass, on the other hand…

Firm.

He clearly didn't miss a squat day.

A black handgun was tucked in his jeans.

I gulped.

Guns freaked me out in a very serious way.

So the fact that he casually waved one around and kept one on his person made me so nauseated I almost puked down his back.

He walked a few more feet then set me down and jerked open a door. "This is where you'll be working."

About twenty different screens faced us; it was like the inner workings of a control room.

The screens showed the back of the house and several of the rooms and common areas.

"Okay." I nodded. Freak. Did he have a camera in my room, too? I made a mental note to only change in the bathroom. Then again, someone like him? Constantly armed? Probably had cameras in the freaking shower. "Is there a computer I can—"

"A computer will be provided," he interrupted. "Those..." There were at least seven free-standing metal files. "...are all the old records of transactions, payments, court cases, pay offs—"

Did he just say pay offs?

"—everything you need to know about our business dealings and our past is in these files. This key..." He held out an old-school-looking key. "...is how you access them. If you make a copy of it, I'll slit your throat."

He looked as if he meant it.

With shaking hands, I took the key. "Noted."

He crossed his bulky arms. "I don't want you here, but I also don't have much of a choice, unless I feel like killing the boss and taking his spot." He didn't even flinch at the idea, just smiled down at me.

Did he say boss?

"I suggest you get started."

He turned to leave.

"Wait!"

His back flexed beneath his shirt before he turned to look over his shoulder. "Yes?"

I had so many questions.

Mainly, was I allowed bathroom breaks and food?

"I'll need sleep. Bathroom breaks. Food. Water..." I tried to steady my voice. "You can't just assume I'm going to lock myself up in here until I finish."

"Of course I can." He smiled.

I hated that smile.

It was spiteful.

Smug.

It was also gorgeous.

Beautifully cruel.

As if he only smiled to mock people, never to convey joy or laughter. What the hell had happened to this beautiful man to make him so cold and bitter?

"And if I don't? Do I get my throat slit? Or will you just pull that gun on me again?"

"See." He performed a slow clap. "You're getting the hang of it. This is my house, my world, my business. I don't want you existing in any of the air around me. As far as you're concerned, I own it. I own you. Finish the damn job, and then you can leave."

"That's—" I clenched my fists. "—that's abuse!"

His eyes flashed. "You don't know the first thing about abuse. Try not to throw around words you aren't capable of understanding."

Fear trickled down my spine.

This man. He would hurt me.

It was in every fiber of his body, in the way he carried himself. He didn't make light, empty threats.

He meant every word.

"I'll… try," I finally managed, when all I wanted to do was yell at him for being such a jackass. I suddenly wished I had taken karate so I could at least make him hurt and make a run for it. Was this punishment from Nikolai? Was this why I got paid so much?

Because I was going to end up dead anyway?

At least from starvation and lack of sleep.

"Bathroom." Chase pointed to the right. "And the only reason I'm even allowing bathroom breaks is because I don't want your filth getting all over a room that cost me over a million dollars to set up."

I frowned and looked around. "But it's just cameras and—"

He held up a finger. "First off, don't insult the room. It's rude." A ghost of a smile appeared on his lips. "And things aren't always what they seem."

He left it at that.

Left me.

With all the files.

And when I stopped hearing his footsteps down the hall, I finally released a few tears and slunk to the floor.

Trapped.

In a prison I'd signed up for.

And afraid for my life.

CHAPTER ELEVEN

"Look." I spread my palms flat against the table. "I've been here for six hours. I voluntarily walked into that door and took that assignment for my own reasons. I promised you eight hours, and when that ends, this is over. I'm grabbing my gun and walking out that door knowing that you'll have nightmares of my face. It's really the only reason I keep smiling with my entire family murdered. Hey, there it is, that look. Right. There."

— *Notes from interview with Agent P, FBI*

Chase

THE SHAKING WOULDN'T go away.

No matter how many times I tried to tell myself it wasn't real, it was just a waking nightmare. I'd see my reflection in the mirror and stare, in disbelief, at the man looking back at me.

It seemed like a sick joke.

She was the first woman I'd touched in over six months. I'd been annoyed, so I'd lifted her over my shoulder.

And I'd been an idiot.

Because I'd forgotten.

I'd forgotten the softness of a woman's skin.

The way her rounded hips felt against my fingertips.

I squeezed my eyes shut, reached for the bottle of whiskey, and took a swig. I'd forgotten.

And now my hands were shaking.

My body pulsed with awareness.

And I hated myself for it.

I hated that I'd responded.

Reacted.

Hated that she'd brought it out in me.

Hated.

She was the exact opposite of Mil. She was soft, didn't talk back, and stared at me as if I was seconds away from ending her life. Her innocent eyes took everything in with fear and trepidation. She would run from me if she could.

Whereas Mil… Mil had pushed back.

Always pushed back.

Pushed me to the point of insanity most days.

Because she'd never listened to me.

It was her downfall.

It had ended up being her death.

Thinking that for one second, she could move the chess pieces in ways to benefit her.

It was a competition between us.

In the bedroom.

Out of the bedroom.

Both of us always trying to one-up one another.

We had laughed about it in front of others.

But behind closed doors, when she thought I was sleeping, I'd see her working on her phone; I'd see her order men to ruthlessly kill people that didn't deserve it, just to prove a fucking point.

She ruled…

Her throne.

There was no room for love.

Love made you a pathetic, weak target.

Never again.

I took another swig and braced my body against the kitchen counter as the deafening silence of the house slowly started to drive me insane.

The doorbell rang. I grabbed the bottle and walked slowly to the main entry and jerked it open.

The UPS guy took one look at me, then at the bottle, and dropped the package off without as much as a "Hi."

He was lucky I didn't shoot him for trespassing.

I glanced down at the plain brown shipping box and froze.

Mil De Lange was typed out in bold, black letters, no return address, and no other information.

I should have been worried about a bomb.

A distraction.

Being a target.

Yet, the only thing I could manage to conjure up was bitterness at those bold letters.

She couldn't even take my last name…

I kicked the box at least three times before I calmed down then pulled out my knife and slit it open.

A bloody hand holding a cell phone waited inside. I pulled the phone from the hand and held it to my ear.

"Knew you'd be too curious," the familiar Russian-accented voice said on the other end. "I've been told you've lost your soul."

I sighed into the phone and kept my attention on the driveway, just in case it was a trap. "I've been told you never had one to begin with, Andrei."

"Ah, so you do remember me."

"Yeah well, hard to forget a dirty Russian."

He chuckled as if I hadn't just insulted him. "Look, I have a business proposition for you."

"Not interested." I almost hung up.

Would have.

"I have eleven De Lange associates saying they'd love to switch sides and come work for me. I shot one of them. You're holding his phone. Keep that, and the hand, as proof of my… loyalty."

"Loyal? You?" I snorted. This from the guy who'd tried to take out all the bosses last year? Who allowed my dead wife to work for him? To get in so deep, she couldn't find a way out? Yeah, right. Loyal.

"How badly do you want the men?" he asked in a calm voice. "How bad does your blood roar to take out every last one of them?"

I gripped the phone so hard my fingers went numb.

"Thought so…" He chuckled. "Shall I send them over?"

"You must have a lot of faith in my ability to kill that many men without getting killed first…"

"Think of it as a test."

God, I hated how much I liked his brain.

"Oh, and it's already too late. They should be arriving in five minutes."

I dropped the phone as two SUVs started making their way down the long driveway.

With a curse, I ran back into the house, grabbed my phone, and dialed Dante. "Ten headed my way, armed."

"Shit." He started firing off instructions.

I wasn't afraid to die.

I welcomed it.

But I refused to die by their hand.

And I wasn't completely sure I could take every last one of them out without getting at least two bullets to the chest.

I dropped my phone and sprinted toward the camera room.

The pretty woman was bent over a few files.

I shoved her out of the way. No time.

I hit the button beneath the desk, and the floor split open and lit up into the hidden room beneath.

Guns. Guns. More guns.

I grabbed two semi-automatics, extra magazines,

and a few grenades, just in case.

When I jogged back up the stairs, the woman was pushed up against the wall with tears in her eyes. "Wh- what's going on?"

"Stay in here," I ordered. "Do not, under any circumstances—"

She ran.

She fucking ran.

CHAPTER TWELVE

"I think you're asking the wrong question. Greedy bastards, all of you." I rolled my eyes. "They will end you, your family, the clerk at the grocery store, the nice old man who rings the bell for the Salvation Army. Men like us have no souls. Don't you get it? We. Don't. Care. And you should remember that, when you go home and kiss your wife, we don't hesitate because we have hearts. We hesitate because we like to see the fear in your eyes before we take your last few heartbeats." I smiled as his face went pale. He's lucky he wasn't already dead.

— *Notes from interview with Agent P, FBI*

Luciana

I RAN LIKE hell down the hall, didn't even grab my shoes — let him have the stilettos. By the time I reached the front door, two black SUVs were pulling up.

It was like a gift from God!

I could plead my case; I could grab a ride out of this hell-hole.

And do what?

I couldn't go to the police.

I just needed to get out.

I gripped the handle to the front door just as the first man hopped out of the front seat.

Completely armed.

With so many weapons strapped to his chest, I couldn't count them. One by one, men followed in tactical gear as if I was in some sort of warzone.

And behind me, I smelled whiskey.

Chase took a swig out of the bottle, calmly placed it on the table nearest to the door, and nodded to me. "You know how to shoot?"

"A camera," I said dumbly. "I can shoot a camera."

"Huh." He loaded the gun and pulled back the hammer. "And here I thought that was a lost art, camera shooting." He smirked as if it was the funniest thing he'd heard in years. "Unless you want to get shot, I'd hide. The pantry has fortified cement walls that semi-automatics can't even break through."

I backed away toward the wall and eyed the kitchen. "You have cement walls for your food?"

He eyed me very seriously. "Food's a big deal. Gotta keep it safe." He shrugged. "Plus, it's connected to a wine cellar."

Ah, there we go.

He nodded. "I'd run now."

I was paralyzed with fear — fear of him, fear for him — which felt so misplaced I'd laugh hysterically if I wasn't afraid I was minutes away from losing my life.

With a sigh, he charged toward me, grabbed my arm, and shoved me in the general direction of the kitchen.

A gunshot rang out. He closed his eyes and shook his head. "De Langes shoot first, ask questions later."

The name had my eyes widening briefly.

He hesitated, flinched, stared through me, then bent down, and whispered in my ear, "Run. Now."

I ran; I sprinted into the kitchen, opened two doors before I found the pantry, and managed to shut the door as three more gunshots rang out.

Hot tears ran down my cheeks as I plugged my ears, hugging my knees to my chest and telling myself that it was all a bad dream.

A really bad, horrible, dream.

CHAPTER THIRTEEN

"Dante Nicolasi is Chase's best friend." I tried not to show emotion, but I hated Dante more than I hated anyone in this God-forsaken world. He'd stolen from me — and nobody stole from me. Nobody. "He's Chase's protégé. The guy gets off by killing people, and I don't blame him. Maybe he'll smile when I kill him. Yeah, I bet he will."

— *Notes from interview with Agent P, FBI*

Chase

ANOTHER BULLET WHIZZED by my head, and I sighed in disbelief. "Pieces of shit never learn, do you?" I pointed my gun at the door as it pushed open and started my rapid fire to the chest, head, chest, head; the automatic trigger just kept going while I aimed.

Three of the men fell, while another grabbed his arm and hid behind one of the chairs; it was my favorite chair.

Was being the key word.

I didn't give a shit about destroying it as I fired at least fifty rounds into the cushions, causing stuffing to float into the air.

He finally collapsed behind it, blood trickling down his leg. "Who's next?" I turned as one of the De Lange men charged me. I fell flat on my back as his fists flew across my face.

"You!" He hit me again and again in the jaw while I smiled. "You killed seven! Seven of us! They had kids!"

I spit out more blood and nodded. "And I had a wife. Life sucks. Get in line."

"You can't kill—" Another hit to the face.

I let him, let him get out his rage, knew what it felt like to need a punching bag so damn bad. It wouldn't matter. In seconds he would be dead by my hands.

"—an entire bloodline! We know what you're going

to do, and I'll die before I let you touch my family!"

I shoved him off me as another bullet whizzed by. I fired in the direction it had come from, hitting the guy directly in the right cheek, and he floated backward against the window, shattering the glass on contact.

Huh, I thought it was double-paned?

Either it wasn't, or he was just heavy as hell.

I charged the smart-mouth and got him to the ground just as another one of the bastards tried to grab me from behind. Luckily, that was when my front door opened, and Dante made his way in, guns blazing.

I hated that the look on his face was joy.

I hated that mine matched it.

Death. Death. Death.

What the hell had I allowed him to become?

And why did I still blame myself? That I let him feed the darkness I'd been afraid of my entire life, only to let it consume me in the same way.

The rest of the bodies fell at Dante's hand; he didn't even break a sweat as he made his way around each body, checking pulses.

"So..." I grabbed my attacker by the shoulders and tossed him against the chair. "...you want to talk about fair? You want to talk about rage? Protecting your family? Where the hell were you when your boss decided to take it upon herself to go to the Russians? Where were you when she was in so deep she couldn't see worth shit? Where. The. Fuck. Were you?"

He stared me down. "If you think for one second that any one of us would have challenged your wife—"

"Dead wife."

"Dead..." His jaw shook with rage. "...wife..." He glared. "...then you didn't know her as well as you thought you did. To defy her wasn't an option. She didn't give a warning. My brother was shot in the head three times for arguing with her. He was her right-hand man. She had no loyalty. And she would stop at nothing to re-establish the De Lange line to its original glory. So we let her."

I jerked away from him, hating the words he was saying, hating the truth that dripped from each and every one.

I wanted the lie.

The lie that said she'd gotten caught.

That she'd gotten in too deep.

Not the truth that she'd never been a good leader.

Never fought fair.

"Arrogance," I croaked, "gets you killed, and betrayal... well, that just sends you to the pits of hell, doesn't it?"

His chest rose and fell as he whispered, "I'm ready to meet my maker. Are you ready for the guilt of sixty men, sixty heads of the Family, on your shoulders?"

I stared him down. He was around forty years old, with a strong jaw and dark brown eyes. He had a wedding ring on his left finger.

"Fifty-one," I whispered, holding the gun to his head. "And now... fifty."

I fired two rounds.

He crumpled at my feet.

The crunch of glass alerted me to Dante's presence. He stared down at all the bodies. "This is the second massacre that's taken place in your living room in a week, Chase."

I snorted out a laugh. "Kind of fitting that the house she had to have built would be filled with corpses."

"Death—" Dante gripped me by the shoulders then slapped my right cheek. "—is never worth laughing over. It will always be unnecessary."

"And yet, necessary," I argued. "Andrei sent them, along with a bloody hand attached to a new iPhone X."

"How was it?" he asked.

"Bloody."

"No, the iPhone, been wanting to grab one..." His voice trailed off.

I rolled my eyes. "Focus. I only used it for a few seconds. We need to get cleanup here."

"Already called it in on my way over." He lowered his voice and looked away as three SUVs pulled up. I recognized each of them. I refused to feel guilt.

The first person in the door was Trace.

Not Nixon.

She looked around the room, doing a slow circle, and then finally faced me, and in that moment, I was transported back to a time when I was babysitting her in her dorm room.

When all she wanted was an ice cream cone and to watch *Twilight* a billion times before reading her vampire novels.

Tears filled her eyes.

And for the first time in six months — I felt.

I hated her for it.

I felt the heartbeats now silenced around me.

I felt the blood on my hands.

I felt the shame in her eyes.

The guilt in mine.

The anguish in the space between us as she continued to stare as if she was searching for the old Chase, as if she was trying to find one redeemable part of my soul still existing.

But no matter how long she stared, we both knew the answer, didn't we? That man no longer existed.

The space between us felt heavy with words left unsaid.

With pain we both refused to acknowledge.

Mistakes I'd made against her.

Mistakes she'd made against me.

And I wondered again, would this have been our ending? Had Nixon not lived? Had I gotten to her first? Had she chosen me instead of him?

A solitary tear slid down her cheek, falling in slow motion to the body at her feet, and I wondered in that moment, if maybe her tears would cleanse my sins, if her kiss would do the same. If any part of her would redeem me, if maybe just in touching her, I'd feel like myself again.

I slowly made my way over to her and dropped my gun onto the ground.

She held out her hands to stop me, just as Nixon barged through the door followed by Phoenix, Sergio, Tex, and a man I'd never seen before in my entire life.

His hair was shaved short against his head, and he had enough muscles to make me wonder if Tex had already tried to beat the shit out of him just to prove he was stronger. He was at least six-foot-four and looked like the last time he'd smiled was when he'd had gas as a diapered baby.

"Vic—" Tex spat the name, and pointed. "—is here to make sure we get alerted next time you get a nice little present in the mail. He's going to be staying in the pool house and running security detail for the next few weeks. He's good at making himself invisible. You'll hardly know he's here."

I rolled my eyes. "I can handle myself."

"Ten De Lange associates were just sent to your house to assassinate you." Tex's voice shook with rage. "We could have lost you!"

"That's what this is about?" I looked around the room at my brothers' faces. "The way I see it, I'm going to die anyway, because I won't stop. You know I won't stop. I'm going to kill them all, every last one, and I know what that means if the commission says no. We all know what that fucking means."

"Don't—" Tex clenched his teeth. "—don't force my hand."

"I didn't," I whispered. "She did, by forcing mine."

Phoenix walked around each body and then did something I'd never seen him do; he covered their faces, and then he faced Tex, bracing his shoulders, and said in a clear voice, "I officially denounce the De Lange name."

The room fell silent.

I was so stunned I couldn't speak.

"Phoenix—" Nixon moved, but Sergio put his hand on his shoulder and held him back.

It was Frank who finally spoke. "That is your choice to make, and yours alone. Either way, Luca would be proud."

Phoenix checked his watch and then looked back to Tex and whispered, "Note it, in the Family records, at seven fifty-two on January fifth, the De Lange Family is officially on its own."

He walked out.

"You..." Nixon shook his head, disappointment marring his features. "...you did this."

Shame filled me as I looked around the room of men who had families, loved ones who no longer had the protection of the Nicolasis.

A mafia family broken and bruised.

In desperate need of leadership.

Who'd just lost their final hope.

The heir to the throne just denied them everything.

And I knew Phoenix hadn't just done it for me.

He'd done it because of her.

And that hurt the most.

A legacy lost — because of greed.

CHAPTER FOURTEEN

I laughed. Oh shit, he was serious? "No. I don't think there's a chance in hell Chase will ever be the same. Tell you what, you bring in that pretty wife of yours and watch me shoot her in the neck then tell me if you don't feel altered?" Idiot.

— *Notes from interview with Agent P, FBI*

Chase

THE BODIES WERE cleaned up. My house looked like a shit hole. We taped the front window as best we could, and I made a mental note to call someone in the morning.

Trace was the last one standing.

Everyone else had left, including Dante and Nixon, though Nixon had left begrudgingly, with one last threatening look my way. I might be insane, but I would never touch a hair on his wife's head.

At least that was what I told myself.

"Wine?" I asked.

"Whiskey," came Trace's quick response.

She followed me into the kitchen and waited in silence while I grabbed two small glasses and poured a generous amount in both. Then we clinked them together.

She gulped hers in one sip and slammed it down onto the granite counter. I was surprised the glass didn't shatter between her slender fingers. "When does this end?"

"When it ends." I shrugged and forced myself to lock gazes with her.

"Don't..." Tears filled her eyes. "Don't let what happened turn you into a monster, Chase."

I laughed at that. "Trace, I've always been more

monster than man. I was just too afraid to admit it, too afraid to claim it."

She looked down at her hands. "So, this is the new you, the real you?"

"This is the me you get," I finally said a few seconds later. More silence hung between us. "Not the same guy who kissed you in college and tried to steal you from his best friend. He was a weak boy—"

"Stop." She squeezed her eyes shut as fresh tears spilled over onto her cheeks. "Chase, just stop!" Her hands moved to her ears as if that would stop the truth from entering the universe.

I gripped her hands and drew her in for a hug.

She sighed against my chest as her tears stained the front of my shirt, mixing with the blood already there. "I miss you."

"No. You miss what we had. But that's been gone a long time, Trace. I think it died the day you broke my heart."

"Don't you dare—" She shoved hard against me. "—blame this on me!" She screamed, "I loved you! I LOVED YOU!"

"You loved him more," I said quietly.

She shook her head. "It's late. I need to go. I love Nixon, but I feel like I've lost my best friend. I lost him… I did that. Not you."

I frowned. "How the hell did you lose me? I was here the whole time."

She smiled sadly up at me. "No… you're really good at it though — this whole funny act, nothing bothers me, I'm Chase Abandonato, I just really love sex with Mil, we argue because the sex is so good. I saw it. I saw the toll it took on you to pretend. To pretend that things were okay, to pretend that you weren't worried about her, to pretend it didn't wreck you when you tried to help her, and she rejected you. Mil was one of my best friends, but she led separate lives. Her work life... She was another person, not the best person, and then the mask would come back on when she was back home." She shook her head. "Did you ever even love her?"

I was silent, then I poured more whiskey and wiped my mouth after I downed it. "Does it matter anymore?"

"I think so, yes."

"I loved her as much as she allowed me, and that's the truth."

It was the most I'd talked about Mil since her death. My chest ached in places I didn't think was possible for the human body to hurt.

"And if she was standing in front of me right now, I'd shoot her in the heart, so she knows what it feels like to suffer every day, knowing the one person you'd always wanted doesn't want you back — and the one you tried to give the rest of your heart to rejected it as a whole."

Trace covered her mouth with her hands.

"Go." I jerked my head to the door. "We're done here."

"Chase—"

"Go!" I roared.

She ran out of the room crying, making me feel like an ass.

And when the crying wouldn't stop, I turned to yell again, only to realize it wasn't coming from Trace, or the living room.

But the pantry.

"Shit!" I ran to the door and jerked it open just in

time to get slapped in the face.
   Twice.

CHAPTER FIFTEEN

"Your time is almost up, and I'm getting itchy, happens when I haven't killed in a few hours. Better start unfreezing my assets like you promised last year when I started this job, or you'll be sorry I walked in the building."
— *Notes from interview with Agent P, FBI*

Luciana

I DIDN'T REALIZE the shooting had stopped until I started hearing shouting in the kitchen. I held my breath for what felt like hours, as more warm tears slid down my cheeks. I didn't want to die, and yet that felt like my reality, my only option, to get shot in the head next to the pasta and Annie's Organic Fruit Snacks.

I cringed when the screaming continued.

It was a woman.

She was sobbing.

Angry.

And by the sound of it...

So was he.

Was Chase going to kill her? The way he was going to kill me?

I bit my lip until I tasted blood, and then a door slammed. I jumped to my feet and searched for something blunt to hit him with. Maybe I could make a run for it if I aimed right between his legs?

My eyes were too blurry, my concentration too shot, so when the pantry door jerked open, I did the only thing I knew how to do well.

I slapped him twice.

And fell to the ground in a screaming mess as

my hand stung like a thousand bees had taken flight directly into my palm.

Chase dropped to his knees next to me and grabbed my hand between his. I was too weak to pull away; he already had me, didn't he? I wouldn't survive the night, would I?

Maybe this whole job with Nikolai was a way for him to get rid of me.

Maybe the whole sociopath rumor was right.

And I'd done something wrong.

Something to piss him off.

So he'd sent me here as a penance.

Better someone else get their hands dirty than America's favorite Doctor McDreamy.

Disgusted, I looked away as Chase held my hand close to his face. "I think you broke your thumb. Who the hell breaks her thumb slapping someone?"

I tried to jerk away and winced in pain as something sliced through my wrist.

"Stop. Pulling. Away," he said through clenched teeth.

And then he was standing and pulling me to my feet, and once again I was getting heaved over his shoulders as if it was my new permanent spot, or maybe he just hated my germs on his floor.

I closed my eyes when I saw one body bag.

Where were the rest of them?

Not that I needed to know.

The door opened, a man with a shaved head and angry snarl heaved the bag over his shoulder and quietly clicked the door shut behind him.

"That nice man with the angry grunt is Vic," Chase said with an irritated sigh. "Think of him as the new bodyguard for the house. Nothing and no one will come through him, unless it's me of course. Apparently, he's good at blending in."

I gulped as Chase sat me on the counter and pushed himself between my knees, clearly not realizing I was ready to bite his face off if he got any closer.

"Barely sprained..." He held my hand closer to him then tilted it over. "...not broken. That's good." He gently placed it on my lap and walked over to the freezer and grabbed a pack of frozen peas and tossed it to me. "Ice up."

I'd never iced anything in my life.

And I even though I wasn't naive, I wasn't exactly used to icing bruised body parts; I was more of an observer in life, not really a participant.

He was all participant.

No observing.

We couldn't be more opposite if we tried.

I pressed the peas to my thumb and held back a cry, only to pull it off. "It's cold."

His eyebrows shot up. "Hence the frozen part."

I tried again.

Clearly making him lose patience since he sighed, marched over to me, and pressed the peas against my thumb harder than my pain tolerance was wanting to allow. "Tight, hold it tight."

I nodded.

"And tell me..." He licked his lips. Not a scratch was evident on his body that even showed he was just in a gunfight. "...why the hell did you slap me?"

"You," I found my voice. "...trapped me in a pantry while people yelled and bullets whizzed by my face!"

"Whizzed by your face?" Why did he look amused?

"YES!" I yelled. "Within an inch of my nose!"

"This nose?" He pointed to my nose and smirked.

"It's not funny!"

"You were safe." He swallowed tightly and looked away. "Anything else you need, princess, or can I go sleep off my body count?"

"B-body count?"

"All dead." He seemed pleased.

"That's horrible." I couldn't help the tears that welled in my eyes. "You killed them all? Why?"

His eyes narrowed. "Would you rather I let them get to you? In the pantry? Did you feel like a good rape tonight? Or maybe just some torture before they killed everyone you hold dear right in front of your eyes? Because I guarantee you, that's what they had planned, maybe even worse. The De Langes show no mercy." He leveled me with a cold stare. "And neither do I."

I could have sworn that when he walked out the door, he whispered, "Not anymore."

CHAPTER SIXTEEN

"Tick-tock." I grinned and put my hands behind my head. "I give you information. You give me power. That's how this works. Plus, who else is gonna kill the Italians for you? The government?" I laughed. He didn't.

— *Notes from interview with Agent P, FBI*

Chase

THE SCREAMS, ALWAYS the screams.

Always their eyes.

The last few seconds of their lives as I take their souls from this earth, begging me to change my mind when they know in the same breath, I won't.

That was the thing about human life.

You don't truly treasure it until you're about to lose it.

And you don't ever really believe you'll lose it until it's too late.

I jerked awake as the sound of a gunshot went off.

And more blood stained my hands.

It wasn't there.

Her blood.

But I felt it all the same.

Just like I felt the empty spot to the right side of my bed where I used to turn and check, at least a dozen times during the night, to make sure she was safe, to make sure she was home.

The first few months, I'd truly believed I'd found something incredible out of such sadness and horror.

And then it all fell down.

The veil.

The mask.

She'd only given me parts.

When I'd wanted it all.

I'd begged for it.

Demanded it whenever I took her body, only to have her close her eyes at the last minute, as if refusing me the most important part of her.

She'd never surrendered the way I'd wanted her to.

And yet I'd tried.

Damn it, I had fucking tried!

I threw a pillow against the wall and put on a pair of sweats. I was just reaching for the bottle of Jack I kept at my bedside when I heard the crying.

The gut-wrenching sobs that, for once, didn't come from my own throat, or my own nightmares.

I opened my door and listened.

I quietly checked every guest room I could think of.

Where the hell was she?

Finally, I made my way downstairs and into the kitchen as the sobs grew louder.

With a curse, I slowly opened the pantry door and flicked on the light.

And there she was.

My new employee.

Huddled in the corner like I'd found her earlier.

"What the hell are you doing?" I hadn't meant for it to come out so gruff and demanding, but I didn't exactly have patience in spades anymore.

"Y-you—" She choked out the word. "—said."

"I said?" I shook my head. "I said what?"

"Y-you."

She stuttered so hard I felt a pang in my gut; it was fleeting, but it was there.

"Y-you."

"Shhh." I moved to my knees, held out my hand,

and very slowly pressed it onto her right shoulder. "I got the *you* part and the *said* part. What's next?"

Her big brown eyes locked with mine. "Safe." She finally got the word out. "Safest." Big fat tears rolled down her cheeks as her body shook beneath my palm. "In house, I need..." Her lips trembled. "Safe, I need safe. I need safe." And then the words wouldn't stop coming as they flew out of her mouth over and over and over again like a broken record.

I'd looked terror in the face more times than I could count.

I'd never seen it reflected so raw in another human.

The knife in my chest twisted as she eyed my hand as if I was going to break her neck, and then she flinched away from me and tried to push herself against the wall, tried to blend in so I couldn't see her. The shaking got worse.

She was in shock.

I wasn't stupid.

I also didn't want to help her.

I had no desire to help her.

No warmth in my heart.

Nothing.

I'd done that before — rescued the girl — and she'd broken my heart. Sometimes the world didn't need a prince. Sometimes it needed a mercenary.

I was the latter.

I shut the door anyway.

Still shaking, she didn't look at me, just kept repeating "safe" over and over again.

I didn't know how to do this anymore.

How to put anyone at ease. I didn't know how to lie, how to tell her she was safe, or that everything would be okay, because I didn't believe it enough to sound convincing. My life was proof of that.

I hung my head and finally got out the only thing I knew to say. "What's your first name?"

She didn't answer right away.

"I'm Chase..." I inwardly rolled my eyes. "...Abandonato."

Yeah, dip shit, she knew that, too.

What? Was I going to confess I liked long walks on the beach and Netflix?

Next, I was probably going to say, *"Oh, and my personal vendetta is to wipe out an entire family dynasty and get myself killed. Hey, could you pass the box of pasta?"*

"I'm not..." I bit down on my lower lip. "...I'm not good at this."

A wave of shiny hair fell across her left cheek; she peeked out beneath it, and with trembling lips finally said, "Luciana."

"Of course." My smile felt bitter. Of course she'd have a pretty name like that.

"And still going with Smith?"

She started shaking again as if I'd just pulled a gun on her by way of saying her last name.

"Alright then, no more name talk." I eyed the fruit snacks next to her knees. "Luciana, do you like fruit snacks?"

I pointed.

She frowned.

"I only carry the orange box. It's the only flavor worth having. Could you grab me some?"

She eyed the fruit snacks, then me, then the fruit snacks.

Mold grew faster than this woman's thought

process. And she was supposed to help the Families? I had my doubts. Then again, she'd just witnessed a killing spree.

Leave it to Nikolai to send us someone who had no idea what the hell we were involved in.

With shaking hands, she reached for the box, gripping both sides before slowly passing it over to me. I grabbed two packs and handed her one.

She took it.

"It's not poison," I joked.

She didn't laugh.

Right, like she'd believe the man who just shot up ten people. Yeah, I really sucked at this. Bad.

No wonder everyone kept warning me not to kill her. It was an actual possibility, wasn't it?

At any given time.

I'd snap.

And she'd be on the receiving end of it.

What the hell were they thinking sending her here first?

"You're in shock." I tried again. "The sugar will help."

She held the fruit snack to her mouth and completely missed. Frustration welled up. Could she not even feed herself?

On her second miss, I scooted closer, grabbed a few of my own fruit snacks and literally shoved them into her mouth and pressed a palm over her lips. "Chew."

Her eyes flashed.

"I'm trying to help." I used the gentlest tone I had, which probably still sounded like metal grating metal, but it was all the tenderness I had left in me.

All the tenderness *she'd* allowed me to keep.

RACHEL VAN DYKEN

Her lips moved against my hand, slowly at first, and the first spark of life in my soul lit.

I jerked my hand away and clenched it into a fist, but the burn remained.

The burn of a mouth I'd never touched.

The burn of a memory I'd long ago shoved into the furthest recess of my mind.

The burn of a woman.

The sweet burn of being possessed... and possessing.

I closed my eyes then looked the other direction.

A cold hand pressed against my forearm. "Thank you."

I jerked away. "I'm not your friend."

She nodded.

I stood and held out my hand.

I was surprised when she took it.

Even more surprised when I didn't flinch away from her touch as I walked her out of the pantry and up the stairs in silence.

Her eyes took in all the rooms that lined the two different hallways.

I crossed my arms and waited. "Pick a room."

She shook her head and started backing away, but no chance in hell was I letting the guys catch wind she slept in the pantry, even if I didn't really care. I knew they'd just make my life harder with the commission — with my life's goal.

With a grunt, I hung my head and started walking toward the room farthest from mine. It was the only one that was finished, with a nice queen bed and attached bathroom suite.

It wasn't painted yet, but at least the bed had sheets,

and she had towels in the bathroom.

She walked in.

I grabbed the knob and closed the door, only to have her jerk it open and run right into me, her hands pressed against my chest, her mouth inches from mine.

She gulped as more tears filled her eyes.

I wasn't used to weak women.

Women who were afraid of everything.

The last person who'd given me a look of complete terror had been Trace, and I hadn't been man enough to deserve it then — to fix it then. There sure as hell wasn't a way I deserved to be the hero now.

I slowly peeled Luciana's body away from me. "Sleep off the shock. You'll feel better in the morning."

She shook her head no.

"You're safe," I gritted my teeth. "You can even lock your door and—"

She tried rushing past me.

"Oh no, you don't." I grabbed her by the waist and spun her around. "No pantry."

"But you said—"

"Fuck what I said!" I roared, and she flinched. Great. Just great. I tried calming my racing heart, and the way her wide eyes penetrated to the darkest places my conscience still somehow existed. "Just... sleep. Please."

She snorted. "It's too big."

"The room?"

She nodded. "I'll just grab a pillow for the pantry in case people come by again... and guns—" She gulped. "—guns g-go off and—"

"Why me?" I muttered before grabbing her hand for the second time that night, and leading her back down the hall to my room.

I slammed the door louder than usual once we were inside, stripped out of my shirt, and climbed into bed, leaving her standing there like a statue.

I closed my eyes and murmured, "Either sleep with the monster who can slay all ten dragons, or go sleep alone in the pantry where I guarantee they'll hear you shaking first."

I smirked as I heard fumbling, a few stumbles, shoes flying, and then the weight of someone climbing into bed next to me.

I froze.

It was too familiar.

Too close to home.

I squeezed my eyes shut.

Never again.

Never. Again.

She fell asleep an hour later, while I prayed to whatever God still cared for me to end my life so I wouldn't have to live in this purgatory anymore.

And when sleep finally did come, and I woke up, I did the one thing I swore I'd never do again...I turned around and looked for dark hair splayed across the pillow next to me.

And found it.

And fucking hated my treacherous body for sighing in relief.

There would be no relief.

Not anymore.

Never again.

CHAPTER SEVENTEEN

"I give you the Italians. You let me keep my shit." I held out my hand, and the dumb bastard shook it as if we were in a business deal where he wouldn't end up dead, where I wouldn't end up killing every single person in that room.
— *Notes from interview with Agent P, FBI*

Luciana

I STARTLED AWAKE and fell off the mattress and onto the floor. It was only a short drop, but it was enough to jar me conscious in a really unpleasant way.

I rubbed my elbow and sat upright.

The bed was empty.

Except for a small indent on the far left side where the killer had slept for God knew how long.

I told myself not to hyperventilate.

It was either hide in the pantry and keep getting yelled at, or sleep next to the only human in the house who knew how to use a gun. I just wasn't sure if he would rather point it at me than the men who came flying at him last night.

He'd said De Lange.

But I refused to believe it was the same last name.

This was America; millions of people had similar last names that had nothing to do with one another. My best friend from high school was from Norway, and when they migrated they changed their name from Ghjangsto to Jacobsen, because the first was too hard to pronounce for the Americans, and she had absolutely no relation to the other Jacobsens who owned a contracting company, or even that one director in Hollywood.

Coincidence.

That was all it was.

I stared at the empty space. The space of a killer, one I had voluntarily slept next to last night. I'd convinced myself I'd had no choice, that I was safer in the arms of someone who would kill me painlessly than downstairs waiting for the ones who'd rape me and make me suffer.

Not the best odds on either end.

I gulped and tried to calm my racing heart.

I just needed to finish this stupid job and move on.

I stood and stared down at the bed, at the imprint and the way he kept at least two feet of space between us, as if I was the crazy one with a gun.

As if he was using every inch of space to put invisible walls between our bodies. And I'd done the same.

I was staring at a chasm.

Separating me and him.

And for some reason, it made me stare harder.

Made me pause.

It made me wonder, what caused a man that beautiful, a man that strong, to turn into a murderer? He could walk down the street and get a modeling job by simply breathing. And he was in a crumbling mansion, on a mattress, on the floor, sleeping as far away from me as possible.

I don't know why I did it.

Months later, I'd realize.

But in that moment, the moment where he'd given me safety when I'd needed it most, I felt like I owed him something, even if he was a scary son of a bitch.

I knelt on the mattress and carefully made the bed as best I could then smoothed the pillows down and stood and surveyed my work.

"What the hell are you doing?" his voice croaked from the door. Chase was shirtless, his jeans were so low-slung it was almost indecent, and his smile didn't reach his eyes; it was mocking, not welcoming. Tattoos ran deep across his abs and into the lower part of his stomach.

I looked away. "Sorry, I was, just making the bed."

He snorted out a laugh. "Unnecessary, I'll just be in it again."

"I know." Why was I arguing? "But it's nice to get into a clean bed and—"

"Nice?" he interrupted. "Does it look like I care about nice?"

At one time. Yes, I wanted to say. Because he didn't seem like the type of guy who lived in filth, broken glass, and blood.

He reminded me of Nikolai in so many ways.

"Maybe," I whispered before I could stop myself.

"Just because I let you sleep on an inch of my mattress doesn't mean you know jack shit about me," he sneered. "Shouldn't you be working?"

"Yeah." I tucked my hair behind my ear. "I'll just be... going over... the files..."

"Great." His eyes narrowed in on the bed and then me.

I stopped breathing altogether when he eyed my no doubt disheveled hair and state of disarray. I probably looked like hell.

Chase took steps toward me until I could taste the whiskey on his breath. "Then go."

I side-stepped him and ran as fast as I could out of the room. He was the devil.

I didn't understand him.

And I hated that I wanted to.

He made me curious.

And that was a terrifying feeling to have in my situation.

CHAPTER EIGHTEEN

"Come out, come out wherever you are," I whispered as I left the room, then gave one parting middle finger to the camera.

— *Notes from interview with Agent P, FBI*

Chase

I STARED AT that damn bed longer than I should have.

Maybe because it seemed so foreign to me.

Having something done for me, rather than I doing it for someone else.

I was a creature of habit. I'd always been that way, so I'd been irritated as hell when she didn't get up at six like I always did, and then even more angered to realize that I was watching her sleep, a woman I still wasn't sure should stay living.

So, disgusted with myself, I ran downstairs and made coffee, poured a healthy dose of whiskey in mine, and managed to clean up the rest of the glass in the living room before going to kick her out of my bed.

But she was up.

And she was… fluffing the damn pillows as if she owned them!

Rage took over.

Simmering into anger.

And then, such a deep-rooted sadness that it hurt to breathe.

"I'm like your bitch." I laughed when Mil ran around the bed and grabbed her gun, strapping it to her chest and pulling her sweater over it. She looked so sexy when she was serious, which was almost all the time now that she was boss. *"Why am I doing the chores again?"*

She winked and then kissed me on the mouth. "Because...
Mama's gotta go bring home the bacon."

Normally I'd laugh, but it hit a nerve. I grabbed her
wrist and pulled her back. "You realize we have millions
upon millions of pounds of bacon, right?"

Her smile was forced as she jerked away. "You do. I don't.
My family doesn't. This is my responsibility."

"And what about us?" I challenged. "Our responsibility
to each other? What's mine is yours?"

"Not this again," she muttered.

"The hell?" Now I was pissed.

"This!" She waved her arms wide. "Chase, I'm a boss I
can't just take a—"

I felt as if I'd just been punched in the gut. "A what? A
made man's money? A cousin to the boss's money? What?
What were you going to say?"

"Nothing." She looked down. "Look, I'll be back later
tonight. I love you, okay?"

Her smile was back.

God, I hated that smile.

The one meant to make me think about sex, about how
good it was between us in bed, when I'd never felt so much
distance between us, outside the physical relationship.

"Yeah," I whispered. "Go."

And I made the bed.

Again.

I washed the blood out of her clothes.

Again.

I couldn't look at myself in the mirror.

Again.

I shoved the memory away and kicked one of the
pillows askew. I hadn't needed shit from Mil, and I
didn't need shit from Luciana.

I walked out of the room with a purpose and was quickly halted in my tracks when Luciana screamed.

I reached back and grabbed the gun from the back of my jeans and slowly made my way down the hall until I stopped at the bedroom she was in.

It was the one where I'd tried to convince her to sleep last night.

She was completely naked except for a blanket she held in front of her olive skin.

I dropped my gun to my side.

And then she pointed a shaking hand at a mouse.

Was there anything this woman wasn't scared of?

I sighed and hung my head. "You screamed because of a mouse?"

"It ran over my foot!" she yelled at me, showing spunk for the first time since she'd made her way into my house, my life.

I tilted my head. "You were trapped in a pantry for God knows how long, slept with an assassin last night, and you're screaming over... a mouse?"

"You're an assassin?" she repeated in a weak voice.

"What the hell did you think I did? Shoot people for my own personal enjoyment?"

"I-I thought that was a one-time thing... like terrorists."

I burst out laughing; it wasn't pretty sounding.

And it didn't sound the way I remembered, easy.

Her eyes narrowed. "What?"

"Finally," I mumbled. "Get angry, never get sad."

She frowned as I nodded toward the mouse. "Sadness doesn't beat the fear, princess."

The mouse moved.

She ran behind me.

I tensed when she put her hands on my biceps.

I stared straight ahead, well aware that the blanket she'd been holding was still within eyesight, which made her completely naked.

I sucked in a breath through my teeth and pointed my gun at the mouse. "Sadness gets you stuck. Fear does the exact same thing. If you're fearful, you run. If you're sad, you're paralyzed... and nobody wants that life. It's better to get angry, to charge straight ahead, guns blazing." I fired a clean shot into the mouse and turned to face her, my eyes straight ahead. "You should get dressed now."

She looked down, covered her breasts, and then closed her eyes as crimson washed over her face. I might have been dead inside, but I still had some semblance of life in me, because I wanted to look.

I didn't.

But I wanted to.

And I hated that want.

The feeling it brought.

The memories right along with it.

"Scream again over a fucking mouse, and the next gunshot goes here." I put the gun to her head and winked. "When I hear you scream next time, I'm going to assume someone's trying to kill you. Got it?"

She nodded, her eyes still clenched shut, as I walked toward the door and slammed it behind me.

Memories of her soft lips punished me the entire walk back to the kitchen for more whiskey.

CHAPTER NINETEEN

"I could justify anything. I would justify anything. I lost my soul a long time ago. I have no fucking desire to find it."
— *Ex-FBI Agent P*

Luciana

I SQUEEZED MY eyes shut as his heavy footsteps echoed down the hall. When the sound finally went away, and I knew I was safe, I opened them and slowly reached down and grabbed my blanket.

Mortified.

Terrified.

He'd just threatened to shoot me for being afraid of a mouse, which made me wonder if he realized how petrified I was of him, what would he do?

I shuddered at the thought and purposefully started to mentally prepare myself for whatever nightmare lay ahead of me for the rest of the day.

I'd finally calmed myself down.

My breathing returned to normal, and I'd managed to ignore the mouse guts in the corner of the bedroom.

The sound of something shattering against the ground had my pulse skyrocketing to an alarming level, followed by another shatter, and then a loud boom.

And then yelling.

So. Much. Yelling

Followed by silence.

Had one of the guys come back from the dead?

Or had more been sent?

I was torn between wanting to jump out the window to make my escape and doing the decent human thing and making sure Chase was still alive.

I finished getting ready and greedily searched or any sort of weapon, just in case the bad guys were back and I had to make a run for it. My eyes landed on a vase in the corner. I grabbed it with shaking hands and slowly made the dreaded trek down the hall, managing to find every freaking creak in the floorboards as I did it.

His room was empty.

I exhaled and peeked down the stairs.

Nothing.

Silence.

I took the stairs slowly, ready for someone to pop out at any time, then turned the corner and walked into the kitchen just as a shadowy figure loomed in the doorway right in front of me, backlit by sunshine streaming in from the kitchen window.

"Aghhhh!!" I just reacted, sending the vase across his face so hard it split in my hands then fell to the ground in pieces.

"Shit!" Chase stumbled into me then braced himself against the wall. "What the hell are you doing?"

"I-I thought you were one of the bad guys from last night."

He scowled. "At least you got part of it right. I am bad, but not from last night." He winced as blood trickled down the side of his head by his right ear.

Tears filled my eyes. "Are you going to kill me now?"

He didn't even blink when he whispered, "Maybe."

And then he leaned in closer. "I don't like when others make me bleed."

"It was an accident! I thought something happened to you, and then I thought—"

Was it my imagination or did his face soften a bit? Just enough for the permanent angry scowl to diminish.

More blood fell, and my guilt tripled. He wasn't nice. Not by a long shot. And he was rude.

Mean.

Angry.

But he was still a person.

And I'd grown up in a home that put human decency above all else; it was probably why I hated violence so much. I felt it was unnecessary and always bred more violence, so why encourage it? Support it?

He pressed a palm to his head and turned around. "Do your job, Luciana."

I sucked in a breath.

The way he said my name.

The way my stomach fluttered when my body had no damn business reacting to anything that murderer was doing.

Cursing, he started rummaging through one of the cabinets and jerked out a first-aid kit.

I hung my head, stepped over the broken glass, and made my way over to him, then wet one of the cloths by the sink and held it to the side of his face.

He jerked away so fast you'd think I'd shot him. "What the hell?"

"Geez, you're like the Beast from *Beauty and the Beast*. It's just a little cut."

His eyebrows shot up. "You hit me with a fucking vase."

Man had a point.

"'Tis but a flesh wound," I tried joking.

It fell completely flat.

My cheeks heated as I held the cloth out to him. He eyed it, then me, then it. "What's your game here?"

"Game?" I repeated, completely lost. "What do you mean game?"

"Four times." His eyes locked onto me with that same intense look I didn't think a person could ever get used to. "Four times I've offered to shoot you."

"Three," I corrected like an idiot who was begging to stay on his bad side.

"Huh, must have just thought it that last time."

Comforting.

I gulped as he took a step closer and then another, until he was inches from my face, until I could see the flecks of gold in his bright blue eyes and see the faint scar on his chin, the ink from a chest tattoo peeking out from his t-shirt.

"So I'll ask again, what's your game here? You don't know me. You don't like me..." His eyebrows rose a fraction of an inch.

I slowly reached across the small space between us and grabbed the wet cloth from his hand and then, very gently, placed it on the side of his head. I held it there while he stared me down with nothing but confusion and anger in his eyes. I didn't back down.

I probably should have.

Any rational human would back down, stop poking the bear, but my conscience wouldn't let me. I'd been the one to injure him; it was my job to heal him, right?

No words were said between us as I held it there; a full minute went by, then finally, he pressed his palm against the back of my hand.

I hadn't realized I was shaking until I drew back and grabbed the antiseptic. I pulled the cap off, dabbed a bit on the cotton ball, and moved his hand away.

He winced at the first contact, and part of me wondered if it was the antiseptic or my touch; both seemed to garner the same reaction from him, as if he either wasn't used to being touched or just greatly despised any sort of human contact. Maybe that was how all murderers were?

I tried not to think about it.

Or about the way his plump lips parted on a gasp when I kept rubbing the blood away.

I went for another swipe when he grabbed my wrist and whispered in a rough voice, "Enough."

I nodded, quickly stepped back, and turned around, unsure why my stomach still felt as if it was at my knees, and why my fingers buzzed with awareness of his skin.

I was almost completely out of the kitchen when he called out, "Why?"

"Why what?" I didn't turn, just waited for his response as I stared down at the hardwood floor and tried to breathe normally.

"Why help? Why clean up the blood?"

Emotion built up inside my chest until it hurt to breathe and I had no idea why, no idea why the intensity in the room had shifted, why I suddenly felt dizzy, or why his question felt heavy with deeper meaning. I looked over my shoulder and answered honestly. "When you're the one who causes the pain, you do everything in your power to make it better."

His eyes closed briefly before he clenched his jaw.

"Most people aren't like that."

I smiled sadly. "I'm not most people."

"No," he said in a gruff voice, "you're not."

I couldn't read his expression.

I took it as a compliment, even if his intent was to insult me, because I didn't want to allow his words to penetrate, to hurt. Something told me that if I let those words in, the man would follow.

And the last thing I needed in my life was an obsession with a guy who killed people for a living — and offered to do the same to me.

I gave him a curt nod and walked back down the hall toward the tiny jail cell, aka office, and shut the door quietly behind me, only leaning against it when I was able to catch my breath and analyze why the heck I was freaking out, and why my heart still felt both tight and fluttery in my chest.

CHAPTER TWENTY

"Sometimes, all the monster needs is to be awakened.
And then... fed."
— *Ex-FBI Agent P*

Chase

My pulse throbbed right along with my head. I tried not to think too much of it, tried to grasp the anger at having Luciana attack me with a vase.

Instead, it was like the old Chase was pushing through in a weak attempt, because my lips twitched.

I didn't laugh.

But something inside of me built, as if I wanted to.

As if I wanted to run after her and piss her off more, scare her, just to get a reaction that would make that feeling come back, the warmth and fullness that spread through my chest when her shaking hands lifted to my temple.

When she tried to tame the untamable.

It was stupid as shit.

And a bad mark in her favor if she thought I was anything but tame.

But she still tried, despite the bark and bite.

Despite the fear.

And my respect for her grew an inch.

Not a lot.

But enough to make me realize that maybe, just maybe, there were some good ones left in the world who didn't deserve to see all the darkness inside.

I promised myself to try.

I knew I'd fail.

But at least I was going to make an effort not to shoot her, so I counted it as progress, and then I took the stairs two at a time and heard her whistling.

Fucking. Whistling.

I finally did it.

I smiled.

And kept walking.

CHAPTER TWENTY-ONE

"I would send them all. I would keep sending them until justice was served, until he broke from the inside out, until they had no choice but to end him, and in return, end themselves."
— *Ex-FBI Agent P*

Luciana

FOUR HOURS WENT by.

Four hours of pure hell as I poured over the family records for the last two months. Right. Months. I was still in 2017 when my stomach started cramping. I adjusted my sitting position as I hovered over the computer and grabbed a protein bar out of my purse.

When the bar didn't satisfy me and another pang hit again, I shot up from my chair and checked my phone.

It was the third.

Right. On. The. Dot.

Shit.

I'd been in such a panic to get here I'd completely forgotten what time of the month it was.

I checked my watch; it was well past noon.

I got a lunch break, right?

Right?

Where I could speed into town, grab tampons, and speed back without being shot?

Anxiety washed over me.

Now I knew why I'd been more sensitive lately. Geez. Not that I wasn't still petrified, but I needed to stop tearing up in that guy's presence before he added it to the list of things that made him want to end my life.

I snatched my purse from the table and ran down the stairs, only stopping at the kitchen to see if Chase was still there.

He wasn't.

Wine was.

A glass was next to a bottle.

I hesitated.

My stomach cramped even more.

I had no idea where any Tylenol was and had nothing with me, but wine... Wine would calm me down a bit.

I poured half a glass and chugged it then made my way into the garage.

The lights flickered on the minute I walked out.

I chewed my bottom lip and tried not to pass out.

Seventeen.

I counted seventeen foreign cars.

Five motorcycles.

And a G-Wagon that looked new.

How much money did this guy have?

Was that what assassins got paid these days?

I gulped and kept walking, trying to find the least expensive car just in case. I didn't have time to look for the one he drove the most; I expected that one to be his favorite and knew the mileage would be proof of that, but I knew if I was gone longer than an hour, he'd think I'd bailed.

My eyes flickered to the black Benz that was nearest the front of the garage. It didn't have a speck of dirt on it. I opened the door and sat against the cool leather and started searching for the keys only to realize it was a push-button start.

"Please let the key-fob already be somewhere in here." I pushed down the brake and tapped the button. The car roared to life. I tapped the garage door button, and it slowly lifted.

The screen in the car said Maybach. I wasn't sure if that meant it was super expensive, and I'd just made a mistake, but I didn't have time to worry about that.

Besides, I half expected Chase to be waiting outside, gun pointed.

Instead, I encountered just empty space.

I put the car in drive and prayed.

The car jolted forward, and I was off.

The gate opened as I approached.

I stopped, grabbed my phone, and asked Siri the closest grocery store location. Relief washed through me when she announced it was only two miles away.

Perfect.

I could be in and out in minutes and grab a few more snacks on top of that.

I set my phone down, took a hard right, and out of pure fear, gunned the car until I was going around eighty down the back road.

I gripped the soft leather wheel with both hands and nearly missed the stop sign. The car swerved. I hit the accelerator after I checked both ways and floored it. "Please, please, go faster!"

The sound of sirens followed my plea.

I glanced in the rearview mirror as first dread slammed into me, and then complete panic.

I didn't even know where his registration was, his insurance. My sweaty palms carefully pulled the car over to the side of the road. I frantically searched the glovebox and came back empty.

"Shit, shit, shit." I started hyperventilating as I closed the compartment.

Tap, tap. The police officer knocked on my window. It took me a few seconds to even find the stupid button to get it down, and when I did, he looked less than pleased.

"Goin' kinda fast." He ducked his bald head into the car, making me jerk back against the console. He eyed me up and down. His black vest said *Police,* and it was bulletproof, intimidating, just like his piercing brown eyes. He sniffed the air. "You been drinking?"

It was on the tip of my tongue to confess I'd had half a glass before jumping into the car because I had cramps and was nervous about living with a potential serial killer. But I kept silent. And shook my head no.

He eyed me again, sniffed again, then leaned back. "I don't believe you."

I finally found my voice and cleared my throat. "I'm sorry, and I know you're only doing your job, I'll admit I was speeding. I just don't have the longest lunch break." If any lunch break. "And I wanted to make it back to work in time." *So I don't get a gun pointed at my head.*

His eyes narrowed. "I'm going to need you to get out of the car, miss."

My worst nightmare was coming to life. I would never drink and drive, and I wasn't the type to ever get pulled over, even when I'd lived in Seattle. My sad little Honda was still in Seattle in storage, just in case.

Maybe it was because the car I was in was expensive? Maybe because it wasn't mine?

Or because I was going eighty in a fifty-five.

Regardless.

I panicked.

"We're just going to do a few…" He licked his lips and stared at my boobs before looking away. "…easy tests."

"O-okay." I tried to keep the tremor from my voice as he fired off instructions.

"You're going to count your steps to nine, then pivot, count to nine again, and stop. You must go heel to toe — no space — do you understand?"

Now he was just being insulting. I clenched my teeth and started counting out as I walked.

I finished and stared him down, crossing my arms. Unbelievable, he still seemed pissed at me!

"Alright then." He held out his leg. "You'll stand like this and count one-one thousand, two-one thousand, until I tell you to stop."

I gritted my teeth. Would he want me to chew gum and pat my head at the same time next?

Just get it over with so you can get to the store and get back.

I got all the way to sixty-one-one thousand when he finally had me stop and then turned and said something into his walkie talkie.

I passed. I wasn't drunk. I knew it. He knew it.

"May I go now?" I asked in the sweetest voice I could conjure up.

He laughed and shook his head. "Miss, there is no chance in hell you're leaving here without getting a ticket. Not only were you speeding, but you smell like wine. Nah, I think I'm gonna take you back to the station for a blood test."

I felt my face pale as my body swayed.

He seemed to enjoy torturing people.

I normally loved cops. I did. I respected the tough job they had, but this, this wasn't just a cop doing his job; this was a bored power-trip.

And a bit of something else.

"This your car?" He nodded his head to the car.

"No." I crossed my arms. "I borrowed it."

"Stole it, you mean?"

"Please don't put words in my mouth," I said sternly.

He made a motion with his fingers for me to turn around. I tried to keep the tears in, the ones of mortification that it was that time of month, and I'd have to ask this douche bag for something once I got to the station, and tears of fear that I was going to be there forever because I had nobody that would bail me out.

I hung my head just as the metal clasped against one wrist.

And then a car sped down the road and stopped right in the middle of it.

It was red.

A red Maserati.

Something I'd only ever seen in magazines and on TV.

Chase stepped out of it and leaned against the side. "Officer Hank."

The officer dropped my hands. "Mr. Abandonato, good to see you."

"I wish…" Chase's voice dripped with hatred. "…I could say the same."

Hank paused.

I trembled.

"Sir?" Hank said to Chase. What the hell? Why did

he call Chase *sir?* "Is there something I can help you with? I just gotta get this one in the car, then I'm all yours."

"There is, Hank. There really is. Why don't you stop what you're doing first, though, so I have your full attention."

Hank dropped my hands and shoved me against the car then snickered. "Yeah well, drunk soccer moms aren't really important anyway."

I rolled my eyes and stared straight at the ground.

Chase chuckled as if he agreed.

I hated them.

Both of them.

And then Chase lunged.

I sucked in a startled breath when he gripped Hank by the neck with one hand and walked him backward toward his own police car before slamming him against it. "I'm only going to say this once." He pulled out his gun and held it to Hank's temple. "You ever mess with one of my employees again, you'll be visiting Jesus with your next breath, and you know I won't stop there. I'm a changed man, Hank. I don't just take you. I take everything that means something to you. How is your wife, Hank? Your two kids? They still getting straight *A*s in school? That first grade teacher can be a bitch sometimes..."

Hank shook beneath Chase's hand. "They're wonderful. Thank you for the Christmas card last year."

"I take care of my own. Don't I, Hank?"

"Yes, sir."

"Why thank you, Hank."

"You're welcome, sir."

"Now, Hank…" He tightened his grip. "…I hate being upset, and I'm feeling really upset right now. Care to ask why?"

"I arrested an employee. I had no idea. I would never—"

"Hank—" Chase scratched the back of his neck with the point of the gun. "—take a good hard look at the car she's driving."

Hank looked.

I gulped.

"That car cost me a hundred and sixty-five thousand dollars."

I swayed on my feet. No wonder it drove so well. Damn thing was like owning my own house.

"Now…" Chase kept talking. "…do you really think that anyone around these parts owns a car like that?"

"No, sir, I wasn't thinking. I wasn't thinking at all."

"Been drinking on the job again?"

Hank gulped.

"Uh-huh," Chase smirked. "This is what you're gonna do, Hank. You're going to walk over to the lady, apologize to her, and beg her to forgive you, or I'm going to shoot you in the kneecaps to remind you who I am. Pray she's feeling gracious, because I'm sure as hell not."

He released a sick-looking Hank, who moved toward me with a complete different attitude and then, very carefully, got on both knees and looked up at me with tear-filled eyes. "Please forgive me, ma'am. Please."

Power filled me.

Fast, swift.

I looked over his head to Chase and saw his approval, the way he nodded his head at me, basically saying that it was my call to make.

My decision.

This man's body.

His life.

I wasn't a killer, though.

I just didn't realize how addicting the feeling of power would be when given to you by someone who had it all.

"You were just doing your job," I whispered. "You're forgiven."

He exhaled and closed his eyes.

"Go away, Hank..." Chase sighed. "...and tell Janice and the kids hi."

Hank stumbled toward his car, jumped inside, and sped off so fast that I blinked and he was gone.

"Th-thank you," I whispered.

Chase made his way toward me, gun still out. Great, now the police officer was gone, and I was on an empty road with a guy who even the law ran from.

Oh, and I still needed tampons.

Could my day get any worse?

"Answer yes or no." Chase was so close to me I could taste the wine on his breath, the same I'd had earlier. "Were you running?"

"No," I said quickly.

"Yes or no." He leaned in until his lips grazed my right ear. I sucked in a breath. "Did he touch you?"

I exhaled slowly and shook my head no. "He just scared me."

"Yes or no." He stayed that way, our cheeks almost pressed together. "Should I kill him for you?"

"No," I said quickly. "He has kids."

"Everyone has something, Luciana. Kids, a dog, a job, a life — doesn't mean that people walk through life without getting punished. Some consequences are just bigger."

"No, he looked scared enough."

"Alright." Chase's breath fanned against my neck. Why did he have to be so pretty to look at? Why did I want to reach out and trace the tattoos down his neck into his shirt? "Now, why the hell were you leaving in the middle of a work day?"

"Lunch break," I said quickly.

"There's food at the house. Try again. This time, don't lie. I don't deal well with liars."

That was an understatement. My cheeks heated. This was bad, so bad. "I, um, woman's troubles, and I didn't prepare for… them. And forgot."

Could I be any less eloquent?

He jerked back like I'd slapped him and then got a funny look on his face before nodding to the car. "Get in. I'll drive."

I didn't argue.

He was the type of man a person just listened to.

And I was too exhausted to argue, to tell him it wasn't necessary, and to be honest, I was still so freaked out I could pass out at any moment, and doing so at the wheel sounded like another great way to get in trouble.

Once I buckled up, he peeled out and onto the road.

And hit a hundred miles an hour right past another cop who waved at him like it was totally normal.

I shook my head and whispered under my breath, "Who are you?"

"The devil," he replied. "Welcome to my hell."

CHAPTER TWENTY-TWO

"Everyone has darkness — I'm the master at wielding it."
— *Ex-FBI Agent P*

Chase

I DON'T THINK I could've been more shocked if I'd tried — and I wasn't a man who was easily surprised. I'd immediately assumed she was running to the cops, not getting harassed by one.

Every man in that police station owed me a favor.

And I respected each and every one of them — except Hank. Hank was the one officer I had the most trouble with, questioning everything, and not knowing when to shut up when he was told to.

Not that I was going to tell Luciana, but that was his third strike, meaning there would be a follow-up, and while I wouldn't kill him, there would be blood as a reminder of who he was.

Of who I was.

King.

I might not be boss, even though it was my birthright, but I had the city of Chicago at my fingertips. That was how Nixon had wanted it — let him lead in the background, let me do the smooth talking.

It worked.

Until I forgot the smooth part.

Now I talked with my gun.

Which only got us more friends.

Less enemies.

But at the cost of every human part of me that still

remained.

Lost in my thoughts, I didn't even realize we were at the grocery store until Luciana started unbuckling her seatbelt.

I followed her into the familiar store.

The same one that Mil used to frequent when we needed groceries or when I needed her to grab something for dinner.

Luciana paused and started reading the signs for the aisles.

I checked my Rolex and sighed then made my way to Aisle Two and increased my pace before standing in front of so many pink and purple boxes I wanted to shoot every last one and then torch them for good measure.

I grabbed a tampon multi-pack and the pack next to it then held them up to her. "We done now?"

Luciana's face couldn't physically get any redder if she tried. It was endearing, that look, and the way it snaked around my insides making me lose my breath for a second.

She nodded without looking at me.

"Luciana," I called, "you promise this is all you needed?"

She chewed her lower lip causing the red to fade to a pale white as she bit down harder and harder. "No."

Honesty, huh? Imagine that from a woman. "Okay, so what else do you need?"

"Tylenol, protein bars." Didn't see that coming.

"Let's go." I jerked my head toward Aisle Eight and after that, Aisle One, and then made my way to the front of the store before dumping everything onto the belt.

"Mr. Abandonato." The cashier cleared his throat.

"Ricky." My curt response.

Luciana was silent as he rung her up; when she reached into her giant black purse, I stopped her just as she pulled out a shiny purple billfold that looked like it had seen better days.

"I've got this."

"You aren't paying for my—"

I stared her down.

"—tampons," she finished with a blush and hoarse cough.

"Apparently..." I swiped my Amex smoothly through the card reader. "...I am."

"Did you need your receipt, Mr. Abandonato?" I hadn't looked away from Luciana; I found her too fascinating. The way she blushed over something so insignificant was astounding to me.

And then she lifted her head and said, "Thank you, Chase."

Her thank you was like an arrow sailing through my body. I physically flinched, not because I was offended, but because it had been so long since I'd heard a thank you for anything.

"Don't you like it?" I was giddy with excitement. The Maybach had been on a pre-order for six months before it was finally delivered for Mil's birthday. "It's black like your soul," I winked.

She just stared at the car and then back at me. "Chase, I don't know what to say."

"Say you'll get naked in the back seat. They recline." I pushed a button.

Her smile didn't reach her eyes as she put a hand on mine. "It's too much... I can't drive around in a car like this when the rest of the Family is struggling as much as they are."

A sick feeling built in my stomach. "Mil, they know we're married. They won't give a shit, and if they say anything, I'll just kill them."

She laughed at that.

She always did when it came to life or death.

"Alright," she said in a small voice.

But no thank you.

She drove it once.

And died six months later.

"Mr. Abandonato?" Ricky called. "I was sorry to hear about your wife."

Luciana's eyes bulged.

Ah, taken down by a cashier at Fred's.

Too bad I actually liked Ricky.

"Don't be," I said, putting on my sunglasses. "I'm not."

I drove in angry silence the entire way back to my car, didn't even say goodbye as I jumped out of the Maybach, Mil's car, and left Luciana on the side of the road.

"Thank you." Her words echoed.

Bullshit.

All women wanted was my face, my body, or my money. They didn't want me. I knew that now.

I knew what to expect.

Expect them to fall in love with the idea of me.

But the real Chase?

Never fucking enough.

Never. Again.

CHAPTER TWENTY-THREE

"Your only job is to kill or be killed. Have fun."
— *Ex-FBI Agent P*

Luciana

By the time I got back to my prison, there was no sign of Chase. The garage door was open, so I quickly drove in, cut the engine, grabbed my bag, and made my way into the kitchen, only to see him sitting there drinking.

Again.

I walked past him.

Or attempted to.

When his arm snaked around me. "Next time you leave without telling me, I'm putting a bullet through your hand, so every time you text, you think of me."

"That won't be necessary," I said quickly. "I-I'll text."

He shoved my hand away and gulped. "Good."

Would it always be like this? Hot and cold? Strategically placed eggshells scattered all over the house like grenades, just waiting to go off with one misstep?

I squeezed my eyes shut and started to walk but then stopped. It wasn't just curiosity, it was more like I was trying to find something — anything that would show me he was human, that he cared. I mean, murderers don't just buy tampons for an employee, do they?

Maybe his humanity was all gone for the day.

He'd used it up after walking down that aisle.

But he'd walked down it as if he was familiar.

He bought the tampons as if he had no shame.

The word *wife* burned across my line of vision until I finally just blurted out. "What happened to her?"

Aka did you kill her like you're going to kill me?

The room fell into a sick heaviness that had me ready to claw at my neck for air as the sound of him standing and then walking over to me slammed into my ears.

He didn't touch me, but I felt him, the thickness of his body, the heat of his breath as it fanned against the back of my neck. "I didn't kill her."

"I didn't ask that."

His laugh was humorless. "You didn't have to."

I shivered as he pressed a hand onto my right shoulder.

"Someone beat me to it."

That was all he said before walking past me and leaving me alone in the kitchen ready to hyperventilate into the nearest paper sack.

I clutched the grocery bag in my hand and steadied my breathing then made my way back up the stairs to my office.

I didn't see him the rest of the day.

CHAPTER TWENTY-FOUR

"You find the weakness. You tap in to it, you call to it, beckon it, make it believe that you're its opposite — strength. Then you rip it away. You steal. You leave them more broken than before."
— *Ex-FBI Agent P*

Phoenix

I DIDN'T SLEEP.

Correction, I hadn't been sleeping, unless Bee held me, unless I could see my son a few dozen times a night and know he was breathing. I woke up at least three times an hour just to check on him.

I always brought my gun.

I was always ready to kill.

And I hated that I had so much weakness in my soul, my blood.

I made my way into Nixon's house and sighed when Frank sat down the newspaper and stared right through me.

"So." Frank reached for his coffee. His silver hair was combed back, his jaw clean-shaven, a scarf wrapped around his neck into a knot, and the guy was wearing a suit.

Always a fucking suit with this one.

"So." I pulled out a chair and sat my ass down in it then put my Glock on the table, one of five that were on me, and leaned back. "Good morning?"

He shrugged. "You realize what this will mean?"

I looked to my left, out the window, the same window I'd looked out when I was a kid, when my dad would beat me into submission and expect me to do the same to all the young girls he sold on the black market. I used to look out that very window and wish for a better life, one where I didn't taste fear on my tongue every day, one where I didn't crave the evil that crept through my veins just begging to be set free.

I was not a good man.

Never had been.

Never would be.

But I held on to the truth that somehow, my mentor, Luca, had seen something in me worth keeping, and because of that, I would die to my old self.

I owed it to my family.

I owed it to Chase.

I owed it to Mil.

My son.

My brothers.

I tapped my tatted knuckles against the wood table. "I know what it means to cut ties from my birthright and take on the Nicolasi name."

Frank wiped his hands over his face, aging before my very eyes. "The commission, they will have to do the break. There will be a blooding."

I nodded. I knew what it meant for the five Families.

It would cut us down to four.

"Cut out the poison," I whispered. "Kill one to save them all."

Frank's blue eyes pierced through mine like a knife. "This will only encourage the commission to allow Chase to attack the De Lange bloodline. This will end in more death than we've seen in a hundred years, Phoenix. Your chess piece could destroy us all."

I stood. "You're wrong."

His eyebrows shot up.

"You forget," I smirked. "I know everything there

is to know about the Families, about our enemies, our friends. My fucking chess piece is the only hail Mary we have. It's our only hope to bring life back to the dead."

"We aren't talking about the De Lange dynasty anymore, are we, Phoenix?" he said wisely.

I grabbed my Glock. "No. We're talking about what it's like to be a man broken from the inside out, with no hope of finding his soul again. We're talking about giving him something to live for, to fight for—"

"The way Luca did for you," Frank finished thoughtfully.

I gave him a jerky nod. "Her blood stains my hands — I get to live with that — but her betrayal? It fucking stole his soul."

Frank let out a long breath before taking a sip of coffee, standing, and offering his hand. "You have my blessing, son."

"Thank you." I squeezed his hand back.

He gripped tighter. "Not that you needed it. We all pretend to have a leash around you, but I know the truth. Men like you cannot be controlled, only placated."

I snorted out a laugh. "You're getting so wise in your old age."

He waved me off with a smile. "I'll tell the others. Nixon won't be happy."

"Nixon can kiss my ass." I shrugged.

"Morning, Phoenix." Nixon walked into the room with low-slung jeans and a white t-shirt. "Why am I kissing your ass?"

"Ah, I'll let Gramps fill you in."

Frank scowled at me.

The door slammed as I left the house and sucked in the cool morning air between my teeth. It was the first time in a hundred or so days I felt like myself.

The first time I had hope beyond the weekend.

The first time, I knew, I was returning the favor given to me.

And I could have sworn I smelled cigar smoke swirl around me in that moment, following me like a warm cloud the entire walk to my car.

CHAPTER TWENTY-FIVE

"Hit him where it hurts the most — his heart, and if his heart is no longer there, you hit him in the second worse spot. His head."
— *Ex-FBI Agent P*

Trace

I T HAD BEEN three days since I'd seen Chase.

It was slowly killing me.

Maybe that was why I was driving to his house again.

Without telling my husband.

Guilt gnawed at me so harshly that it was getting harder to breathe the closer I got to the iron gates.

I was a fixer, yes.

But this was more; it went deeper.

I kept having nightmares that one day I'd visit Chase and I'd be too late; he'd be on the ground, a bullet to the head, or worse, hanging from the stairway with a rope around his neck.

The nightmares wouldn't stop, and every time I woke up Nixon, he didn't have anything calming to say, nothing that made me feel like he wasn't freaked out about the very same thing.

The only difference? He was boss.

He had more on his plate than the fact that his brother and best friend was having a hard time. I only knew because he shared his burdens with me.

We still had no idea where Andrei had gone and had quickly gotten word that all of his assets had miraculously been unfrozen.

Which was impossible.

And yet? Shipments for Petrov Industries started going out last Friday.

Drugs and weapons mainly.

It was driving Nixon crazy that we had a very calculating enemy out there, who knew everything there was to know about us, thanks to Mil.

It kept him up at night.

So while he was concerned for Chase...

He was more concerned for our little girl, more for me. The fact that Mo was pregnant — would probably send him over the edge.

Things changed when you brought in innocent lives.

They had to.

I pulled up the long driveway, cut the engine, and then made the short distance trek to the front door, not bothering to knock. Knowing Chase, he was probably stewing in his office or in the kitchen drinking.

His two favorite pastimes.

"Chase?" I called, making my way through the living room and into the kitchen.

He was perched up on the barstool with a bottle of wine in front of him.

No glass.

Great, he was just drinking from the bottle.

"How drunk are you?" I asked, making my way around the granite island.

He shrugged.

"Ah, so drunk you forgot how to speak?"

He scowled and reached for the bottle. "Brave of you to come back."

"The only thing that scares me is the fact that you haven't had a shower in five days."

"Bullshit!" He stumbled to his feet, swaying in front of me. The man was cut like a freaking brick. Every sinewy muscle was on display beneath his dark t-shirt. I looked away. His gaze was too intense, his meaning clear. "I showered this morning…" He frowned. "…I think."

"Right." I licked my lips. "Have you eaten?"

His brows furrowed.

I inhaled deeply. "Okay, only alcohol, no food, got it. Why don't you sit back down, and I'll make you a sandwich."

"Why don't you get back in your car, and I won't call Nixon and tell him his wife's entertaining second prize?"

I slammed the fridge door shut. "Does it make you feel better?"

"What?" His grin was sloppy drunk, stupid. At least he was grinning. "Mocking myself? Yes, it does."

"Mocking me." I slammed a hand onto the counter, and he jumped. "Mocking our friendship, what we had—"

"We were never friends, Trace," he interrupted. "Friends don't kiss friends. That's not how friendship works, trust me. Otherwise, I would have been friends with fifty girls in college…" His voice trailed off. "No, I don't kiss friends. Apparently, I only kiss girls that belong to someone else and ones who betray me. Fucking awesome track record, huh?" He lifted the bottle to his lips again.

I stomped over to him and jerked it out of his hands. He stumbled against me, his hands going to my hip.

Sadness swept through my body, making it hard to breathe as his pain-filled gaze dropped to my lips.

I couldn't give him what he wanted, what he thought he wanted, what he thought would make the pain go away. It would just make it worse.

I knew that.

He leaned down, his forehead touching mine. "Please leave."

I shook my head.

"Leave," he said again. This time, his voice cracked; torment rolled off him in waves.

I gripped his biceps, righting myself as he leaned down and brushed a kiss to my cheek.

"Leave."

I sucked in a breath. "Who's going to take care of you?"

"That—" came my husband's voice, "—isn't your fucking problem, is it?"

I jerked away so fast I knocked over the wine bottle, spilling it into the sink, as a drunken Chase collapsed against the barstool and stumbled to the floor.

Nixon's anger was so palpable that the air was thick with it.

I gritted my teeth. "I was trying to help. I know your hands are full with Petrov—"

"Just like your hands are full with my cousin?"

I don't remember moving.

But I did.

I slapped him so hard across the cheek my palm stung.

And then I gasped with tears in my vision as Nixon closed his eyes and then grabbed my hand and placed it where I'd slapped him. "I deserved that."

"No..." I felt like complete shit. "...you didn't."

"You," Nixon whispered, "I trust."

"And Chase?"

"Complicated," Nixon finally said, his blue eyes locking on Chase as he lay still against the hardwood floor. "I'll get him upstairs. Why don't you look around for his new employee, make sure she knows he's passed out. I'm not letting you play nurse."

I rolled my eyes. "So the new girl gets the honors?"

Nixon's mouth curved into a smile. "Remember when that was your title? New girl?"

I stood up on my tiptoes and kissed the corner of his mouth. "Remember when I mooed in front of the entire student body, and Phoenix drugged me, and you pushed me away into that one's arms?" I jerked my head to Chase. "Or how about the time that—"

He covered my mouth with his and kissed me hard then pulled back. "Okay, you made your point. We all have shit."

"We're a freaking reality show, Nixon," I sighed. "And Chase is clearly the producer's pick, the one who stirs up trouble to get ratings," I said, making light of the situation so I wouldn't crumple against my husband's chest.

Nixon kissed the top of my head. "It will get better. I promise."

They were the words I needed to hear. "How do you know, though?"

He pressed a finger to my lips. I parted them, tasting his skin. "I have to believe that we've been brought to this point, not to just collapse from within, but to grow, to become greater than before. The legacy our parents left behind was one of complete brokenness. I think we deserve to give our children something more, don't you? I think the universe owes us at least that."

I nodded silently.

"Come on," Nixon sighed. "I'll heave him up to his room. Damn guy still weighs a ton, even with a diet of wine and whiskey."

I made a face while Nixon knelt and grabbed Chase's body.

"Go grab Luciana and fill her in."

I saluted him and made my way up the stairs.

CHAPTER TWENTY-SIX

"Money talks. And so do the dead, just not in the way you think."
— *Ex-FBI Agent P*

Luciana

I RUBBED MY eyes.

Then stared at the number again.

Payroll and finances for the last year couldn't be right.

Could they?

I stared at the tax forms and investments then stared down the rest of the numbers; nothing financially made sense.

There were fifty different companies, all owned by a Chase Abandonato Winter, and every single one of them had money circulating through each other.

Money laundering wasn't a new concept, but the way he did it was... fascinating.

And the way he paid to get it done...

Unheard of.

He was able to clean his own money because he owned banks, not just small branches, but one of the biggest banks in the United States.

I frowned harder.

If the numbers were correct and not a typo, the guy had pulled in almost two billion last year, and paid out close to nineteen million to people in his different companies, mainly his bank, and a few people named associates.

Associates?

Like business associates?

My fuzzy brain tried to put everything together, but the stomach cramps, mixed with my exhausted eyes and the fact that I was staring at more money than I'd ever seen in my life, had me a bit thrown off.

I wasn't stupid. People who shot people, or were attacked like he was, didn't just get paid blood money. Either he was Jason Bourne, or they were part of a crime organization that apparently even the government turned a blind eye to, if the whole scenario with the cop was anything to go off.

My chest felt heavy.

I pressed a hand against it and jumped out of my seat when a knock sounded on the door.

It opened.

Trace, the woman from before, the one who did nothing but aggravate Chase more, the one who seemed to deny him everything, was standing in the doorway and, for some reason, I felt anger.

And an unholy protection over the man who'd kept me from getting wrongly arrested, from the man who was more foe than friend.

But so broken that if I didn't defend him...

Who would?

Who?

I glared.

She seemed taken aback, and then her pretty, deep brown eyes narrowed into tiny slits. "Do we have a problem here?"

I licked my lips. "No, just working."

She crossed her arms and looked around the room.

I knew what she saw, tons of folders open, papers scattered. It was chaos, but everything had its place, and only I knew the way.

"Nixon sent me," she said, just as Nixon walked by with Chase hanging over his back. "We need to add another fun job to your description."

Great, just great. The last thing I needed was to be next to the guy for an extended period of time. I didn't trust him.

And if I were being completely honest, I didn't trust myself.

I clearly had some major Stockholm Syndrome going on if I felt any ounce of protectiveness over the guy, but there it was.

My stomach sank when his head fell over Nixon's shoulder in a deathly sleep, his face pale.

I tried to move past Trace, but she held her arm out, blocking my path. "If you hurt him…"

The threat was there.

And rather than scare me…

It just pissed me off. "Look…" I clenched my teeth. "…I don't know who you are, but from what I've seen so far, I'm not really that impressed."

"You don't know the hell that guy's been through," she hissed, her head ducking toward mine.

"I know that seeing *you*," I whispered harshly, refusing to back down, "isn't making it better."

She jerked as though I'd just slapped her, and tears filled her large eyes, threatening to spill over any second.

Nixon's voice interrupted our exchange. "She's right."

Trace's face fell more as a tear streaked down her

right cheek. "I can't lose him, too."

"Too?" I asked, looking between the both of them.

"She was my friend, too," Trace admitted, staring down at the ground. "Guess you don't really know who your real friends are until their loyalty is tested, huh?"

I had no clue what she was talking about.

Nixon just sighed and pulled her into his embrace, studying me over the top of her head. "Make sure he doesn't suffocate from his own vomit, and if he wakes up screaming, try singing."

"Singing?" I repeated dumbly. "How's that going to help?"

Nixon, for the first time since I'd met him, looked ashamed as he kissed the top of Trace's head and whispered, "His mom used to sing."

"Okay." *Used to* being the key phrase.

Because she was no longer here? Or because she was out of the picture?

They both turned.

I clenched my hand into a fist and called after them, "What are you?"

"Vampires," Trace called back with a completely straight face, about the same time Nixon said, "Zombies."

They shared a smile.

I huffed in annoyance.

"Follow the trail, Luciana," Nixon finally said, not so helpfully, and they made their way back down the stairs, leaving me with the devil himself.

CHAPTER TWENTY-SEVEN

"Inaction is sometimes the greatest action one can choose."
— *Ex-FBI Agent P*

Chase

"I LOVE YOU," I whispered into her hair, ducking my head against her neck, only to find a speck of blood. I retreated. "Mil?"

She sighed and wrapped her arms around my neck, then sucked my lower lip. "Make me forget."

"That I can do," I said in a hollow voice. It's what I'd been doing for the past six months.

Making her forget.

When all I really wanted was for her to remember all the reasons we were good for each other, and all the reasons to fight for what we had. In a world full of ugly, sometimes all you had were the broken pieces of love to cling to. But if you ignore them too long...

I shuddered.

And she let out a moan as I gripped her ass.

I loved sex as much as the next guy.

What I didn't love?

Was a one-sided relationship where she gave me her body.

And I gave her my everything.

I tossed and turned as the memory faded to black, as blood started dripping from my hands, her emotionless eyes looking up at me, gone.

She was gone.

Gone. Gone. Gone.

I squeezed my eyes shut and wrapped my arms

around my body, if I held on tight enough it wouldn't hurt so bad, if I could just squeeze out the pain. If I could just find peace.

From anything.

Suddenly a small voice filled the room. It was pretty, soft, the melody made my breathing all but pause, and then there were hands on my face. They matched the softness of the voice. I wasn't used to soft.

I was used to harsh realities.

Darkness.

Being used.

Tossed aside.

The big joke.

Ignored.

But this, this touch, it felt... more like giving than taking.

I didn't understand that concept.

The one where I wasn't the one always emotionally empty, physically exhausted, mentally on edge.

I clung to the wrists that belonged to those hands as my thumbs caressed the soft skin beneath her fingertips and on the backs of her knuckles. And when she sang a little louder, I gripped a little bit tighter, as the nightmare faded into the darkness. I squeezed my eyes so tight I saw flecks of light.

Maybe I was finally dead.

Maybe she was an angel.

But for the first time in years, I wanted to be the taker, the one who stole all the light, all the good and kept it for himself, for just one second.

Maybe I'd have peace.

Maybe she'd let me, this angel.

So I pulled her closer to my chest and inhaled the air

around her neck, and when it wasn't enough, I tugged that hair, wrapping it around my right hand, exposing the softness near her collarbone, and pressed my face against the warmth.

A heartbeat.

Steady.

And the song that fell from her lips.

About a man finding love where it was once lost, right in front of him, I'd heard it before, one of those sappy romantic love songs that made me scowl.

But when a woman sang it.

It sounded perfect.

Like it could happen.

I didn't realize a tear had fallen from my face as wetness hit me on the chin, and then I realized.

I wasn't the one crying.

My angel was.

CHAPTER TWENTY-EIGHT

"We mobilize after the commission… when they are at their weakest."
— *Ex-FBI Agent P*

Luciana

I DIDN'T SLEEP a wink.

He was heavier than he looked, if that was even possible, and every few minutes he'd stir and say, "Emiliana."

I wanted to believe it was his mother's name.

But I knew that was foolish.

It was her.

His dead wife.

It had to be.

I didn't want to ask, but so many questions burned in my brain; if he missed her so much, why did he say he wished he could have killed her?

I didn't know.

Maybe I didn't want to know, considering he was this torn up about her and still wished her dead? It didn't really bode well for letting his personal feelings get between him and his murdering jobs.

I shuddered just as he clutched my wrists tighter and moved to his back, pulling me on top of his body so I was straddling him.

At least I was in pajamas. I'd been too afraid to leave him alone, so I'd grabbed one of his old t-shirts and a pair of Nike sweats and tossed them on before singing him back to sleep.

The only time he looked peaceful was when I was singing.

I sang until I was hoarse.

And then tried singing some more.

When I finally lost my voice, I started rubbing his face and down the sides of his sharp jawline. A person could cut steel with a jaw like that. He had such perfectly sharp features it was intimidating to stare straight at him, almost like my eyes couldn't take in everything at once and needed a time out.

I stilled across his chest when he shook his head and then opened his eyes.

I was on top of my employer.

With his clothes on.

In his bedroom.

Straddling his body.

I was so going to get fired.

"You." He jerked up then winced as he placed a hand to his temples.

I quickly reached for the water on the nightstand, along with the medicine, and held it out to him.

With a curse, he grabbed it out of my hands and swallowed both pills dry before chugging the entire glass and setting it back down on the stand.

This was not good.

His blue eyes were crisp.

Angry.

I seriously could do nothing right with this guy.

And I was still stupidly straddling him because I was afraid to move.

"Choose your next words carefully..." he rasped.

Damn him, he had no right to sound sexy after

being hung over and passing out last night. He didn't even smell! It was bordering on ridiculous, inhuman. Of course, vampires made sense now.

"Did you sing to me last night?"

I wish I was a better liar. Then again, lying didn't necessarily mean he'd let me live. I hung my head and gave him a slow nod.

"How long?"

"What?" I whispered nervously.

"How long," he repeated, "did you sing?"

I self-consciously pressed my hand to my throat. "Whenever you needed it the most." All night. Words left unsaid.

"So the angel sang the devil to sleep..." he whispered, closing his eyes. "...at the risk of her own damnation."

Was he still drunk?

I frowned, tempted to feel his forehead for any sign of a fever.

"Luc." It sounded like Luke; I wasn't sure I liked it. "I'm going to need you to get off of me before I take it as an invitation."

I scurried away so fast I took every blanket with me.

Of course he would be naked.

Of course.

That was just the kind of luck I had.

He didn't seem to mind, just laid there with his eyes at half-mast, a smirk crossing his harsh features, and a body straight out of Mt Olympus.

"You're staring," he pointed out.

I looked away and pressed a hand to my face. "Sorry, I just— I'll just go get back to work then."

I jerkily walked toward the door, only to have his hand reach out and gently grasp my wrist. "Thank you."

I was so shocked my jaw nearly came unhinged from my face. "For what?"

He dropped my arm, turned away, and whispered, "For the peace."

"Anytime," I said over the golf ball lodged in my throat.

"Luc?" He turned to me, eyes sad. "I won't hold you to that... Better not to make promises you can't keep."

There was more to it than that, more meaning, something deeper. I opened my mouth to pry, but he was already turning his body completely away from me, as if he was putting that invisible barrier back up between us.

CHAPTER TWENTY-NINE

"Predators stalk their prey. The good ones are patient for hours, days, months. I have been patient for years."
— *Ex-FBI Agent P*

Chase

THE SOUND OF my text messaging going off woke me up from another dreamless sleep, one where I felt music surround me, rocking me off to sleep.

I gripped my phone and stared down.

> **Nixon:** You alive?

My head throbbed. I remembered Trace coming over, leaning in, oh shit, I groaned into my hands and then fired off a quick text.

> **Me:** No bullet holes, and it's not like you to miss.
> **Nixon:** I didn't.

I checked my body for blood, not one of my prouder moments, and came back empty.

> **Me:** So you poisoned me?
> **Nixon:** The thought crossed my mind at least a dozen times when I grabbed that glass of water — but I decided it would be too painless.
> **Me:** So does that mean torture is on the menu?

He added Tex to the conversation, then Sergio, Frank, Phoenix, and, of course, Vic. Apparently the guy was getting closer to everyone though I barely saw him on my own property.

> **Tex:** Catch me up. Who poisoned who?
>
> **Me:** I'm alive.
>
> **Tex:** I'm suddenly disappointed...
>
> **Phoenix:** Nixon should have killed you.

I growled and gripped my phone in my hand so tight my fingers turned white.

> **Me:** I was drunk.

Dante's name popped in on the chat.

> **Dante:** You're always drunk.

It stung.

The entire conversation stung.

And lately I hadn't given a shit, so why did it matter now? Was it because I actually got a decent night's sleep without nightmares? Is that what sleep did to a person? Make them more human? Or was it the single tear from the most deserving to the least of them all?

She'd cried.

I remembered that much.

And I wasn't threatening her.

Which meant something was making her sad.

And all fingers pointed at me.

Me.

I was making her cry.

Or they were tears of pity.

And for once I didn't actually care, because pity

was, first and foremost, grown out of a deep-rooted longing to care for another human, and I couldn't ignore the fact that one tear was more emotion than I'd been given in a very long time.

Too long.

The anger built up again. Against her, against myself, against the situation that I tried to control, tried to make better, only to end up losing myself so completely that I'd become obsessed.

I didn't want to apologize.

I wanted to fight.

I wanted to yell, shoot.

Instead, I replied.

> **Me:** Nixon, you're well within your right to end me, alcohol or no alcohol.
>
> **Sergio:** Guys, CNN just said Hell froze over. Think Chase had anything to do with that?
>
> **Me:** MIDDLE FINGER EMOJI, YOU ASS HAT!
>
> **Tex:** There's an actual emoji for that, you dumb fuck.
>
> **Me:** Not a big enough finger... Not a big enough anything, if you get my meaning.

Hell, was I joking? Seriously? Maybe I should sleep more often...

> **Dante:** Funny because last time I heard you say...
>
> **Nixon:** Shhh, Dante, let the grown-ups talk.

Dante sent an actual middle finger emoji, making me smile at my phone for just a second .

Me: Why are we all on a group text?

Nixon started typing.

I waited, my nerves already overtaxed from having a woman spread across me not five minutes ago. If I was being honest, I'd admit that my body still felt hot to the touch, that the hair on my arms stood on end, still, at the sight of her in my clothes.

I shut that shit down immediately.

She might as well be Delilah to my Samson.

All women were.

> **Nixon:** The commission is set for a week from tomorrow. The Families are flying in from Sicily. They will also be performing the bloodletting ceremony in order to strip Phoenix from the De Lange line.

Stunned, I just stared down at my phone.

Nobody said anything.

So I typed with shaking fingers, just seeing the name made me see murder and blood.

> **Me:** Why?

Phoenix was quick to answer.

> **Phoenix:** Because you're my brother. And my sister is dead to me.

I closed my eyes as anxiety slammed into my chest.

He started typing again.

> **Phoenix:** Because when I was the worst of them

all — when I hurt Trace — when I hurt my brothers, myself, countless women, people — when I was covered in so much shit I didn't even want to live, someone gave me a purpose, a reason to drop the knife I held next to my own throat. A reason. Don't prove me wrong.

I tried to swallow the ball of emotion in my throat, but it refused to go down. None of the guys said anything.

I very slowly typed out my response.

Me: Thank you.

Frank typed next.

Frank: This only changes Phoenix's bloodline. What you do with that, with the rest of the De Langes, will still be voted on.

Me: Understood.

Nixon: Think you can stop killing people for a bit?

Me: No promises.

Dante: Good thing he doesn't have a hamster.

Me: Jackass.

But I was smiling.
Down at my phone.
As if I was looking at a naked picture.
I quickly frowned.
Mil had loved to tease me like that.
At first, I'd adored it.
And then it just felt — fake. As if I was being used because of how much I wanted her, how much I wanted

to please her.

Men were fools.

All of us.

Driven by desire while getting slowly bled dry.

I tossed my phone onto the bed and managed to stand without wanting to take a jackhammer to my head to remove the pain.

I stared down at the three empty bottles of Jack littering my floor and shook my head. One thing was for certain; the alcohol was hindering my sleep.

Which left only one more option if I had any hope of resting and being at my best before I took every single one of those bastards down.

I peeked my head out the door.

My angel.

And a fucking truce.

CHAPTER THIRTY

"Patience, patience, burn from within. I watched them without them knowing and found great pleasure in moving my first piece."
— *Ex-FBI Agent P*

Luciana

"THANK YOU." CHASE'S voice jolted me out of my intense stare-down with the Final Will and Testament of Emiliana De Lange.

I immediately tensed and slid the folder underneath the pile and turned.

"For what?" I asked, trying to sound casual when my heart was thudding so fast against my chest I was sure he could both see and hear it.

Our eyes met.

He looked... different.

Dangerous still.

Naturally too sexy for words.

And clean.

I narrowed my eyes.

"Do I pass inspection?" He was smiling.

Why was he smiling?

Was this a trick?

I grabbed the closet thing I could find, which just so happened to be a pen, and held it out in front of me, pointed at him.

His eyebrows arched. "Either you're a better fighter than I am, or you really think a pen's going to keep me away."

"Don't." I held it between us. "Just, say what you need to say, and then…" I gulped. "…go away."

He crossed his arms and stopped walking. "I just came to say thank you, that's all."

I lowered my arm. "For what?"

His eyes drank me in. "The first sleep I've had in six months."

My chest tightened as I looked away. "I'm sure that was the alcohol."

"Nah, that was the singing."

Heat flooded my face, and I knew I was blushing, embarrassed that I'd literally sung a murderer to sleep for a solid six hours while trying not to fall asleep on his hard chest. It was both the best and worst night of my life.

The best because I genuinely felt like I was singing the demons away.

The worst because I figured he wouldn't remember, and he'd just wake up as haunted as before, never changed, never free, and for some reason, it mattered.

It really mattered to me.

I didn't know what to say so I stared down at the ground. Best not to look into his crystal blue eyes; they made me feel things, nice things, not angry things, and with how hot and cold he was, I knew I needed to keep my walls up.

"I wanted to thank you with something else." He moved again.

Oh no. Hell no.

I lifted the pen and shook my head slowly. "All done and thanked! You can go now, I should, should, um…" Could I be any less eloquent? "…get back to the grind." Oh, God, what was next? Punching his shoulder and calling him slugger?

His grin only widened.

He. Was. Epically beautiful.

Men weren't supposed to look like him in real life, with light eyes, dark, perfect olive skin, strong jawlines, hair I wanted to dig my hands into, and a body just made for magazine covers.

"Grind, huh?" He pressed his lips together. "Alright, well, I guess I'll just eat by myself then…" He started backing away just as my treacherous stomach grumbled. He grinned back at me. "Hiding a T-Rex in here, or are you hungry?"

I covered my face with my hands. "I didn't eat breakfast."

"Well then…" He made a motion with his hand. "Follow me."

"Chase…" I gulped. "…you don't have to, really. I know you… I know you don't like me… or people for that matter."

"Today I'm making an exception," was all he said before leaving me to decide my own fate.

Ugh. I was starving.

With a little mental slap in the face, I followed him out of the room and down the stairs in silence.

The kitchen smelled like rich pasta and homemade bread.

He must have a personal chef or something.

And then he went over and started stirring sauce on the stove. I frowned so hard my vision blurred. He moved to pull bread out of the oven, and I immediately wondered if I was on a hidden camera show, the ones where they ask you what you would do if someone murdered a dozen people in front of you, and then asked if you want to break bread.

Obviously, I was the dumb one in the situation.

I was still living with him!

I slapped my hand against my face and gave myself a hard shake as I walked over to the stove. It smelled like spaghetti with a heavy dose of basil, and I sniffed again.

Chase froze next to me as I dipped my finger into the sauce and licked it.

Completely out of habit.

I winced. "I'm so sorry. I just, I used to do the cooking and I just, I'm so sorry I won't touch anything else, I swear. Your house, your kitchen, your food, your—"

He slapped a hand over my mouth and then pulled it back and pressed a finger to my lips. "You talk too much when you're nervous. Talking usually gets you killed." His lips twitched. "But since this is a thank-you day, I'll give you a free pass."

I exhaled.

"Holy shit, I was kidding." He shook his head. "Go ahead, take another taste."

Still breathing heavily, I dipped my finger deeper and then sucked it off.

He jerked his head away like the motion offended him.

It needed more salt. I didn't tell him that though. You don't tell the man with the gun that his cooking could use more salt. No, you just strategically find it on the counter. Bingo. Grab it, and then tap some out.

He turned on my last shake of the sea salt.

I froze.

He stared at my hand, the one I was probably going

to lose after dumping salt into his sauce.

Because that was what they did to kitchen criminals like me who sent steak back when it was overdone or, God forbid, asked for ketchup!

"I, uh…" I had nothing. Absolutely nothing. "…didn't get much sleep last night…" Even as I said it, I wanted to gag myself and then jump off a cliff. That was my excuse for the salt?

"Ohhhhh…" Chase crossed his arms. "…so this is a thing, you sleepwalking your way to work and then just picking up salt and shaking it all over the place?"

"Sure?" I tried.

"Lie," he whispered, and then he dipped his finger into the sauce and licked it so slowly my heart fluttered at least a dozen times before he was finished. "Huh, needs more salt."

My hand was still hovering. He tapped the back of it a few times causing more salt to come out before very gently guiding me away from the stove and toward the table.

What had just happened?

A glass of wine had been poured for me.

One for him.

We sat next to one another as he served me, and when he lifted his glass, I numbly lifted mine and clinked it against his before taking a giant gulp.

"So, you cook?"

"Two years of culinary school," I said proudly. "Before law school, I never really knew what I wanted to…" My voice trailed off as he stared at me like I was a naked unicorn.

He took another gulp of his wine.

Then another, still staring me down and then finally

he got out, "You. Cook?"

"Yeah." Didn't we just have this conversation?

He put his glass down; his hands were shaking.

Why were they shaking?

I'd done something wrong again. I just didn't know what.

"Look, if you could just tell me the rules, then I'll know better next time."

A frown furrowed his forehead. "Rules?"

"So you don't get angry with me," I said stupidly, feeling like a kid.

"The problem," he said in a quiet voice, "is not that I have rules, because even if I did, you would have already broken every single one. It's in your nature. You can't help it, just like you couldn't help the salt. Rules won't save you. They never do. All you have is this..." He tapped my chest with a finger. "...and this." He cupped my face then caressed my temple. "Two things to get you through life. Fuck the rules."

Okaaay.

"And I'm only angry ninety percent of the time."

"And the other ten?" I just had to poke him.

He grabbed his fork and started digging in. "I'm sunshine and rainbows." He sighed. "Would you believe me if I told you I used to be the funny one?"

"No," I said, probably too quickly.

He looked bitterly down at his plate. "Yeah, that makes two of us."

I didn't move.

"Eat, Luc. It's not poisoned, just a truce."

"A truce?"

"An 'I'm sorry for being such a dick to you.' And when you're done eating, I have a mutually benefiting proposition..."

"Let's hear it."

"Eat first."

"I'm too nervous now."

He leaned back and crossed his arms. "Sing the devil to sleep... and I'll help you with your work so you can get your ass out of here and onto the next Family."

"Tame the beast, and I get extra help?" I toyed with the idea. "And you promise not to... threaten me anymore?"

"I promise..." He gulped. "...that I'll try. It maybe habitual at this point in my life."

I rolled my eyes. "You're in your twenties. Nothing's habitual yet."

"When you start killing at twelve, it sure as hell is."

It was my turn to start choking.

"So, what do you say?" He leaned in, his forearms bracing against the marble table. "I help you. You help me?"

I was quiet.

"And maybe the more I sleep the nicer I'll be... you never know. We could become... friends."

I stared over at his clear blue eyes and said the first honest thing that came to mind. "You and I will never be friends. Don't insult confession time with a lie."

He looked stunned, and then his face completely transformed, as if he respected my truth more than the terrified lie.

"Cooks and calls my bluff..." He lifted his wine glass. "Happy Friday."

CHAPTER THIRTY-ONE

"And so it begins."
— *Ex-FBI Agent P*

Chase

I'D WORKED ALONGSIDE her for a full week, answering more questions than I'd ever answered in my entire life, and still, she never asked what we did.

It was Monday. My body ached from being on my hands and knees going through old family records like it was actual fun, but she needed to see everything, to know everything, to freaking file everything.

"What's this?" She pulled out my black folder.

I jerked it out of her hands. "Nothing you want to read, trust me."

"But it has your name on it?"

"Right." She was wearing red lipstick. Why was she wearing red lipstick? I shook my head. "Which means I know everything inside it. It's not relevant."

She finally relented when she found my birth certificate.

Seriously? How much shit was in these old filing cabinets that Phoenix had dropped off? It was like he wanted my suffering to know no end.

I jerked the paper away from her. "Also irrelevant since it doesn't matter anymore."

"Your father?"

Ha! I made a mental note to shoot Phoenix in the toe later. "Not much of a father, trust me."

"Was he cruel?"

"Cruel?" I repeated incredulously. "He wasn't even my real father. He groomed me as second-in-command to a dynasty I was supposed to fucking lead, and when it came time to lead it, I said no, I stepped down, and I wonder, every day, if she'd still be here if I'd had taken my position as her equal."

I stopped talking.

What the hell kind of air was I breathing?

Truth serum?

I quickly jumped to my feet, needing an escape. "I'm going to go into town. Did you want to take a break and go with me?"

Luc stood and straightened her white blouse; I looked away when a part of her bra showed through, and she retouched the front and pulled on her long cardigan. Everything about her was the opposite of Mil.

Every. Damn. Thing.

Mil wouldn't have been caught dead in a sweater.

It was leather.

Gucci.

Prada.

Everything that told people she had power, and she'd wield it however she wanted.

And then there was Luc in a cream sweater and a Burberry headband.

I almost laughed.

Almost.

She was the type of woman who went to PTA meetings and wanted seven children. The kind I could see wanting to start a family right away so she could get started on all those fun art projects with fingerpaints.

A familiar ache filled me.

I shut it the hell down.

"So?" I asked in a gruff voice, needing to leave more than my next breath.

"Sure, let me just get my purse."

"No need." I was already leading her out of the room. "Whenever you're with me, your money's no good anyway."

"But—"

"It's in your job description. Trust me."

She was silent as we got into the car and drove into town, past the marketplace we'd visited earlier, and toward the Whole Foods close by.

It used to be rare for me to be out without security.

And now it just felt normal.

I'd like to see someone try to attack me. On my worst day, I could end them with a simple snap of my fingers.

I shook off the uneasy feeling creeping along my skin as I touched the small of her back and led her into the store.

She grabbed a grocery cart as if it was normal to go shopping with me, and then, very strategically, wiped it down with an anti-bacterial wipe.

I watched in complete shock and amusement as she even cleaned the buckle for the invisible child that would be sitting there.

"It clean now?" I mused at least three minutes later.

She made a face, her tawny brown eyes focused in on the cart as she lifted her chin in a challenging look. "It's always good to be safe."

"Safe." I snorted, walking next to her. "Safe isn't real. You know that, right? It's just what we tell people so they feel better about their shitty lives and actions.

You will never truly be safe. You're already dying."

"Wow…" She patted me on the arm. "…you should have been a life coach."

"Are you…" I stopped walking. "…teasing me?"

She stuck out her tongue. "I do have a sense of humor. I just choose not to demonstrate it with the man who has a gun."

"How very… safe of you." I grinned.

She rolled her eyes, but she was smiling, and again, so was I. It felt good, to smile more than once a day, to talk with someone who wanted nothing from me, who looked at me like I was basically one second away from hurting her but trusted me anyway.

I didn't know that kind of trust.

Wasn't even sure if it really existed.

And yet she gave it to me day in and day out, without reservation.

It made no sense whatsoever.

And the more I thought about it, the more confused I became.

"Is it okay if we get grapes, or is that going to offend your delicate sensibilities?"

I stared after her. "Get the color right, and we'll see."

She scrunched up her nose. "Who eats green grapes?"

"Good answer." It was my turn to pat her on the arm. She was making it too easy to talk with her, too easy to exist when I'd been doing nothing but living in hell.

She made me feel like I could breathe without feeling angry, guilty, bitter. But it only lasted so long before it crept back, reaching down into the deepest parts of me, demanding to be set free.

"Are you... okay?" She reached out.

I jerked back, like an ass. "Yeah." I gave my head a shake. "I'll take the cart and meet you back here in a few minutes."

I needed to get away.

It wasn't real.

She was a paid employee and petrified of me.

That was why she was a nice person. She literally had no other option. God, I was stupid.

I weaved my way down the aisle aimlessly, grabbing cereal and a few other things that interested me.

I was about five aisles away from produce when I felt it.

My body went on high alert as I jerked around.

Empty.

Nobody was watching; nobody was following.

I discarded the cart and reached into the back of my jeans for my Glock, slowly making my way down the aisles, pointing, looking, pointing, looking.

And then I heard it.

"Where the fuck is he?" a man's gruff voice called out.

And then crying.

Sobbing, actually.

"I-I don't know who you're talking about!" Luc cried.

I rounded the corner. A man was holding her at gunpoint next to the grapes. Bad idea, such a bad idea. I almost felt sorry for him, and then I locked eyes with her and nodded.

"Look at me!" he demanded. "You have five seconds to change your tune before I shoot you in the head."

More tears fell.

And he started counting.

"One. Two. Three…"

She stilled.

Her eyes closed.

"Four. Five."

He didn't shoot.

I knew he wouldn't, but she didn't.

He needed information.

And he'd torture her, before killing her for it.

I very slowly walked up behind him and knocked him in the back of the head. He fell to the ground with a grunt. I sighed and grabbed him by the ankles and pulled him into the nearest employee entrance.

Luc followed me in stunned silence.

Once we rounded the corner, and there was nobody in sight, I pulled him into one of the large freezers.

"Keep the door semi-open, Luc." I didn't look at her, couldn't focus on anything other than ending this guy's life without anyone hearing the gunshots.

I fired two rounds into his chest; head would be too messy, and I didn't want blood everywhere.

I quickly covered him with some blood from the meat, and then tossed the meat around him so it looked like he stumbled in there and either froze to death, or was drunk.

I didn't necessarily need to stage the scene, but I had been told to stop killing until the commission, and my guys knew that I didn't care about cleaning up my own shit, so if they got wind of this, they'd wrongly assume it was another dispute, not me.

I refused to chance it.

My right to kill them all.

I grabbed Luc's trembling hand and shut the freezer door behind us then started pulling her back toward the main employee door, only it flew open the minute I reached for it.

I turned Luc in my arms and slammed my mouth against hers. She jerked in response as I kissed down her neck. "Help me out here."

She clung to me, wrapping her arms around my neck as she slowly parted her lips. Her body was cold, like she was seconds away from passing out, but her mouth? Red hot.

I had never planned on kissing another woman again.

Plans changed.

I just didn't know my reaction would be so swift.

So violently unreal that I was the one having trouble selling the kiss because I wasn't used to being kissed in that way.

With hopeless fucking abandon.

As if it was a goodbye.

She tasted like cherries, her tongue smooth against mine, not dominant, just subtle as if she was taking her time exploring every inch of my mouth, taking the opportunity and running with it.

So I let her. I braced her against the wall and moaned when she dug her fingers into my hair and grabbed hold.

"Um, sorry, sir. Sir!" A young guy tapped my shoulder. "You guys can't be back here."

Tap, tap, tap. Where the hell was my gun again? *Tap, tap, tap.*

I finally pulled back only to see Luc's lips a swollen red, her headband askew, and her chest rising and falling so hard you'd think I'd just challenged her to a race.

"Got it," I said hoarsely. "Sorry, we just... got carried away."

"Newlyweds?" He said the absolute wrong thing I needed to hear in that moment.

I completely shut down and muttered, "Something like that."

I didn't reach for her hand.

I didn't comfort her. Even though her skin was pale, her lips bruised, her entire demeanor shaking with fear.

I didn't have anything left but confession and a hell of a lot of anger that her one kiss...

One innocent kiss...

Had undone me so completely.

That I almost hated her more than I loved the kiss.

Hate was easier for me.

Resentment came second.

I resented it all.

The way she responded.

And the way my heart finally soared to life after taking a direct hit so many months ago.

I hated that, for the first time since letting go of Trace, embracing my life with Mil, my soul decided to jumpstart and point out the obvious.

That Mil would always love herself more than she loved me.

And that I had allowed it.

Because I'd been so desperate for love.

Not real. Not real. Not real.

I was silent the entire way home.

CHAPTER THIRTY-TWO

"It's easy to bait a monster. All you need is to gain their attention. Their loyalty follows once you feed the beast. Easy. So. Damn. Easy."
— *Ex-FBI Agent P*

Luciana

IT WAS NEARLY impossible not to touch my mouth after that kiss — but I managed it. His lips were hot to the touch, his skin rough like he'd skipped a day shaving, and his mouth... It was almost enough to distract me from puking over the sight of him shooting that man; the only reason I wasn't freaking out was because I was happy to be alive. I'd literally thought he was going to kill me before Chase swept in and then, it just happened so fast I was still trying to convince myself it wasn't real.

But that kiss?

Had made it real.

All of it.

I crossed my arms and held myself as he pulled into the driveway of the mansion.

His mouth had tasted like the best mistake of my life.

The minute our tongues touched, I knew it was a kiss I would never forget, a kiss I'd compare every other kiss to until I finally admitted there would never be anything like it again.

Nor anything better.

Damn it, of course the guy with all the money and

too many guns kissed like he knew my mouth better than I did. I shivered again as Chase killed the engine.

Wordlessly, he got out of the car and slammed the door.

I wasn't sure what I had done wrong, just that something had pissed him off, whether it was my lack of kissing experience, the fact he actually had to touch me, the body in the freezer, or all of the above. I had no clue.

I just knew I was partially at fault.

Or at least he would see it that way.

With a huff, I silently got out of the car and followed him inside, half expecting more alcohol to be set out on the counter, only to find a glass full of water and him staring into it like it was going to tell him his future.

"I'm sorry," I blurted.

He flinched and then looked up at me with hooded eyes. "For?"

I moved from one foot to the other and said in a small voice, "For getting grapes."

There, that sounded good.

After all, the grapes started everything, right?

He gave his head a shake. "Unbelievable."

I held out my hands in front of me. "Next time you can just go by yourself. I'll be more careful about my surroundings and—"

"Shut up. Please." He slammed a fist onto the granite and then braced his massive body against it.

I jolted.

"I'm not pissed about the grapes, and since we're confessing, I'm not even really pissed about the body, just add it to the rest of the ones I've buried in my back yard."

My eyes widened.

"Shit, I was joking," Chase said quickly. "It's not you…"

"But it is…" I nodded. "It's okay. I just wanted you to know that whatever I did, I won't do it again."

"How do you know not to do it again if you don't even know what you did?"

He had me there. I chewed my lower lip.

"Do me a favor?" He approached slowly.

"Okay." I dropped my arms and waited while he braced my shoulders and lowered his face.

"Don't pry."

Not what I expected.

"You mean…" My eyes narrowed. "Don't pry when it comes to—"

"Me," he finished. "Don't ask me questions that you know I probably don't want to answer. I'll keep helping you with your work, just… anything personal is off-limits, got it?"

I wracked my brain trying to think of what I could have possibly asked that was too personal and came up with nothing.

We'd been kissing.

And then the guy asked if we were…

Understanding dawned.

Chase could see it. I knew he could because he suddenly looked away and walked out of the room as if someone was chasing him.

"Got it," I whispered under my breath. "Don't ask about her."

"Ever," came his loud voice as he poked his head around the corner. "Are we doing this or not?"

He still wasn't smiling, but at least he didn't look

miserable anymore.

"Sure thing." I nodded and checked the time on the microwave. "Are you free to work for a few more hours?"

"Well..." Chase sighed. "...that depends. Anyone attacking us?" He looked around; the house was deathly silent. "That would be a no, so yeah, got a few hours I can spare."

"You're kind of a smartass," I mused, following him out of the kitchen.

He was quiet and then laughed like it was a secret joke. "You have no idea, Luc. No idea."

CHAPTER THIRTY-THREE

"Tick. Tock."
— *Ex-FBI Agent P*

Chase

I COULDN'T GET the word out of my head.

Or the feeling in my chest when that punk kid had said it.

Newlyweds.

It brought too many memories.

So many memories.

Of her walking down the aisle toward me, Luca holding her arm, her bawling in the bathroom, and me holding her hand. I'd sworn I'd protect her with my gun, with my blood, I'd sworn I'd give all I had to give, all that was left.

The anger boiled beneath my skin, filling my lungs, making me dizzy the more I thought about it, and then Luc had to go and steal it right out of my body by apologizing for grapes.

Grapes, for shit's sake.

Grapes.

Fucking. Grapes.

I was too stunned to respond right away, and then seeing her stern expression as if she truly believed that if she just acted a certain way, did certain things, watched her surroundings, she would be safe from the world. Safe from me.

It was the biggest lie of all, the fact that she sought me for safety, when I was the one with the gun.

With the anger.

With all the reasons and justifications to end lives.

And yet she was trying to placate me.

Trying to calm me.

As if she could sense that the rage was so out of control I was having trouble not breaking the glass in front of me.

I shoved the word out of my consciousness and continued pulling files from the last few court cases that we'd settled. I handed them over.

She looked down. "Were any of these settled in court?"

I fought to keep my expression blank. "Why would we settle in court when we can settle outside of court?"

"But…" She kept reading. "…if you've never really been to court, why is it so important you have a young lawyer?"

"Youth." I shrugged. "Our guy was getting too old. The job hadn't been much of a challenge anyway, not when you have as much money as we — I — do."

"We?"

The five Families.

Mafia.

The bad guys.

Criminals.

But I went with "Gardeners."

Her eyes narrowed. "Don't bullshit me."

"Did you just say…" I leaned forward and whispered. "…shit?"

"Bullshit. There's a difference, and gardeners don't get paid billions of dollars."

"Sure they do. It's all right here in the fine print." I pointed to the stack of papers. "I mean, I don't just garden. I've got a few banks, schools, universities…"

Her eyes widened. "Is this the deed to Eagle Elite University?"

"Possibly." I shrugged. "I thought Nixon had it."

"You can't just own a university."

"Can't you, though?" I winked, feeling marginally better that she was focusing on the rest of the information and not my past, my black folder, or any of the wills in the corner that were currently burning a hole in my retina.

Every time I looked over at the wills, I started sweating.

I knew what mine said.

I knew what *hers* said.

I swallowed and walked over to the box. It haunted me, that box, the contents.

The white horse lay down on top of the papers. I picked it up.

"What's that?" Luc called over her shoulder.

"This," I held it out. "…is what betrayal looks like. Think of it as a certain swift death. You ever see this outside of your office, know that I'm minutes away from shooting you. Know that you need to run as fast as you can, and pray to God I don't catch you." My voice shook as I sat it back down on the top folder, Mil's Last Will and Testament, and turned.

Luc was completely pale.

"What?" I said gruffly.

"I'm sorry."

"Wow, two sorrys in one hour…" I rolled my eyes and started walking toward the door; I needed another break.

"I mean them both."

"Yeah?" I called over my shoulder. "And what's this sorry about? Your heavy breathing?"

Her answer was swift. "For whatever haunts you. I'm sorry."

"It's not your burden."

"Something tells me it shouldn't be yours either."

The anger was back.

I wanted to lash out, to yell at her to mind her own fucking business, but the damn doorbell rang. With a grunt, I shoved away from the door and ran down the stairs just in time for it to open wide, revealing Dante and El.

"What the—"

They walked right past me. "Sorry we're late."

"For?" What the hell? More cars pulled down my driveway, and I groaned. "What the hell, D?"

"You don't look drunk." He slapped me on the back and then ran his hands over his buzzed head. Damn guy looked so much like Luca it was scary. It also made the guys want to rough him up a bit, me included; he was too damn pretty. No guy should look that pretty.

El didn't seem to mind.

Something clanged in my kitchen.

Dante winced. "I'll just go make sure she doesn't burn anything down."

"This house doesn't burn easily, trust me," I grumbled.

"Tear." Dante used his middle finger against his cheek. "Poor sad billionaire can't burn down his own mansion with his anger, and even matches don't work. Alright Bruce Wayne, I'll just be in the kitchen."

I glared.

Little shit.

Within ten minutes, everyone, wives included, were all seated around the table.

Vic made an appearance from the back yard, making me wonder just how long he'd been doing perimeter checks, and why it bothered me that I never even knew he was around.

He grunted his words rather than speaking them, and he was like two of Tex mashed together.

I sat at the head of the table, Tex at the other end.

The wives scattered in between.

But no kids.

"Since when did Family dinner night turn into date night?" I asked aloud. I'd put Luc next to me for protective reasons only. I didn't want the guys asking her questions, and the wives were even worse. God save us all from Italian families with the questions and food and questions and food.

I refused to look at Trace.

And she refused to look at me.

Nixon was staring down at his plate as if it was speaking to him.

And Phoenix was drinking wine as if it was water.

He wasn't a drinker.

Then again, neither was I until I lost my shit.

"Since we all had kids," Nixon finally answered. "And speaking of kids?" He cleared his throat and nodded to Tex.

Tex had a mouthful of pasta and grimaced. "What?"

"Anything you want to tell me?"

Mo stilled.

Finally, the attention was away from me and on someone else.

I still hadn't touched my food.

Trace and Mo had brought it so I didn't have to cook; it was as if they knew that cooking for all of them only brought pain.

So why the hell was I able to do it for Luc?

I tried not to think about it.

Tex coughed a few times and then elbowed Mo who elbowed him back.

"They're pregnant," Bee blurted, then covered her mouth with her hands. "Sorry, it's the wine."

Phoenix wrapped an arm around her and pulled her close, whispering into her ear, causing her face to flush.

God, even the worst of us could still get a woman and make her blush.

Why did I get the rat?

The one who betrayed this.

These people.

My blood.

I stood.

Tex leveled me with a glare.

I sat back down.

Not because I couldn't go head-to-head with him, but because I couldn't leave Luc to the wolves.

"How far along?" Sergio asked.

I rolled my eyes. "You would ask that."

"Bite me," he snapped.

"Mature." I lifted my wine glass to him while he flipped me off.

Dante put his gun on the table and pointed it toward Sergio who just burst out laughing like *"Yeah, I'd like to see you try."*

Don't get me wrong, I wasn't even sure D had a conscience anymore, but Sergio had age and experience over the guy, plus, he knew what it was like to live with demons.

Sergio and I had more in common than I wanted to admit.

Both of us had lost our wives.

His had been taken.

Mine had made a choice.

The wine went sour in my stomach.

"Fifteen weeks." Mo grinned at Nixon. "And stop looking so grumpy. Don't you want to be an uncle?"

Nixon tossed back the rest of his wine. "Yes, but that means you touched her!"

He pointed at Tex, who gave him an incredulous look. "You've heard us having sex and this? This is what bothers you?"

Phoenix covered Bee's ears.

While Dante suddenly choked on his wine, and El patted his back.

Trace grinned at them then locked eyes with me over the table.

Shi-i-it.

I owed her an apology about as much as she owed me one.

"Excuse me." She stood and dropped her napkin on the table, then approached me.

Everyone fell silent.

Our drama was real.

Our past was shitty.

I exhaled and stood, but not before Luc touched my thigh and squeezed.

I almost knocked over my wine.

She had no reason to be nice to me.

No reason to care.

And yet there it was.

A thigh squeeze.

I wanted to direct the hate I felt toward her; I wanted her to feel the pain that constantly thrummed in my chest, but you can't hate someone wearing a headband. You just can't.

I did a double-take when I saw her grab the small pearl necklace from beneath her white blouse.

Fuck me, did she have nylons on, too?

I didn't have time to look without everyone wondering why I was staring her down, so I followed Trace down the hall and out the door.

I shut it quietly behind me.

It was bitter cold outside.

Neither of us was wearing a jacket.

It made me just as numb on the outside as I felt on the inside, this feeling, the cold seeping into my bones; it was an everyday thing for me. Torn between feeling something and then nothing. Not caring, just existing.

"You were always on my side," Trace whispered.

I flexed my fingers, shoved them into my pockets, and listened.

"Even when Nixon was a complete jackass to me, even when the rest of the guys were asses, when the world was against me, you weren't." She wiped at her cheeks. "I've always loved you."

Hell, not this again.

I almost went back in the house.

"But not in the way you deserved, Chase. And I know you know that. You're not stupid."

I hung my head as the past rejection came back, stinging me in the ass. It had nothing to do with her being right, I just hated the reminder it brought.

"I saw the way you looked at her and thought... this, this is how it was always supposed to be, and I think, for a few brief moments, you thought the same. Everything finally made sense."

"And then it didn't," I answered for her.

She nodded. "And then it didn't. And then I watched someone I love just... lose his light."

"Bullshit. I've never had a light."

"Like the freaking sun, Chase."

"Cute." I rolled my eyes.

"My point is this..." Trace turned to me. "I feel responsible for you the way you felt responsible for me a few years ago, because when you had Mil..."

I flinched at the name.

"...I wrongly assumed you were fine. I turned a blind eye. I justified not asking if things were okay, and I refuse to be the shitty friend again, the shitty person who says they love you but never asks you the hard question."

"Oh yeah, and what's that?"

"Was it anything other than sex? Was there a soul connection? Because what I feel for Nixon, it's in my soul. What I feel for you, well, that's just my heart telling me that you're one of the best people I've ever known, and if the woman you're with can't see that, then she deserves to die."

"A bit bloodthirsty, Trace."

"Mafia changes people." That was her answer?

Warmth spread around me as I stared at her, really stared at her, I wasn't attracted to her anymore, not in that way, but I did love her, I loved her so fucking much it was ridiculous.

But she was right.

She'd always been right about the way we felt for each other.

Kissing her had felt like... cheating on my best friend, and if I was being completely honest, cheating on the woman who would one day own me the way Nixon owned her.

Sadness came then.

Anger followed closely after.

"Trace..." I clenched my teeth. "...I'm not..." God how did I even say this? "If I don't get approval from the commission—"

"Don't say it," she snapped as tears filled her eyes.

I pulled her in for a hug. "They'll have no choice." I grit my teeth against the cold. "I'd make the same one if I was in their position. Just make sure Nixon gives me a clean shot. Suffering sucks. I've been doing it for the last six months."

"Chase!" She beat at my chest with her hands.

I held her close.

She hit me harder.

I clutched her tighter as she burst into angry tears. "You can't just stand there and tell me that you're going to give up!"

"I'm not giving up," I whispered hoarsely. "I'm just being honest with you, maybe for the first time in my life. I swore an oath I mean to see through however I can, and nobody, not even a girl from Wyoming who took down the great Nixon Abandonato, is going to stop me."

She wiped her tears and shoved me one last time. "I didn't take him down."

"You own his heart and his dick. Be honest, Trace."

She shoved me again, this time more playful.

"Promise me one thing." Her big eyes filled with more tears.

I nodded.

"Just think about what you're really gaining by all of this and what exactly..." She opened the door as laughter hit me in the ears and chest. "...you'll be losing."

"I've already lost it all," I whispered.

More laughter trickled from in the house, feminine laughter. "Hmm, doesn't sound like it, does it?"

She patted me on the chest and walked back into the kitchen, leaving me leaning against the door wondering what the hell had just happened and why I actually felt better, rather than worse.

CHAPTER THIRTY-FOUR

"There's nothing better than when plans finally come to fruition. Send someone else. It's time."
— *Ex-FBI Agent P*

Chase

"She's wearing a headband," Dante said between bites of cake. "You saw it, right?"

"And pearls," I added as I watched her laugh with the girls. I narrowed my eyes as she tugged at the necklace again. She hadn't been wearing it before dinner. Had she put it on so she would look nice? Why the hell did I care?

"You're staring again," Dante mused.

I rolled my eyes. "Just trying to figure her out."

"Ah, so he's curious?"

"No, he's just..." I grit my teeth. "I don't need to explain myself to you. Say one more thing, and you're going to end up missing a tooth."

He shrugged. "Wouldn't be the first time."

"Or the last," I grumbled.

"You seem... different," he said a few seconds later, just as Tex and Sergio approached arguing, because that was just how they lived their day-to-day lives.

I shrugged.

Tex jerked his head toward Luc. "You guys catch the pearls on that girl?"

I groaned.

Sergio crossed his arms. "Nikolai says she's the best."

My body froze as a bit of trepidation ran down my

spine. I'd forgotten about that part. "Nikolai Blazik." I said his name out loud, wondering why it bothered me that he'd sent her.

Sergio snorted. "She graduated with honors and has been working as a junior associate for the last two years, stays late, arrives early, has literally no life, not even a cat."

"Parents?" I asked, curiously.

"Adopted. They may as well be her grandparents."

"Hmmm." I frowned. "Is her last name really Smith?"

Sergio gave me a pointed look.

"Yeah, that's what I thought."

"But we can trust her?" Dante piped up as Nixon and Frank approached with a bottle of wine.

"Nikolai is very... specific." Sergio took the wine from Nixon. "If she had dirt on her, I'd know it, and I'm guessing she'd have at least a dozen guns pointed at her head."

I changed the subject. "I told her we're gardeners."

Sergio spit out his wine while D burst out laughing.

Frank grimaced. "Perhaps you should tell her what we really do."

"Hey, she saw me shoot people. I joked that I was a paid assassin. Why correct her? Plus, I want her to figure it out all on her own. We'll see how good she is or how smart she is when she broaches the subject."

Tex sighed. "Just don't shoot her, okay? She's actually nice."

I made a face. "It's been at least two days since I've threatened her life."

Phoenix started a slow clap, while the guys grumbled to themselves.

I stared across at her again; she met my gaze, her fingers teasing the pearls. I licked my lips and stared at her red mouth. Her and that damn red lipstick.

I refused to think about the kiss.

It had been necessary.

Completely necessary.

No other way.

Right?

My body was dead anyway.

If I couldn't even conjure up a little sexual enthusiasm out of a kiss, then I really was like *The Walking Dead*. But I couldn't blame my dick for not wanting to jump on board with another woman who held my heart in one hand and a knife in the other.

CHAPTER THIRTY-FIVE

"First I end him, then I end them all."
— *Ex-FBI Agent P*

Luciana

I PLACED MY mom's pearls, the only thing that was left with me at the orphanage, into the box and hid it away in my suitcase. Maybe it was stupid, but whenever I was nervous, I wore them and told myself that they were magic.

It had been my only solace through foster care.

But because they were real, I always had to keep them hidden.

And for the most part, I never wore them, just touched them when I would cry myself to sleep and dream about a different life with parents who loved me, a big house, maybe even a dog.

A loving family.

A smile.

I squeezed my eyes shut.

My adoptive parents said there was no background information on my biological parents; it was as if they'd never even existed.

Maybe it was better that way. It just fueled the fantasy I had about them being royalty, or rich, or maybe just alive and waiting for me.

I stripped out of my skirt and blouse and carefully hung them up in the large, empty closet, then grabbed a pair of pajama bottoms and a tank top.

Time to sing.

I knocked on his door twice before he rasped for me to come in.

I'd been singing to him for two nights.

And both nights he'd fallen asleep within minutes, as if my voice was magic, which I knew was the furthest thing from the truth; it was passably pretty, but I wasn't going to be getting any record deals anytime soon.

"Hey." I inwardly groaned. Could I be any more awkward with him? During the day I at least had something to do with my hands. I was working myself to the bone, but at night? At night my thoughts were scattered. "You ready?"

Chase walked around the corner, the fireplace was on, the bath water running on the other side in the bathroom. I'd never really seen his room with the lights on.

It wasn't small by any means, but it didn't seem like a master bedroom, even with the walk-in bathroom.

He had a towel wrapped around his waist, giving me an insane view of his abs and all the ink taking over his skin.

"Hey." Chase typed something out on his phone as if it was normal for him to walk around half-naked in front of all his employees. "I ran the bath for you."

I tilted my head at him. "I'm sorry?"

"Bath. You." He pointed at me, then behind me. "I'm gonna go shower in the other room, figured you could use some time to relax. Oh, and there's champagne."

"What?" My jaw almost fell to the floor.

"Hearing problems?" His eyebrows shot up. "There. Is. A. Bath. Running. For. You. In. The—"

I held up my hand. "Can you not ruin a nice thing

by being an asshole? Please?"

His lips twitched and then fell into a full-on grin that had my clothes ready to just fall off my body in wonder. Seriously, I even held onto my tank top to make sure it didn't disintegrate into a puddle at my feet.

He sauntered by me, his deep *V* distracting every molecule in my body, and then he stopped once we were shoulder to shoulder. "You blushing because you called your employer an asshole or because of the towel?"

I swallowed and met his gaze. "A bit of both, I guess."

He nodded. "When it comes to sex, trust me, you're safe."

"You said safe wasn't a reality."

He just shrugged and walked by me.

That wasn't helpful. Not at all.

"Thank you!" I called.

He turned and leaned a muscled arm against the doorframe. "It was a long night, always is during family dinners. You looked exhausted."

I felt exhausted. I self-consciously tugged at my tank top. "I was adopted so, I don't... I'm not really used to all of that."

"I know," he whispered.

Of course he did.

We stared at each other for a few more seconds before he pointed. "You should probably make sure that it doesn't overflow."

I nodded, a bit breathless, then turned around and made my way toward the bath.

The bastard had even lit candles.

I wanted to throw them. How dare he go from threatening to kill me to drawing me a freaking bubble bath?

I clenched my teeth.

It was impossible to stay mad at someone that attractive.

Add the whole bath thing on top of it…

And I was seriously the girl I never thought I'd be, the one that made justifications for his horrible actions every time he did something nice.

With a huff, I peeled my shirt over my head and dropped my pajamas then hopped in.

"SHIT!" I yelled and stood then bumped my head on the low chandelier causing me to stumble a bit against the wall, which naturally led to me pressing my hand against the fireplace and slipping onto my ass as hot water sloshed all over the sides.

I quickly stood again, just as Chase rounded the corner, an amused expression on his face. "You gonna make it?"

I covered my breasts.

He didn't seem to care.

Was he gay?

There was literally no reaction at all. He stepped forward and examined my head then, very slowly, leaned down, inches away from my belly button and then lower, and flicked on the cold water, his eyes never leaving my face.

My breathing picked up as he felt the water then stirred it around my ankles, never once looking away from my face.

One minute felt like an hour. He stood again, so close to me I could almost feel his towel brushing against my thighs. "You should be fine now. Should I stay just in case?"

"I think I got it," I croaked.

He winked and walked off.

Winked.

He. Winked.

I was so shocked that he wasn't yelling or throwing things that I gaped after him like he'd just grown three heads.

Either he was softening me toward himself before shooting me...

Or the Grinch actually had given him back his heart.

I slowly sat in the tub and moaned out loud when the hot water massaged my tired muscles.

I had been sitting for maybe one minute when a knock sounded at my door.

"Yeah?" I called.

"Jets, right side, black switch."

"Thanks!"

He didn't say anything else. Ugh, maybe his heart was still on vacation, or he was definitely killing me.

At least I'd be warm.

I closed my eyes and let my guard down a bit especially after the glass of champagne. He'd left the bottle, so I poured another and wondered what kind of psycho would try to burn this place down when it had a bathroom like this?

Several bathrooms like this.

I yawned and stretched with a smile on my face and then frowned because I was thinking about him again.

About his grin.

About his eyes.

He wasn't mine to have.

He wasn't anyone's.

If there was anything I'd learned about Chase, it was that the world, in his mind, owed him everything — and he was hell-bent on settling that debt.

CHAPTER THIRTY-SIX

"Guilt was not something I was used to. It wasn't in my makeup. Not something the mafia teaches you. No, the mafia teaches you survival. My father taught me how to live and how to kill. And I was a good student."
— *Ex-FBI Agent P*

Chase

On the outside I was calm.

Confident.

Still angry.

Still an asshole.

But my heart? It beat so wildly that I pressed a hand to it and leaned against the wall in the spare bathroom. What the hell was that?

The almost painful feeling that stretched my chest wide. The one that made me think I was having a heart attack.

Naked.

She'd been so naked.

I'd only acted unaffected because I was in shock.

Complete shock.

Eight months, and I'd told myself I would never touch another woman again, promised myself I'd leave this earth with her blood on my hands, that it would consume me in every way.

And now I was thinking about her wearing those damn pearls.

And nothing else.

I dropped the towel and stepped into the shower then braced one hand against the wall as my body pulsed with need. I clenched my teeth. Unbelievable. She wore headbands!

I killed people.

She had pearls.

I reached for myself and gripped.

I wasn't going to live past my last few kills.

I moved my hand as water pelted my back. Her parted lips… that wide-eyed innocent look that made me even wonder if she'd ever had sex before or if she'd just been too busy being proper to even think about it…

I let out a grunt of frustration.

My hand was a pathetic substitute for that mouth of hers.

It was painful, removing my hand, staring at the wall, and quickly flipping on the cold water.

Any other woman, and I'd be satisfied.

Any other woman, but not her.

No, not her.

"Fuck!" I slammed my hands against the tiled wall and grit my teeth as freezing water hit me from all sides, cooling me off but doing nothing about the fact that I was going to impale her if I got too close.

I smirked, even though it wasn't funny. To think I'd thought she'd broken my dick, too.

After all, *she'd* taken everything else.

Why not take that?

Have the last laugh?

I squatted down and let the water hit my face, chilling me to the bone. If a cold shower didn't do it, I wasn't so sure she should sing to me tonight; the last thing I needed was for her to think I had her in my room because I was seconds away from screwing her.

"Agh!" I stood and washed my body, rinsed, then grabbed a towel and quietly made my way back into the bedroom to grab a pair of pajama pants. Tonight was not the best night to just wear black Stance briefs to bed.

I'd literally just pulled up my pants when she walked around the corner, clothed, with her skin looking dewy and pink.

I wiped my face with one hand and stared.

She didn't move.

Her hair was in a knot on her head, and her face was bare, no makeup.

And I'd never seen anyone so innocent-looking, so pure, in my entire existence; it made me want to lock her up like a psychopath and put a full-time guard on her just in case someone saw what I saw and took advantage.

She had long legs.

Full hips.

And breasts that, I knew for a fact, would spill over my hands, and then some. I averted my eyes for the first time since she walked out and grabbed a chair. "You can just sit... here."

I placed the chair a few feet away from my bed.

Away from temptation I didn't need.

And then turned off the lights and went to lie on the mattress. I pulled the down comforter over me and heard the sound of the chair scraping across the floor until finally settling about an inch from my body.

Great. Just. Great.

I exhaled slowly and managed to relax my body. Luc moved to the chair but must have tripped on something because one minute she was standing next to me and the next minute I was getting kneed in the junk and seeing stars.

"SHIT!" I roared as she covered her face and

stumbled back to the chair.

"I'm so sorry! I was just trying to— never mind. Maybe this is a bad idea. Do you need an ice pack? Peas?"

I couldn't help it. She'd offered me fucking peas.

I lost it.

I laughed, and for the first time in I didn't even know how long, it felt like a real laugh, as if it came from some place good, not from the darkness.

"So you're not hurt?" she asked when I stopped laughing.

"You pretty much just took my dick off with your knee. What do you think?"

She hung her head.

I reached for her, hesitated midway, then just went with it as my fingers tilted her chin toward me. "It was an accident."

"So you're not... going to..." She eyed the gun on my nightstand.

"For rendering me sterile?" I joked. "No."

She made a face. "I didn't knee you that hard."

"My balls went into my spleen. Trust me. You did."

Even in the dark, I could make out her blush.

I tried not to react to it.

Told my body it was finally losing its last grip on reality, but I couldn't resist. I cupped her face again with both hands.

Her breaths came out in short, ragged exhales as if she was having trouble sucking in enough air.

I leaned in just as a loud crash sounded downstairs.

Well, that did the trick.

I grabbed the gun and pointed it at her. "Stay."

"But—"

"Stay!" I yelled it this time and shut the door behind me.

Another crash and then whispering.

They must have been trying to gain my attention, or they were literally the loudest and worst associates on the planet.

I flicked on the lights.

Nothing happened.

No wonder.

Either they'd cut the lights or— Thunder sounded in the distance.

Well, at least I had my answer.

I waited for someone to make an appearance at the bottom of the stairs. After a few seconds, there was no more talking. Well, shit.

I walked down quietly and turned the corner into the kitchen then felt movement behind me. I turned and shot.

Direct hit to the head.

The guy fell to the ground. Just as Vic approached from behind, blood covering his face as he gave his head a shake. "They cut the power." He rasped, "Bastards ran from me—I had it handled."

"That why you look ready to pass out from blood loss?" My eyebrows rose while he gave me a fuck you look and raised his gun just as another guy popped out from the left, the bullet hit him between his eyes, but Vic was still looking at me, his face indifferent.

"Lucky shot."

His lips twitched. "I never miss."

My front door opened, and there he was.

Fucking Andrei Petrov.

Clapping.

CHAPTER THIRTY-SEVEN

"There is no prey, only predators, lots and lots of predators, and the people stupid enough to invite them in."
— *Ex-FBI Agent P*

Luciana

I HEARD TWO gunshots, then talking.

He'd told me to stay, but if they were talking, surely that meant one of the other guys had shown up, right? The good ones? I frowned. They all shot at each other, but I was beginning to side with Chase. He never attacked them; he was always attacked first. That had to be a vote in his favor, right?

I opened the door and made my way down the hall and paused at the stairway. Chase was just lowering his gun as the tall guy started clapping.

"Andrei," Chase sounded bored. "Tell me they weren't yours. They were loud as shit."

Andrei shrugged. "They were De Lange associates. I brought you a snack. You should say thank you."

Chase grunted his response, while Vic, who stood behind him snarled and then left the room like he didn't have time to talk, only shoot.

Andrei had leather gloves, a long wool coat, and handsome features if I could look past the anger that seemed to wrap around him just like his coat. Was everyone angry who did what Chase did?

I gulped and waited.

"What did you need, Andrei?"

"I need nothing. My assets have been unfrozen. I'm living the high life." He put his hands in his pockets. "No, I'm here for you."

"To kill me?"

"We both know the Italians are too useful to kill."

Italians?

They did drink a lot of wine.

Organized crime.

The payouts.

Two billion dollars.

My mind worked.

Murderers.

Police calling him *sir*.

Dread washed over me as I waited.

"True," Chase smirked. "And the Russians, well, there's only one of you left... How sad. Daddy doing okay in prison?"

Andrei didn't even flinch. "I hated my father as much as you did. You know that."

Chase seemed to soften a bit. "Yeah well, none of us really liked our fathers. They didn't do things right."

"No," Andrei spat, "they didn't."

"I should hate you," Chase said.

"And yet you don't..." Andrei flicked off something from his jacket as if he was inspecting it for lint. "I am sorry she died, but you know I did what I had to do. I did what you would have done — what any one of you would have done. I think that's the problem. You know this business. I know this business. If she was willing to betray you—"

"Stop." Chase clenched his teeth.

"Then..." Andrei shrugged. "...how long before she would betray me?"

She?

"Again, why are you here?" Chase crossed his arms. I could tell he was annoyed.

"Locations." Andrei held out a piece of paper to Chase. "There are fifty-seven individuals left, not including any of the wives or children."

Chase took the paper and examined it. "And what am I supposed to do with this?"

Andrei winked. "Follow your heart?"

"She took it with her," Chase fired back.

Pain sliced through my chest. Ridiculous. No wonder he couldn't even look at me, didn't even flinch when I was naked. The man belonged to someone else, a dead someone else.

Andrei let out an impatient sigh. "Then you're the dumb bastard who let her."

Chase moved, his hand toying with his gun. "Watch it. Still my house, my property. I could end you, and the FBI wouldn't even blink."

"That," Andrei chuckled, "is where you're wrong."

"Oh yeah? Why's that?"

He didn't answer just turned on his heel and then called back, "For what it's worth, I'm glad you didn't have to do it."

Chase was silent.

"Shooting one's wife would not be a nice memory. Better that Phoenix did the hard thing than either of us. Better he end his line…"

I gasped and covered my mouth with my hands, garnering the attention of both Andrei and Chase.

If he wasn't going to shoot me before, he most likely would now. He'd told me to stay. Why hadn't I stayed?

Andrei's eyebrows shot up. "Moving on so soon?"

"Employee," Chase said through clenched teeth. "Who apparently doesn't listen to instructions well."

I trembled.

Andrei smiled at me. "Pretty, though."

It felt like an insult.

His eyes raked over me. "Innocent."

Chase looked ready to murder him.

With a tilt of his head, Andrei looked from me to Chase. "How much?"

"Excuse me?" I stupidly interrupted.

Andrei put up his gloved hand as if he wanted me to stop talking.

"She's not for sale," Chase bit out.

"Five hundred thousand." Andrei examined me again. His blue eyes seemed to look through my thin pajamas. "On second thought... two million. I'm going to wager she's a virgin."

"I'm not." Of course now I would speak.

It seemed to only encourage him more. "I like her spirit."

"She's not a horse," Chase spat. "Stop insulting me, and her, and leave. We're done here."

Andrei shrugged. "Your loss." He walked out the door and shut it quietly behind him.

My knees knocked together as Chase, very slowly, took the stairs one at a time, then faced me at the top of the landing, his breathing even, his eyes crazed.

"I'm s-sorry. I thought it was over and then—"

"When I tell you to stay—" He gripped my chin in his right hand. "—you fucking stay."

I nodded jerkily.

He released me and turned then slammed me against the wall and kissed me so hard I couldn't breathe. The gun was by my right ear pressed against the wall, just like me, and this man, this beautiful, scary man, wasn't shooting me.

He was kissing me.

So I kissed him back.

I wrapped my arms around his neck and held on.

I told myself it was adrenaline.

I told myself that it was his face, his body. It was convenience.

It wasn't any of those things.

It was just him.

I couldn't explain it.

His teeth nipped at my lower lip, and he lifted me with one arm. The gun clamored to the floor as he moved against me, his mouth assaulting mine in a way that had me clinging to his shirt, and then his biceps, as he swept his tongue past my parted lips and into my mouth as if he belonged there. I squeezed my eyes shut as he twisted my hair in his right hand and deepened the kiss. The heat from his body pulsed between us, and I let out a moan. He drove his body against me harder, leaving no space between us. I moved my hands to his hair, tugging at it in an effort to get closer. I'd never been so consumed by a kiss, by another person, and the way his rock-hard body pressed against my softness, my thighs clenched when he lowered his hand to my ass.

My breath caught when he pulled away, dragged a kiss down past my jaw, and bit the sensitive skin where my neck met my shoulder. I cried out just as the door slammed downstairs.

"Chase? It's Dante. Got your 911 text— Oh shit, more bodies... Should we open up our own morgue?

Might be lucrative if you keep this up." He rounded the corner just as Chase released me. I almost fell to the ground, but my jelly legs caught me.

Dante looked between us and then quickly turned around and walked off, a smile on his lips.

"You—" Chase heaved, stabbing a finger against my chest, and then caressing that same finger across the bite mark he'd made on my neck. "—belong to no one."

Not what I expected.

My stomach sank to my knees.

"I'd kill you before I'd let him have you."

He cursed and kicked the wall, making me jump a foot, then stomped down the stairs.

Tears filled my eyes as I numbly walked back down the hall and shut the door to my room, my lips trembling the entire time.

What had just happened?

CHAPTER THIRTY-EIGHT

"Everyone has a weakness. I thought his was dead. I thought wrong."
— *Ex-FBI Agent P*

Chase

My hands shook with rage.

At her.

At myself.

At Andrei.

"Are we gonna talk about it?" Dante asked as he started wrapping the first body in a black tarp.

I glared and stayed silent as I got the bleach and dumped it in the metal tub I'd pulled into the house.

"Because…" The bastard wouldn't stop talking. "…it looked like I walked in on you pre-sex."

I hung my head. "Dante, listen to me very carefully. Hell would have to freeze the fuck over for me to have sex with her. There, happy?" When I turned to face him, it wasn't just him in the room, but Luc, too, and she was holding out my gun, and it was shaking in her hand.

"You dropped this, and since you always have it, I figured…" She held it out to me. Her eyes wouldn't meet mine.

"Luc—"

She shrugged. "You don't owe me an explanation. I'm not yours… remember?"

I took the gun from her hand.

"Good to see you, Dante." She smiled at him.

I hated it.

"You, too." He looked like he meant it.

Her smile fell when she glared back at me and walked off.

Dante and I watched her go.

When she was gone, Dante whistled and then shook his head at me. "You should go apologize."

I looked away. "Not apologizing for telling the truth."

"Shit, sometimes you're an idiot. I take that back. Ninety-nine percent of the time, you're an idiot, I've known you less than a year and still... This shit is..." Dante grabbed the bleach from my hand and motioned to the stairs. "Go apologize. She looked ready to cry."

"Tough shit. Life's hard."

Dante set the bleach down on the floor then sucker-punched me across the face. I wasn't expecting it, so I fell back against the tarp currently covering a dead body. "What the hell?"

"Well, I feel better." Dante cracked his knuckles. "Now, go apologize before I beat the shit out of you."

"You've never been able to before. What makes you think you can now?" I taunted.

He shrugged. "Universe is on my side today. Plus, you're pissing me the hell off."

"Get in line."

"Chase, you can't just..." Dante leaned back against the table. "...you can't just play with girls like that."

"Who says I'm playing?"

"The guilt on your face when I walked in," Dante snapped, "and the look on hers when you turned away."

I ran a hand over my hair and stood. "What? She looked pissed?"

"Nah, worse, man." Dante shoved me toward the stairs. "She looked... hopeful."

"Well, shit," I grumbled making my way slowly up the stairs.

I knocked on her door then opened it.

She was huddled to one side of her bed, her knees tucked underneath her. Eyes closed.

"No chance in hell you're sleeping."

She didn't open her eyes.

I sighed and lay down next to her, putting my hands behind my head. "I built it for her, you know."

Luc didn't move.

"The house."

Nothing.

"It's why I tried to burn it down... Note to self, marble doesn't really melt."

She sighed. At least it was something.

"She broke a very important part in me, something that made me still feel human. Like she just... ripped apart what every single person on this planet thinks nothing of." I hated how true it was. "I fucking lost my humanity, my soul. I'm not a good man, Luc."

She turned on her side and stared me down. Her soft lips pressed together in a thin line. "That's a choice."

"Doesn't feel like it." I stared at the ceiling fan as it slowly went around in circles. "Trust me, if I knew how to find that part of myself again, I would. It's gone. That man... he's dead."

She didn't say anything, just pressed her palm against my chest for a few moments then finally whispered, "No, you're not." And then she tapped her fingers to the rhythm of my heartbeat. *Thump, thump, thump.*

I gripped her wrist. It was painful, the reminder that my heart was there but that it didn't feel anymore, that I was cold, in over my head, dead inside, so fucking dead.

She kept tapping her fingers.

She tapped.

I tried to stop her.

It hurt too much.

My veins burned.

My eyes squeezed shut as memories flooded. Memories of her smile... the way she tasted... the good, the bad, the ugly.

The end.

I sucked in a breath.

Thump, thump, thump.

My heart picked up speed.

And then, she started singing.

To the most undeserving man of all.

I fell asleep with her hand on my chest and her voice in my ear.

CHAPTER THIRTY-NINE

"A patient man can wait as long as it takes to gain the world."
— *Ex-FBI Agent P*

Luciana

EVERYTHING WAS WARM. Especially my body. I moved toward the warmth and froze when I realized it wasn't my mattress or the blankets giving me that warmth.

It was a man.

A jackass, to be more precise.

One who kissed with wild abandon then rejected the girl after — twice.

Not that I thought it was going to go further.

He was too hot and cold for that.

What I didn't think would happen was a threat followed by an embarrassing insult in front of Dante.

I was afraid to move.

I'd been ready to cry myself to sleep when I realized he didn't deserve my tears, and then he had to go and start talking to me, about her. My ears burned to hear more. What kind of woman would ever look at Chase and look away? Or think there was something more in this world?

He was perfect.

When he wasn't an ass.

Or killing people.

Okay, so we all have flaws, but still.

His words burrowed into my heart, splintering it

into tiny pieces, until it almost hurt to breathe. To exist but not really live.

To go day-to-day in nothing but a fog of numbness and pain, never knowing which will strike harder.

I didn't know what to do, to calm him, to help him.

So I'd shown him.

The only way I knew how.

That he wasn't broken.

He was still whole.

Feelings have a way of defining our realities, and he was letting them. He was letting his anger, his pain, dictate his actions. Rather than choosing to fight, he was giving up.

And taking it out on everyone else.

I tried to turn to face his sleeping form, but his arms braced me so tight, I couldn't move a muscle.

He pulled me closer.

And then his nose was on my neck, his lips soon following.

My eyes widened. "Chase?"

Oh good, he was a sleep kisser.

I elbowed him slightly.

He grunted and then turned on his back, easily taking me with him. I yelped once I was straddling him.

His erection pressed against his jeans.

I tried not to look.

It was nearly impossible.

The bulge was just evidence that he wasn't dead. Idiot.

"Chase." I shoved his chest.

He gripped my wrists and pulled me against his body.

"Chase, this isn't funny."

He finally opened his eyes and then shoved me away like I was the problem. I almost fell off the bed.

"What time is it?" He rubbed his face in confusion.

"I would have looked, but I was getting attacked."

He jumped to his feet and with crazed eyes looked around the room. "Who? When?"

I pointed my finger at him.

He frowned, first at my finger, then up at me. "What the hell are you talking about?"

"Just…" I held out my hands. "You got handsy."

His lips twitched. "Handsy?"

I gritted my teeth. "Mock me, and I'm going to go find that gun you're so fond of and point down." I jerked my chin to his package.

He gaped. "Wow, didn't think you had it in you. Then again, you did just try to take my dick off last night, so why not point and shoot? Really."

I couldn't believe I'd just threatened him.

"I, uh…" He licked his lips and then gave his head a shake. "…I gotta go make sure Dante didn't fall into a tub of bleach."

He didn't smile.

"Wait, you're serious?" I asked.

He just shrugged. "Part of the business. No finger prints, no evidence."

"Who were those guys?" I called as he was leaving my room.

"De Langes" was his clipped answer.

Terror gripped me by the throat. I waited for him to leave then quickly shut my door. With shaking hands, I grabbed my cell and sent a text to my mom.

Me: Everything's great. Can you do me a favor and send me my blue box?

Mom: Blue box? With all your school records and foster care information?

Me: I'm feeling... nostalgic. I miss you guys.

Mom: Okay, honey. I love you!

It was a miracle, in and of itself, that my mom even knew how to text at her older age, but the fact that she was well-trained to keep things short when I was working was a huge blessing and mark in my favor. If anyone looked at my phone, they'd just think I was checking in with a parent.

Not digging into my own past.

Just to make sure.

It wouldn't dictate my future...

I gulped, thinking about the bodies downstairs.

...or lack thereof.

CHAPTER FORTY

"All it takes is the removal of one stone for the entire wall to crumble. It must fall. It must."
— *Ex-FBI Agent P*

Chase

DANTE HAD DONE a good job cleaning up the bodies; he was turning into a pro, which a year ago would have worried me. Now I was just thankful I didn't have to bleach off fingerprints and blood. I moved around the room and froze when I saw a figure sitting at my kitchen table.

Drinking my coffee.

Reading my newspaper.

"Can I help you?" I spat. How the hell did Vic move around so quietly without me knowing? It had always been impossible to sneak up on me, and this guy managed to do it in my own damn house.

He didn't look up from his newspaper, just grunted out his response. "Think of me like your babysitter."

"Oh, hell no."

"Hell yes." He took another sip of coffee. "Don't worry. You won't even know I'm here."

I hated how true that was; he was only seen when he wanted to be seen. Just who was this guy and where had Nixon found him?

"You're the size of a bus and drinking my coffee. I know you're here," I ground through my clenched teeth.

He set the newspaper down, and his green eyes raked over me as if I was under inspection, and then he leaned back. Two guns were strapped to his chest. "I'm on patrol. That's two attacks on the Family. Two attacks in one week."

"I handled it." I shrugged.

"And if you can't next time?"

I froze on my way to make coffee. "Then I die."

"Nixon said you'd say that."

"Fuck Nixon."

"He said you'd say that, too."

I exhaled and pressed my palms flat against the granite countertop. "So what? He sent you because he wants me to live?"

"Apparently," Vic said in a low voice, "you mean more to him than he does to you."

"Why would you say that?" Guilt twisted my stomach until I felt like I couldn't breathe.

"Because..." Vic stood and washed out his coffee cup, dried it, then put it away in the cupboard. "...you touched his wife, and you're not dead. Instead, he sent you more protection for the home you tried to burn down a few months ago. I wonder why he's being so generous?"

My expression didn't waver even though I felt like shit. "Because I'm an Abandonato? Because I'm royalty? Because I'm one of the youngest billionaires on the planet? Because I'm ruthless? Because I'm lethal? Or maybe because I'm Family... Either way, he wants you here, so I won't complain. Just stay away from Luciana."

His eyebrows rose slightly. "He didn't prepare me for that one."

"Excuse me?" Okay, now he was pissing me off.

"Huh." He rapped his knuckles against the counter

and gave me a salute. "I'll just be doing a perimeter check. My number's already programmed into your phone."

"How the hell did you do that?"

"Sergio."

I rolled my eyes. Bastard needed more hobbies.

He slammed the front door.

Blanketing me in silence once again.

I stared ahead; the windows to the back yard folded out into a perfect landscape. A firepit, salt-water pool, outdoor living area. I scowled. Only the best for the best.

The house had cost me fifteen million to build.

I would have spent my life savings on it, if it would have made her happy.

"Okay, you can open your eyes now!" I pulled my hands away from her face, ready to burst with excitement. She'd said she wanted a pool, so I'd gone a step further and given her an outdoor paradise.

Mil's jaw dropped. "You outdid yourself!"

I wrapped an arm around her. "I figured you needed your own space, a place to relax… wash blood off your hands."

She elbowed me in the ribs even though we both knew it was true.

"So, you like it?"

She turned in my arms and took my mouth, kissing me deep, then pulled away. "It's perfect, just like you."

I scowled. "I'm not perfect."

"Chase…" She frowned and then gave her head a shake. "You're impossible to even live with sometimes. You're so perfect. I can't even go to the grocery store without women hitting on you, and I'm with you."

"All I see is you," I said truthfully.

Guilt flashed across her face; it was happening more and more, and I couldn't for the life of me figure out what the hell she had to feel guilty about. Our life wasn't the best — but it was better than most. We still fought, but we always made up, and that was all that mattered.

"I know," she whispered. "Sometimes..." her voice cracked. "...sometimes I wish we weren't married."

My stomach dropped. "Why the hell would you say that?" I jerked away.

"Because..." She didn't reach for me. "...you've always deserved more than I'm capable of giving."

She'd never admitted it before, at least not out loud.

We stared at one another in silence.

The truth hanging between us like a fucking chasm.

"Mil..." I reached for her.

Tears filled her eyes. She swiped her cheeks and did what she always did when things got serious. Defaulted. "So, we should try out that pool."

She stripped naked.

And I shoved the uneasiness from my heart, my soul, and jumped in after her.

I'd always jump in after her.

Always.

The coffeepot dinged. I jumped and nearly knocked over the other mug that was set out on the counter.

For the first time in months, I could think about her and not immediately feel the need to torch the house. For the first time in months, I looked out at the pool and felt nothing but bitter sadness for what could have been, if she'd only let me in.

I exhaled slowly and poured myself a cup of coffee then eyed the pantry. Pancakes sounded good. I could make pancakes.

My hands shook.

I'd cooked once since her death. And it had been for Luciana.

It had always been a sort of self-soothing practice, and when Mil died, I didn't want to soothe myself. I wanted retribution.

Maybe it was time to try something else.

My chest ached.

I pressed a hand to it and tried to breathe evenly.

Thump, thump, thump.

I shook my head.

Luc was right.

I wasn't dead inside.

Not yet.

Soon.

But not yet.

I wondered in that moment if Mil would have done things differently had she known her time was almost up.

My time would be.

It was simple logic.

I would wipe them clean.

And I would get taken out for doing it.

Simple math.

Simple all around.

If I only had two weeks to live…

I looked up at the ceiling and smiled as the memory of Luc offering to shoot me this morning replayed in my head.

Pancakes, it was.

I might even get wild and add chocolate chips.

CHAPTER FORTY-ONE

"Put a guard on a criminal, and it only encourages more outbursts. It proves one thing. He's a threat."
— *Ex-FBI Agent P*

Luciana

My stomach growled. I pressed a hand to it and scowled at the floor, imagining Chase eating whatever he was cooking while burying the bodies. Thanks to Nikolai for dropping me into the twilight zone, where gorgeous men kill bad guys and have so much money that even the law backed down.

Gorgeous men — I grabbed a stack of folders and carried them over to the desk — who are used to getting everything with a snap of their fingers, so they take it.

Then freaking insult it within the same breath.

I thought I was over his words.

I thought wrong.

I'd been exhausted last night, hungry for an apology, and a bit terrified that a man with a cruel smile had offered to buy me minutes after Chase's mouth was on mine.

A headache started pulsing between my ears.

Great, just great.

I grabbed another deposition and read it over. Nothing interesting.

And then another stack of payouts.

To the Chicago Police Department.

Color me shocked.

Donations to three of the local hospitals.

And a new cancer wing under the Abandonato name.

For kids.

My eyes widened at the number.

Ten million dollars.

Seven zeros.

Damn it!

I dropped the paper and put my hands on my hips. How was I supposed to stay angry at a guy who shot bad men and donated money to cancer wings?

Unbelievable.

I reached for the next folder when the door to the storage room opened.

Chase stood there, shirtless.

His jeans hung low on his hips.

Mouth dry, I focused in on his eyes so I wouldn't accidentally stare too long at his perfect body.

"Hungry?" he asked.

"Poison?" I countered, pointing at the plate.

He smirked. "Close." He moved toward me. "Chocolate chips, actually. Only poison to dogs and only in obscenely large amounts."

"Kill a lot of dogs, do you?" I said a bit too breathlessly, making me mentally slap myself for allowing his shirtless presence affect me when I wanted to stay pissed at him.

"No…" Chase grinned. "…only people."

"Well, that's reassuring," I joked, even though I knew it was true, I'd seen it firsthand.

"Isn't it though?" He winked. "I wasn't sure how hungry you were so I may have gone overboard." For the first time since I'd walked into that house, he looked genuinely nervous, as if I was going to throw his pancakes back in his face.

The facade slipped.

The cocky, *'I'll kill you for looking at me'* facade.

And in its place, a vulnerability that was impossible not to respond to.

I took the plate and then grabbed the fork and took a huge bite, too huge, but I was starving.

His eyes lowered to my mouth.

"Mmm." I loved pancakes. I tried not to hate him for finding my weakness so easily. "They're so fluffy."

"It's the duck eggs," he said in a gravelly voice.

My eyes snapped open. "Duck eggs, really?"

"I may have ducks."

"Real ducks?"

"No, fake ones that lay fake eggs that I put in real pancakes. Yes, real ducks." He crossed his arms. "They're better to cook..." He gulped and looked away. "...to cook with."

"Do you name them?" I took another bite.

"The ducks?"

I nodded at his curious look. "Yeah."

"Huey, Dewey, and Louie," he said with a completely straight face.

"Ah, so that makes you..." I pointed my fork at him. "...Uncle Scrooge?"

"Insulting the man who feeds you?"

"Pancakes hardly make up for threatening to shoot someone," I said before stopping myself. Great, now he was going to threaten me again.

He tilted his head at me, his expression puzzled. "You're right."

"I am?" I almost felt his forehead to make sure

he wasn't feverish; the dark circles were gone from under his eyes, and he looked... more human than I'd ever seen him, which consequently also meant that he looked so beautiful it hurt to stare directly into his haunted blue eyes.

"Don't get told that often?" he smirked.

I looked away and took another bite, only to realize that I'd literally downed three full pancakes in front of him. Awesome, he's going to think I'd rather eat than breathe. Only partially true.

Chase grabbed the plate from my hands and set it on the desk near the stacks of all his monetary donations.

Children's wing. Hospital.

He moved closer.

I squeezed my eyes shut. Killer. He was a killer.

He slept with a gun and had pointed it at me on numerous occasions. *Just don't look into his blue eyes. Don't look.*

"You have some syrup." His thumb swept over my bottom lip.

I sucked in a breath.

When he lowered his head and then picked up the plate next to me, I could have sworn he was going to kiss me; instead, he was just leaning over.

Stupid, stupid, Luciana.

I'd schooled my features by the time he faced me again. This time his eyes followed my black blouse all the way down to my pencil skirt and stilettos. "You know, you don't have to wear... that."

Was he hitting on me?

My eyes narrowed as I put my hands on my hips. "Listen, sexual harassment is a real thing in the workplace. I'm keeping my clothes on, thank you very much!"

He bit down on his bottom lip and nodded his head. "Women's rights... got it." He turned on his heel and left the room then peeked his head around the corner and winked. "I meant you could wear jeans and a t-shirt instead of high heels."

He disappeared again.

I groaned and pressed a hand to my forehead just as he poked his head around the corner again and said, "Oh, and you still have chocolate..." He pointed to the side of his mouth. "...right here."

I wiped my mouth with my sleeve without thinking.

"Looks like you'll need to change after all."

"This is all I have!" I called back to him and got a credit card thrown at my face in return.

I picked it up off the floor. "Um, I'm not letting you—"

"We leave in ten," was all he said.

And since he had a gun...

And my shoes were so uncomfortable I could cry...

I listened.

CHAPTER FORTY-TWO

"There is no greater feeling than when every plan falls perfectly into place."
— *Ex-FBI Agent P*

Chase

I HATED THAT everything came back down to comparison.

Her easy trusting smiles, even though I'd threatened her and mistreated her, and finally, the way she'd thrown herself into eating the pancakes like she'd never had real food before.

I wasn't insecure in anything.

Except cooking.

Because I'd lived with someone who rarely ate.

Always too busy.

Always on the run.

Always leaving food on the plate.

I would never tell Luc that my anger matched my panic when she'd picked up the plate and examined it. I wasn't even aware it was a test until she passed with flying colors and devoured the whole thing in front of me. I half expected her to start eating the plate.

With each bite, my heart cracked.

And I hated that my first thought was *So that is what it's like… to give something and have someone actually take it without reservation.*

So that was what it felt like.

It was like a match getting lit in my chest, spreading warmth throughout my body. It was addicting knowing that if I did something, she'd actually accept it; she wouldn't argue. Maybe she was too afraid to argue?

But something in me felt as if it had just been put back together again. And it was all over a plate of damn pancakes.

Luc was silent on the car ride; she kept rubbing her hands together as if she was nervous to be riding with me. I couldn't blame her. I was speeding.

I was always speeding.

Why have a sports car and not speed? It made no logical sense.

I parked on the street near Michigan Avenue. Versace was one of my favorite places, but I knew their idea of casual wear was a t-shirt that cost more than a Honda.

"Let's go." I snapped my fingers at one of the guys and tossed him my keys.

"Mr. Abandonato." He nodded.

Luc just stared at me with wide eyes.

As if she wasn't used to money.

As if this wasn't normal when it had been my normal my entire life.

Doors just opened.

People looked away.

Nobody made eye contact.

Just like nobody ever said no to me.

"So…" I shoved my phone in my back pocket then placed my hand on the small of Luc's back. She flinched and, for some reason, it bothered me because I wasn't sure if it was a flinch out of fear or something worse — attraction. I knew what to do with fear.

I had no fucking clue what to do with the other.

I could just come out and tell her not to fall for a dead man.

Two weeks was enough time to form an attachment.

And I didn't want my death being on her conscience.

No tears wasted.

I didn't deserve them.

I never have.

All I knew was that my days were numbered, and when I thought about living out the rest of my time sitting in my giant mansion alone with blood on my hands, I kind of wanted to point a gun to my temple and pull the trigger. But when I thought about Luc…

I could breathe.

A little easier.

"…so," I whispered, "where to?"

"Um…" She frowned at the stores that lined the street and then looked back at me. "…I'm a bit out of my element here."

"What? You don't normally go shopping with mercenaries?"

"Ah, so now you're a mercenary?"

I shrugged.

"Organized crime," she said quietly, "sure pays well, doesn't it?"

I just smiled.

"You're too young, you know…" Her face grew serious. "…to be mixed up in something like this."

I stopped walking. "Luc, I've been mixed up with this since before I said my first word. My cousin and I were forced to kill at thirteen. I had blood on my hands at the ripe old age of eight. Believe me when I say I'm old as fuck."

Tears filled her eyes.

I reached for her. "What's wrong?"

"Nothing." She looked away. "It's just… I think that's the saddest thing I've ever heard."

"Don't waste your tears on me," I whispered. "I'm not worth it."

"I'll decide what my tears are worth," she shot right back and then defiantly stared me down as the first one fell.

Stunned, I watched another fall. I couldn't take it — the guilt, the knowledge that she somehow felt bad for me, wasted her sadness on a life that meant nothing, did nothing but end other lives.

With a trembling hand, I reached out and caught the third tear. "I think that's the first time anyone has ever voluntarily wept for me."

"That just makes me want to cry more."

"Don't." I smiled. "People will think you're breaking up with me, and I don't think my ego can handle the rumor that Chase Winter got dumped on the street by a girl wearing..." I tilted my head. "What is it you're wearing? These clothes feel too old for you."

"It's called a business suit," she scoffed and then frowned.

And that had just slipped. Sharing my last name.
Shit.
Not that she didn't probably already know.

"My mom dabbled in fashion design."

"Winter," she repeated, and then her eyes widened. "WYN BOOTS?"

Did she just scream about boots?

Wow, weakness found.

"You want a pair?" I asked. Or ten?

"I've been on a waiting list for two years!"

"Then this is your lucky day." I grabbed her hand without thinking. She squeezed it before I could pull away.

So I kept holding it as I led her to Gucci.

"Chase." Darla knew all of us by our first names. We all loved clothes, but Sergio was a complete whore about what he wore; his shopping addiction was legendary. Last month he dropped so much money here that they sent him a Christmas ham and a set of keys to the store. Ridiculous.

"Hey, Darla." I kissed each cheek without letting go of Luc's hand. "I'm in need of some boots, jeans, leggings…" I shrugged. "…whatever she wants."

Darla looked between the two of us and then down at our joined hands. "Anything for one of my favorite customers."

"You're just saying that because Sergio isn't here."

She threw her head back and laughed. "True, that man…"

"Hey, don't talk about him in front of me. It hurts my feelings."

She winked. "Alright, why don't you go grab a cup of coffee. This may take a while. Makeup too?"

"Everything."

Why not?

In two weeks I'd be gone, and she'd at least remember me as the guy who set her up with clothes instead of the guy who'd kissed her then tried to shoot her.

"I'll leave you to it then." I gave Luc a reassuring smile and went off in search of Starbucks.

CHAPTER FORTY-THREE

"If it's too easy — it's probably harder than you think."
— *Ex-FBI Agent P*

Luciana

I WAS SO overwhelmed it was hard to think straight. Darla tossed so many clothes at me that I was drowning in them, and every single piece was so soft I wanted to throw them into a pile and take a nap.

He'd been gone two hours.

So I'd had two hours to overanalyze why he was doing this. It wasn't just that he was being nice; it was like he was trying with me.

Was it because of last night?

Or was this just a trick?

Fatten me up, buy me things, make me feel safe, then pull the trigger? I hated how untrusting I was, but he'd proven he was unstable, right? So how did I know this was going to end well?

"Have you, um, known Chase long?" I fished while Darla handed me a long wool pea coat.

She didn't look at me, just nodded. "Yup."

"Years?"

"Does it matter?" She smiled sweetly, but I heard the message in her tone. Stop prying. Stop asking questions.

"I work for him — them." I frowned to myself. "I'm the new lawyer."

"Ohhhhh." She sounded relieved. "I thought, well,

never mind what I thought."

"You thought what?" I put on the coat and examined myself in the mirror. It was a dark green and made my skin look flawless and my eyes more intense.

"Don't worry about it."

I crossed my arms.

"Look, don't get angry. It's just, they're great guys. They..." She looked like she was choosing her words wisely. She couldn't have been much older than me, but she looked wiser, so much wiser. "...they don't bring women anywhere. Ever. And if their wives are here shopping, they have enough security that you almost wonder if the president is visiting."

"Oh." For some reason that deflated me.

"No, no, that's a good thing!" she said encouragingly. "It means you aren't a target. It means you're safe."

Safe. The word burned.

Safe.

Without his protection.

Safe.

I stared at myself in the mirror and whispered, "Safe isn't a reality."

"No," came a familiar voice, "it isn't."

I sucked in a breath as the man from last night grinned at me through the mirror.

"Andrei," I said his name coolly.

He clapped his hands. "Ah, so she remembers my name. I'm... honored."

Doubtful.

I eyed Darla, but she was already walking away helping another customer. And when she turned back, she mouthed, *"Sorry."*

Seriously?

Panicked, I made sure to stay in front of the mirror; there were too many people in the store for him to just take me in broad daylight, right?

"You look different." He tilted his head. "I like it."

"I don't care what you like," I said quietly.

His grin widened. He was younger than I but older at the same time. His icy stare probably had women everywhere throwing themselves at him, but they didn't know what I did. He wasn't one of the good ones.

"I'm surprised, you know…" He shrugged. "…that Chase would leave you alone."

Make that three of us.

I tried not to look affected.

"That bothers you? That you're… just as interchangeable as a light bulb?" He leaned in until his lips were close to my neck. "I could kill you without anyone seeing a damn thing… but I won't. I don't like killing pretty things. I came to warn you."

"Oh?" My voice shook; my knees knocked together. "What's that?"

"The man buying all of these clothes no longer has a soul. You cannot love what you cannot save." He grit his teeth. "And you cannot trust a man who no longer trusts himself."

I frowned. "You're warning me about… Chase?"

"Like I said, I hate when pretty things get injured… and you…" He ran his hands down both my arms. "…are beyond beautiful. Do not trust him. When the time comes…" He bit down on my earlobe. "…fucking run."

I gasped.

And then he was gone.

CHAPTER FORTY-FOUR

"Game. Set. Match."
— *Ex-FBI Agent P*

Chase

WHEN I GOT back to the store, Luc was sitting in the corner, teeth chattering, bags gathered all around her. Her cheeks were highlighted with something shimmery, and a nude lipstick decorated her kissable lips.

But she was shaking.

I set the coffees down and approached.

She jerked back as if I'd pulled a gun on her.

It stung.

And completely confused me.

"Luc?"

"Can we go?" she asked in a small voice.

I nodded and eyed Darla; she wasn't paying any attention to me. Instead, she was folding clothes.

And her hands were shaking.

"Darla..." I stood behind her. "...a word?"

She went completely still. And didn't turn around.

"Look at me," I said in a lethal voice.

She turned, her lips trembling. "Yes?"

"You're going to tell me what happened, or I'm going to break two of your favorite fingers with the rings on. Imagine the swelling. Imagine the pain. They may even have to amputate. And I hate — I really hate — hurting people I actually like."

She swayed and then looked down at her feet.

"Look. At. Me," I said for the second time. I hated repeating myself.

She jerked her face to mine and whispered, "Petrov."

"Fuck." I ran a hand through my hair.

"Maybe you'd keep more employees if you protected them," Darla said through clenched teeth. "We had no protection! He waltzed right in, touched her—"

"He touched her?" I roared.

Darla jumped back while Luc made a noise in the corner.

I was too angry to think.

I grabbed the bags and Luc's hand and dragged her out of the store. When we got to my car, I made sure Luc was settled before I dialed Sergio.

"What's up?"

"Gucci cameras on Michigan Avenue. I want the feed from the last hour. Send it to my phone."

"Hello to you, too. Nice day isn't it? How's the family? Oh good, good—"

"Sergio—" I clenched my teeth.

"Fine," he bit off. "Give me five minutes."

I ended the call.

Luc started shaking next to me.

I reached for her hand, but she pulled it away.

So I reached again and didn't let her.

I squeezed it tight.

When we pulled into the garage, I finally released it, only to see her run out of the car and into the house.

I slammed my hand against the steering wheel then punched it with my fist and yelled.

Maybe I would kill him after all.

After the line was dead.

Maybe I would add one more hit to my list.
Andrei Petrov.
For touching what wasn't his to touch.

CHAPTER FORTY-FIVE

"I thought of his anger. And I smiled."
— *Ex-FBI Agent P*

Luciana

I COULDN'T STOP shaking.

I didn't know what to believe, what to think.

I hadn't even grabbed the bags from the car. Just run away. I'd run away like a scared kid because I was in too deep. Working for a crime organization.

I rolled my eyes.

Get real.

I knew the word.

Mafia.

I was working for the mafia.

Maybe if I said it out loud I'd feel better?

"Mafia."

Nope, not better. Not by a long shot.

I hugged myself and rubbed away the goose bumps on my arms, my teeth starting to chatter.

I grabbed the blanket from my bed, but it fell each time I tried to grab it.

"I'll get that," Chase said from the doorway.

My eyes drank him in.

Was he the devil?

Was he an angel?

Was he both?

I didn't break my gaze from his face when he

slowly walked around the bed, grabbed the blanket, and wrapped it around my shoulders. "A blizzard's coming in."

Great.

I didn't respond.

"If we lose electricity, don't panic. It's just the weather."

I nodded.

He sighed and then sat on the bed. He lifted his arm then wrapped it around my body.

He felt warm.

But the warmth was short-lived, because I'd just been warned by the guy who wanted to buy me to run from the very man trying to keep me warm.

Safe isn't real.

What is safe?

Confusion warred with logic as Chase pulled me further under his spell by just being near me, comforting me.

"I used to be the funny one." He grabbed my hand and examined it like he was looking for scratches.

I let him, too exhausted and petrified to move away.

"I know it's hard to believe, trust me. Everything was a joke. Everything was funny. Life itself was funny. The darkness always attacked, but I never let it in. I was stronger than the darkness. I laughed in its face. But you can only taunt for so long before it finds a chink in your armor and then, it consumes you, and you let it because it feels better than the pain."

I turned to him. "Darkness always feels better. It forces you to ignore the light."

His smile was sad. "There is no light, Luc. Not anymore."

So Andrei was right.

I hung my head.

"I'll admit there are glimpses."

I jerked up. "Like?"

"Like when I watch a girl put away three pancakes in under two minutes."

I almost reached for the pillow and smacked him with it. Instead I said, "Or when you get to name your ducks?"

"Close." His smile grew and then fell altogether. "I'm trying, you know, not to be an ass, but I literally have no clue how to do that anymore. It's a bit foreign."

"I noticed." I squeezed his hand back.

"Would you be more comfortable with me if you knew more?" His eyes searched mine.

"Oh, I know everything. You donate money to the entire city of Chicago. They gonna name you mayor anytime soon?"

He snorted. "Very funny, and you know what I meant."

I shrugged. "It would make me trust you more, yes."

"That something you want?" He seemed a bit dumbfounded.

"What?"

"Trust?"

I nodded slowly. "I want to know if you're going to make me pancakes one day then threaten to shoot me the next. I want to know if you're going to insult me to your friends then kiss me in the next breath."

"To be fair, I kissed you first," he corrected.

"Why?" I blurted. "Why kiss the girl with business attire and pearls?"

His lips twitched. "You forgot the headbands."

I touched my head. "I'm not wearing a headband today."

"Headbands." He shook his head like he couldn't believe it. "The universe is seriously fucking with me."

"What?"

"And to answer your question…" He leaned in. "…I kissed you because I realized you weren't marked, not by me, not by anyone, and I couldn't stand the idea of Petrov thinking that you were for sale, that you could be bought, when I'd already decided to keep you for myself."

I parted my lips. What did that even mean?

"I kissed you, because for the first time in eight months, I wanted to feel something other than soul-crushing pain," he whispered. "And that's the truth."

"Did it work?" I swallowed. Staring at his eyes was painful when I wanted to look at his full mouth.

He leaned in and pressed a soft kiss to my lips, then drew back. "Only as long as the kiss lasts."

"Oh."

"I won't make you promises, Luc. I'm offering you nothing."

I jerked back.

"Because I literally have nothing left to give."

I pressed a hand to his chest; his heart was racing. He still had it; it was still intact, working. But he believed the lie people often did when they were in pain.

That it meant there was something inherently broken within them, when the opposite was true. Heartbreak was just proof it *was* working.

If you had no heart…

You'd feel nothing.

I nodded. "I'm not asking for anything."

"That's the damn problem." He kissed me again. "Isn't it?"

I frowned.

"It's an unfair trade." He licked his lips slowly like he wanted to taste me with his tongue. "Believe me, I know, and you're in way over your head, princess."

"I was in over my head the day I walked in this house."

He covered my mouth with his and laid me back against the bed then threw the blanket off my shoulders, exposing the thin, long-sleeved shirt I'd left the store in. His hands moved down to my hips. I moved against them. The hands of a killer.

I knew one of us had lied.

And that *one* of us...

Was me.

CHAPTER FORTY-SIX

"He was too far gone. Nothing, and no one, would bring him back from the depths of hell. It was a feeling I knew all too well. All. Too. Well.
— *Ex-FBI Agent P*

Chase

I KISSED DOWN her neck, confused by why I wanted to, confused by why I felt so damn attracted to someone who couldn't even defend herself with a weapon if she had one in both hands.

Everything about her screamed innocence, from her clothing to the way she carried herself, and yet, such wisdom in her words, in her perceptiveness, that kissing her felt like a balm to my dirty soul.

It felt like the cleansing I'd never wanted but desperately needed.

I licked her lower lip, encouraging her to open up for me. She grabbed the front of my shirt with both hands. I tried not to tense beneath the feel of her fingertips twining around my shirt, tugging me closer, as if she couldn't get enough and never would. I threw a leg over her small body, straddling her, then dipped my tongue into her mouth, tasting her. Her lips opened wider like she wanted more of me. And I gave.

I massaged my tongue against hers, testing her out, shocked by how smoothly we fit together. Our mouths, neither one fighting for dominance, just existing in a lust-filled haze of want. She responded by arching into me. I almost saw stars. There was nothing this woman wasn't giving to me.

Nothing.

I should have felt guilt.

But I didn't.

Because I'd never felt *this*.

Total surrender.

Emotion shuddered through my body as if I was waking up from a foggy sleep, and with each addicting touch of her small hands on my skin, I felt more and more alive, as if she was shocking me back to life, slamming electricity into my heart, forcing it to beat, even when my brain demanded its silence.

Its utter death.

I growled in frustration, in torment, as I dragged my mouth down her neck and tugged at her shirt, peeling it over her head in a rush of adrenaline and lust. Her lacy black bra barely contained her breasts.

"Are you going to tell me to stop?" I said between breaths, needing her to say no, needing her to push me away more than I needed her to beg me to stay. This wouldn't end well.

And I was the only one who knew that.

She was fucking a dead man.

I closed my eyes as a fatal bliss stared right back at me, challenging me, beckoning me, even though there would only be death.

Darkness.

No light.

No light.

Never again.

"Only if you tell me you're going to shoot me later," she deadpanned, her eyes searching for what I wasn't willing to give, her body responding regardless of the loss of my heart.

I caught my breath and reached for her bra. She lay

back, a look of complete trust in her eyes as she slowly wrapped her hands around mine and pulled it down.

It was sexy as hell.

I never promised her I was good.

And yet she opened up to me.

I ached to taste more.

I leaned down and traced a nipple with my tongue then sucked; my tongue flicked against her pink untouched skin.

Her hips moved.

And then she said it.

"Chase."

I sucked in a breath, not trusting myself to not lose it, to fall off the deep end as the dark dragged me into the depths of hell.

My name.

I shook my head.

Me.

"Chase," she said it again, her small hands moving to my chest as she reached for my shirt.

Why was I letting this happen? Why wasn't I stopping when I swore to myself I'd never slip like this?

Ever again.

But the more she touched.

The deeper I fell.

Over my head.

Both of us were in over our heads.

Two weeks, and I'd be gone, with memories of her tongue on my skin.

I threw off the rest of my shirt and slammed my mouth against hers, picking her up by the ass and pulling her down the bed so I could get a better angle, so I could kiss her deeper, harder. So I could sink into her.

Her kiss devoured me, and with each heated press of her lips, I lost more restraint, more control.

"Chase."

My name again.

Like a prayer I didn't deserve.

A prayer no God would ever answer.

"Chase."

I threw my head back as she gripped my length through my jeans. I moved against her and then flicked open the button.

She hesitated.

I watched indecision war across her full lips, and then she wrapped a hand around my neck and very slowly reached down.

One second.

Two.

Three.

Her fingers felt cold against me. I was so sensitive to her that I ached. Her fingers tightened, not reaching around me by a long shot. I hissed out a curse.

"Shit." Too long, it had been too long.

Had it ever even been real?

Or felt like this before?

Like I was going to pay for my sins, for taking this, knowing what would happen, taking her without question when I didn't deserve it, and never would.

When I opened my eyes, she started to slowly pump me with her hand, the girl with the headband and nylons.

I licked my lips and reached for her breasts again, when she pressed her free hand to my chest and very slowly, shoved me to my back.

In a trance, I watched as she pulled my jeans down and then crawled over my body and lowered her head.

What. The. Fuck.

A kiss to the tip was all it took for me to lose my mind, my control. I moved against her lips on instinct, wanting more of the slick heat of her mouth, more of her tongue sucking, swirling.

She spread her palms against the bed, her breasts kissing my legs, rubbing against my thighs as her mouth moved up and down slowly. I tried to make it last; squeezed my eyes shut as I felt my body demand release.

I gripped her head, holding her in place. My breathing was ragged, so close. "Luc—"

She locked eyes with me over my cock and said, "You have nothing to give? Then let me."

I snapped as she took me deep.

And when I tried to pull away because the feeling was too much, because I was tarnishing her innocence...

She refused to move.

Our eyes locked again.

And I lost control.

Handed it over.

And felt myself orgasm so hard that I was afraid my hips bruised her mouth as I bucked against its heat.

Chest heaving, I stared her down. *What the hell just happened?*

Her voice was husky as she slowly ran her hands up my chest and then kissed my neck. "See any light, Chase?"

"Stars," I said groggily. "I saw stars."

"Told you so." She yawned and lay against my chest.

I pulled her close as anxiety spread over me.

I was a killer. I would always be a killer.

Broken.

Damned.

But for a few brief minutes, she'd done the impossible.

Given me a shred of humanity and light.

And made me feel like a man.

CHAPTER FORTY-SEVEN

"When a plan backfires, you simply try it at another angle. There is no defeat."
— *Ex-FBI Agent P*

Luciana

Did I just give a blow job to my boss?

A murderer?

A guy who even warned me to run from him on numerous occasions?

During a work day?

Not even on my lunch break?

I'd fallen asleep against his chest and woken up alone. Hopefully, he wouldn't fire me for sleeping on the job; then again, if I was going to get fired, pretty sure the blow job would be the thing to do it.

Stupid. So. Stupid!

What had I been thinking?

I wasn't thinking. That was the problem.

He tasted so good, felt so right in my arms, and then the sadness. God, the sadness on his face. I couldn't bear to even look at him while he kissed me like it was this invisible prayer to take it all way, to just… love him. A man I barely knew.

I wasn't one to do *that*. Ever.

I'd done it once and hated it so much that I'd sworn off all men — apparently, all men but ones who should be in prison.

Even better.

I quickly put my shirt back on and the new jeans I'd left the store with and padded down to my office.

Everything was as I'd left it, so I quickly got to work. My eyes kept reverting back to the box that read, *Emiliana De Lange,* right along with the white horse that had been placed on top of it.

My curiosity was going to get me killed.

I shut the door and walked over then picked up the black folder I'd been looking at a few days back.

When I opened it, I nearly threw up.

The girl in the picture...

The one with the dark hair and dark eyes...

Was too pretty for words.

Like the exact sort of woman I would imagine Chase being with.

I self-consciously touched my neck for my pearls, but I hadn't put them on. Then I touched my hair.

No headband today.

This woman wouldn't have been caught dead in a headband.

She had on higher heels than what should be legal, black leather pants, and wore a bright smile on her face.

Huge sunglasses were placed on her head. If I didn't know any better, I'd think it was a cover shot for Vogue.

The information next to it had her age, birthdate, known aliases, and kills.

Kills?

I did a double-take.

Why would she have kills?

"Twenty-seven?" That had to be a typo, right? Or was that normal? Were wives also supposed to join the mafia, like some sort of gang? I kept reading.

Miscarriage.

My heart sank.

And then I read in big bold letters, *RAT*.

I dropped the papers all over the floor.

Rat.

Rat.

Rat.

Pieces started falling together. Why he'd said he wasn't sorry she was dead. Why he was so broken, why—

"Find something interesting in there?" Chase asked casually.

I dropped the papers again as shame washed over me. Great, I asked for trust and now I was snooping, not that my job wasn't to snoop, but I highly doubted this was what he'd had in mind, trying to find out about the dead wife, the competition the—

Was that it? Did I really think she was competition? I wasn't even in the running.

There was no race.

Just the broken pieces she'd discarded and left behind.

The ones she'd been willing to gamble on — and lost.

Anger filled me.

And for the first time since arriving at the house, I got a glimpse into his rage, his darkness.

And I hated her for it.

I put the papers back on the desk and waited in silence for his next sentence, or maybe even a gun getting pointed at my face.

Chase didn't say anything, just slowly walked over to me and stared down at the papers. I squeezed my eyes shut as he slammed his fist down onto them and then shoved the entire desk onto its side, causing all of my files to go flying.

Tears filled my eyes as I kept squeezing them shut, willing it to be over.

But when I opened them, he was gone.

I fell to my knees to catch my breath.

Only to have him come back into the room and join me on the floor in picking up the files.

"We should just burn these," he said in an angry voice. "You've seen enough."

"Or too much," I said before catching myself.

I was seriously just asking to get buried in his back yard, wasn't I?

His cold eyes met mine and then softened immediately. "I'm not going to... I won't hurt you, Luc."

Not physically maybe.

I exhaled. "Okay."

"Shit, do you really think—" He ran a hand through his hair. "Do you think I would do that? Now? After..." He shook his head. "I wouldn't." He placed a hand over mine. "I won't."

I gave him a silent nod and then dropped the bomb. "She betrayed you."

His eyes flashed.

"Maybe if you talked about it—"

"To the help?" he sneered.

I flinched as if he'd slapped me.

"Luc—"

"Go," I said with a sad smile. "It's my job, remember? I'm just... the help."

He stood, crossed the room, then slammed the door

behind him.

While I looked down at her picture and cursed her to hell.

CHAPTER FORTY-EIGHT

"It's almost time."
— *Ex-FBI Agent P*

Chase

I FELT LIKE shit.

It wasn't a foreign feeling, but this time I knew I'd really hurt her, and that was the last thing I wanted to do, for her to think of me with disdain when I was gone. Why couldn't I just get over it and give her a good few days? Give myself a good few last days?

Because I really was broken.

So. Broken.

I wanted to lash out, because it hurt so much to keep in.

I grabbed my phone and looked out at the pool in stunned silence as snow began to fall.

My phone dinged.

About damn time.

> **Sergio:** I cut straight to the times when he touched her and was speaking to her. Don't kill him yet. Your body count is high enough as it is.
>
> **Me:** No promises.

I watched him touch her, scare her. I watched him lick her ear and felt such a possessive rage wash over me that I threw my phone against the wall.

"Shit!" I tugged at my hair and did a small circle in the kitchen. What game was he playing? And how the hell was I going to protect her from the grave?

I went to pick up my phone, thankful that the case had broken its fall, and texted Sergio.

> **Me:** I want security on her until Petrov is wiped from this earth...

Vic chose that moment to walk by with a wave of his gun, as he performed his new ritual of walking the premises before sitting in the garage on his computer watching the perimeter cameras.

> **Me:** Vic. Use Vic.
>
> **Sergio:** Okay... any reason for this? She's under the protection of the Families already.

My hands shook as I typed out.

> **Me:** Not good enough.
>
> **Sergio:** But—
>
> **Me:** Don't argue with me on this.
>
> **Sergio:** Interesting.
>
> **Me:** Don't read into it.
>
> **Sergio:** Too late...

I rolled my eyes as I stared down at my phone and then sent a text to Phoenix, her words haunting me the entire time.

> **Me:** Do you still see her face at night?
>
> **Phoenix:** Her blood will never wash off my hands.
>
> **Me:** How did you come back from it?

Phoenix: From...?

Me: Everything — the rape, the women, the prostitution rings, the need for violence — how did you come back from it?

Phoenix took a while to respond, but when he did, I almost dropped my phone.

Phoenix: I didn't.

Me: What do you mean?

Phoenix: It's a part of me. So I learned to accept it and allowed others to love me through it.

I closed my eyes and set my phone down as memories flooded my mind... her mouth on mine... the trust in her eyes... the surrender of her body.

Me: I'm a piece of shit.

Phoenix: You're just now figuring this out? I've been telling you this since we were twelve....

Me: I'm giving her the next few days off. In fact, I don't want her working on any of the background information until after the commission.

Phoenix: Your call, but can I ask why?

Me: No.

Phoenix: Thought so. Oh, and you're still a piece of shit. Try not to freeze your balls off in that empty house.

I smiled.
It wasn't empty.

CHAPTER FORTY-NINE

"Take down one, take them all."
— *Ex-FBI Agent P*

Nixon

I DRUMMED MY fingertips across my desk as Trace slowly made her way toward me with a glass of wine. She sat in my lap and handed it over. "What has you looking so... depressed?"

"Chase." I swallowed the anger, the resentment, the guilt, and looked away. "What else?"

She shrugged. "Anything I can help with?"

I took a sip of wine. "I love you... more than anything."

Trace frowned and wrapped her arms around my neck. "And I love you, but where is this coming from?"

"I want to murder him." I spoke the words slowly and gauged her reaction. Her eyes widened a bit but other than that, she seemed more confused than anything.

"O-kay..." She drew the word out. "Why?"

"He kissed you."

She smiled and burst out laughing.

I didn't.

"Nixon, that was years ago!"

"Doesn't matter. I still... I can't compete with the friendship you guys have, and I don't want to. Doesn't mean I don't like it. I hate it. I dream about his murder at least twice a day now then feel guilty as hell because he's like my brother. I just... I don't know him anymore, can't predict his movements, his actions.

Nothing about his behavior makes sense to me. He's a loose cannon."

Trace sighed. "That's where you're wrong. You know exactly what it feels like to lose it all."

I shook my head. "What do you mean?"

"If your plan with Luca and Phoenix hadn't worked... You saw me and Chase kiss and didn't know it was a ruse. You saw him shoot me, heard the gunshot... You know that feeling in your chest."

I rubbed at it and looked down. "Yeah."

"That's a sliver of what he's still feeling at having the woman he gave everything to throw it all back in his face as if he wasn't enough."

I listened.

And closed my eyes. "I never want to feel that way again."

"I suspect he doesn't either, and yet..." She lifted a shoulder helplessly. "...all we can do is support him and try to prevent him from murdering another fifty-seven people. He says if you guys say no, he's still...." She didn't finish as tears filled her eyes.

I kissed her forehead. "Then you know what we have to do."

A tear slid free. "Can't you make an exception?"

"No..." My voice shook. "...not in the mafia."

She pressed her hand to mine. "Blood in, no out."

"No out," I repeated, kissing her mouth like she was my drug, because she was. My everything, my heart, my soul.

Pain crushed my body until it was almost too much to bear, and I realized... had our positions been swapped...

Those people would already be dead.

CHAPTER FIFTY

"I have done everything in my power to set things up. And now, I watch."
— *Ex-FBI Agent P*

Luciana

THE SMELL FROM the kitchen interrupted my pity party in the office, I'd started in on the very boring, very tedious notes from the last lawyer and wanted to set the book on fire.

Basically, my job, unless I got fired, was to protect the families at all costs, deal with payouts, bribes, keep the wills up to date, and all the normal things you would assume a crime family would need.

No wonder they were paying me so well.

If word got out...

If one party slipped, if for some reason the FBI or police stopped working with them, I'd be in prison for the rest of my life.

I gave my head a shake and went in search of a bottle of water or soda, something — anything — to dull the ache in my chest and the choking sadness that filled the house.

Chase was at the stove stirring something. I tried not to be affected by his biceps or the tat that wrapped around his neck, but it was impossible. His neck was too huge.

His body too dangerously lethal.

Any woman would stare.

And I'd tasted him.

I felt my cheeks heat as I quickly snatched a bottle of water out of the fridge and opened it, only to take a swig and spit it out onto the floor. "It's snowing?"

"You swallowed earlier. It's the same thing, Luc, only this time it's water," Chase said in a bored tone.

Maybe it was the stress.

Dead bodies.

Prison.

The constant yelling.

Guns.

But I lost my mind.

And chucked the water bottle at his head.

Water sprayed everywhere.

I froze.

Chase stopped stirring and, very slowly, turned around.

With wide eyes, I braced myself on the other side of the counter and waited for him to move.

He did.

So I ran in the opposite direction.

Apparently, too slowly, because he grabbed me around the waist and threw me onto the counter. With one swift movement my ass was bare against the biting cold granite and my leggings were at my ankles.

He gripped my thighs and jerked me down the counter then wrapped my legs around his neck. His icy blue eyes flashed as he purposefully lowered his head, locked eyes with me, then parted my core with his tongue.

And licked.

My mouth dropped open as he swirled his tongue then sucked. His triceps flexed and stretched as he gripped me, working me into a frenzy, finding so many sensitive areas I forgot to breathe.

I squeezed my eyes shut as his tongue dove deeper, only to pull back just when I was ready to fall off the edge.

Or the counter.

Whichever came first.

Another flick of his tongue, and then he drew my bud into his mouth and sucked.

"Chase!" I pounded my hands against the granite. Nothing to hold onto, just him, just this horrible, gorgeous man.

"Open," he demanded, gripping my thighs harder, digging his fingers into them as he moved deeper. His blue eyes flashed with hunger.

I pulled his head down, whimpered, and then lost control of every inhibition I'd strategically put in place as I spread my legs for a murderer and liked it.

The lights flickered out just as he lifted his head and jerked his shirt over his head.

I followed with mine.

My body moved without any mental cues.

Primal.

Everything with this man was primal.

Need.

Want.

No hesitation.

No control.

Just hands removing clothing as fast as humanly possible.

I unbuttoned his jeans, pulling them over his hips. He crawled up onto the counter, his mouth meeting mine in a frenzied kiss as I clawed at his back. More. I wanted more.

He was driving me wild. My heart slammed painfully against my chest as his mouth found mine, eager, wanting. More desperation lit between us as the darkness rolled off his shoulders in waves.

I felt in then.

What plagued him.

And I promised to take.

Every awakening breath stimulated another mind-blowing and meaningful caress of his tongue against my mouth as if he couldn't get enough, and my responses only encouraged his aggressiveness.

He bit down on my lip and then sucked. His knees clamped around my naked hips. His blue eyes sparked, filled with longing, and then, without warning, he filled me so completely. I gripped his arms, holding him still. "That was..."

I could feel him everywhere.

Between my thighs.

Our bodies pulsed together, blood pumping, heat spreading faster than I could control as my muscles flexed to keep him in, to move.

Somehow, in that moment, it was like I could feel his darkness in my soul, as if he demanded I see him and accept him, darkness and all.

Our eyes locked.

My breath quickened.

A sense of foreboding slipped between our bodies, and I shuddered as he made a frenzied glance to my mouth as if he was asking permission to claim me as his.

I wanted this.

Wanted him.

A slow nod was all I gave.

It was all he needed.

"No promises," he said raggedly.

"Okay," I agreed.

His light eyes turned dark with possession as a wave of feral need flashed across his face, as if I was the savior he'd been waiting for all along. I was heady with desire, with the need for him to move, and then his hand moved my hair to the side as he gripped my neck and slid almost completely out of me. I felt the loss so severely I gasped. His hips moved, his eyes stayed locked on me, as if he wanted to make sure I wasn't going to disappear.

His muscles flexed as he flooded me again, took complete control, and I let him. I clung to him as he moved, my nails digging into his hot flesh while he greedily took my mouth over and over again.

Lost. I was so lost to him.

Time didn't exist out of this man's arms.

Maybe it never had.

I shut my eyes in delirium as he thrust deeper, pulling his mouth away from mine, lips parted like he was breathing me in. My skin felt fevered as I grabbed the back of his neck and pulled him in for another kiss and surrendered my body, let go, and gave.

"Luciana." There was reverence in the way he said my name. "Luciana, I'm sorry."

His eyes, I knew, would haunt me for the rest of my life, I just didn't know why. So I held onto the perfect glimpse of Chase Winter Abandonato and the way he filled me.

"You'll always be protected," he whispered. "I swear it. Safe, always safe."

A bead of sweat dripped from his chin onto my chest. My breath hitched as he filled me one last time, slow, deep, perfect.

I fell back against the cold granite as his warmth filled my body, completely taking over every empty space I had.

I couldn't catch my breath.

Didn't want to.

Chest heaving, he whispered against my neck, "It's not nice to throw things."

"So this—" I caught my breath. "—was my punishment?"

He grinned and then slapped my ass so hard I winced. "No, that was."

I laughed and shook my head.

His smile transformed his face as he took my mouth again and again. He spoke against my lips, as if it was normal for us to be naked on the kitchen counter. "Hungry?"

I looked down between our joined bodies. "Starving."

I hadn't realized, until he was grabbing plates, still naked, that he hadn't promised *he* would protect me.

As if he knew he wouldn't be here to do it.

CHAPTER FIFTY-ONE

"Sex never puts things into perspective. If anything, it makes you selfish. It makes you afraid. It makes you weak."
— *Ex-FBI Agent P*

Chase

I WAS DOING dishes.

As if it was completely normal to have sex with my employee on the kitchen counter, eat on it, then clean up.

Something was seriously messed up in me.

And yet, I felt no guilt.

None.

I'd shown her my black soul.

And she'd kissed me anyway.

I had nothing to feel guilty about.

I'd protect her from the grave.

And leave this earth knowing at least one woman found me worthy of something other than being her bitch.

Anger rippled through me as I grabbed another plate. I exhaled slowly and tried to focus my thoughts on Luc's body.

But my brain kept pulling me back to the past. It lingered there too often, like a puzzle I would never figure out but torture myself with for the rest of my existence.

Nobody knew the hell I lived with.

The chaotic thoughts of my own personal tragedy. *What if? What if? What if?*

That was my song.

My chorus.

My blood sang it, even as my anger tried to overtake it.

"Hey," Luc said, making me nearly drop the plate onto the counter.

I tried to appear unaffected by her smile, but it was impossible; the woman seemed to smile over everything.

Especially food.

She'd been so thrilled to have dinner I'd half expected her to get naked again.

"Hey," I said back, my voice less confident than before, my darkness returning, because that was what it fucking did. I never felt the light long enough to hold on; it always slipped away.

Darkness always took over.

Leaving me exhausted.

And angry.

"So I was thinking…" Luc leaned across the counter.

"Me, too," I answered. "I'm firing you."

She jerked back.

I smirked. "I'm kidding. But how about a little proposition?"

"This should be good," she said under her breath.

I smiled, my chest lightening a bit. I liked that she wasn't as terrified as she had been before. I mean, she'd thrown a water bottle at my face with intent on physical harm. That was progress in my book.

Which was completely messed up if that was my way of gauging someone's interest, but whatever.

Luc pulled her hair into a bun on the top of her head and crossed her arms. I liked it, the relaxed look, I liked her naked more but figured if I said that, she'd just think all I wanted was sex.

Which was only partially true.

I wanted to live.

Before I died.

Funny how when faced with your own demise, you see things you never really saw before. Like the few freckles splattered across her cheeks, or the slight curve of her upper lip making it impossible for any sane man to look away without thinking of it wrapped around him.

I braced for her anger, welcomed it, even as I rapped my knuckles against the counter and slowly made my way toward her closed-off form. "Wait until after the commission, then you can get back to work."

"Commission?" She frowned. "Like the city commissioner?"

I tried not to crack a smile.

She glared.

"Sorry." I licked my lips. "I forget you weren't born into terror."

Her face fell as she lifted a shoulder. "Just a different kind of terror, Chase."

The foster system.

I reached for her, not sure what I was trying to accomplish, just maybe the old Chase recognizing the human need for comfort, and the dead Chase awkwardly trying to remember what that looked like, felt like.

I touched her hand.

She squeezed it back then pulled me closer until our bodies were inches apart. I hovered over her, at least a foot taller.

Damn, she was too small for this big world.

Too innocent.

Too dangerous.

Fear lit my blood on fire as I watched her eyes search mine. "So what is it then?"

"Wine?"

"Wine is the answer for everything?" she asked in a slightly more optimistic voice.

"It's flavored water. That's how often we drink it." I grabbed a bottle and two glasses and then moved to the table.

The lights were still off, but it was shockingly bright in the kitchen, probably because of all the snow falling.

"It's pretty, isn't it?" She stared out at the snow as if it was a Disney movie, and we were the stars.

Wrong. Genre.

"Yeah." I squinted out at the snow falling across the damn pool and all the memories of that fucking back yard. "Beautiful."

She rolled her eyes. "You're not seeing it."

"I think I am," I said in a stern voice. "Two inches of snow, covering all the pavers and the pool. Snow I'll need to shovel tomorrow. Snow that will melt into dirty snow. Just... snow."

She gaped at me. "No! That's not it at all! You're wrong."

My lips parted in surprise. Nobody told me I was wrong. Unless they wanted to see what heaven looked like, or hell, depending on the person. "Well then, what do you see?"

She stared out, her smile relaxed, happy. I had no idea what those words felt like anymore. "A fresh start. Blank canvas."

I sucked in a breath.

"Sure, the snow's going to get dirty, but that happens after a fresh start, right? You fall down. You get back up. It's all in how you see the bigger picture. You can blame the blank slate for missed opportunities, or you can embrace it and all the things it has to offer and learn from it. Every fresh snow..." She quirked her lips. "...when I was a kid, at least..." Her eyes met mine. "...was a promise that I could change things, that if the snow got a second chance, so could I."

My heart thudded.

It hurt to breathe.

I broke eye contact and looked down. "People are rarely given second chances in life, Luc."

"Because they're the ones refusing to take them."

Did this damn woman have an answer for everything?

"So..." I changed the subject. "...the commission."

She grabbed her wine, swirled it around in her glass, then took a sip. "Yeah, why is it important that I stop working until then?"

I shrugged. "Burn out?"

She rolled her eyes. "I've been here a little over a week. Nice try."

"Things..." I chose my words carefully. "...will be different after the commission, alright? I won't be around as much." Or at all, if they have it their way. "It's been a hard year, and you make me laugh." Butchering it. I was completely butchering it. "I just—"

She put her hand on my arm. "You want to spend time... with me?"

I nodded.

"As my employer?"

"Hell no," I growled.

"Okay." She looked down at her lap.

I tilted her chin up. Her eyes were worried.

"I won't touch you unless you want me to, I promise. Tell you what, in the mafia we have a little thing—"

She gasped.

I rolled my eyes. "Like you didn't know."

"Nah, it's just weird hearing you say it."

"Even weirder than finding a dead horse head in your bed, am I right?"

She paled.

"Shit, I was kidding." Light spread through my chest then disappeared as fast as it came. Damn, my body felt heavy without it. "In the mafia, we have things called markers. If I give you my marker, it means I owe you a favor, and if I don't own up, then you have a right to take my life."

Her eyes widened. "That seems... severe."

"Life is severe." I looked away.

"So I spend time with you... until this weird commission thing, and I get a favor? Any favor?"

"Exactly."

She seemed skeptical. She should be. "And this commission... it's what exactly?"

"A meeting." I shrugged like it wasn't a big deal. "We have them sometimes when there are disputes within the Families. It's a normal occurrence."

She sighed. "Can I ask you something, then?"

"Sure." Maybe. My breath hitched.

"Why me?"

Because she was the opposite of everything I'd had with Mil. Because she reminded me that I was still human. Because she made breathing hurt a bit less. Because if I didn't make it through the commission, it would be these moments with her that would remind me that humanity wasn't all damned.

That if I could protect her now...

Be with her now...

At least I'd know I left one good thing behind the mountain of bodies I was taking to the pit of hell with me.

"Because you're you," I said, hoping the simple answer would be enough.

Clearly it was. Tears filled her eyes as she nodded her head. "It's nice to be wanted for being you, isn't it?" And then those intelligent eyes flashed to me, fucking seeing through my soul with such laser-like intensity, I almost shoved her away, almost screamed, almost lost my shit.

And then her hand was on my arm as she whispered, "Okay."

CHAPTER FIFTY-TWO

"I'd never been jealous of my enemies — until now."
— *Ex-FBI Agent P*

Luciana

THE SNOW CONTINUED to fall throughout the night. As per our agreement, I sat next to Chase and sang him to sleep, worried as he thrashed in his bed as if demons were dragging him to hell. He woke up twice, yelling her name.

And my heart sank to my knees every time I heard it fall from his lips.

The love he'd had for her must have been otherworldly.

I wondered what that felt like.

What it would be like to have a man love me with such intensity, such boldness that it haunted him.

Once I knew he was fast asleep again, I stopped singing and caressed his face; it finally looked at peace. A feeling of dread filled me as I wondered if that would be the only time he'd actually find it.

When he was asleep.

Forever.

The thought had me rubbing my chest.

He should be my enemy.

Instead, I was starting to think of him as a friend, as someone who saw past people's exteriors and searched for the good and bad on the inside of their hearts.

I had no idea why he was asking me to spend time with him.

But after hearing his screams at night...

And feeling the darkness in his gaze and touch — I knew I had no other choice.

It didn't help that I'd had a nightmare of him screaming at me to run, only to have that Andrei guy shoot him in order to protect me.

It was the stress of this strange new world.

With a sigh, I stood to leave, only to have Chase snake his arm around me and pull me back down to the bed. "Sing them away..." he begged, agony lacing his voice.

"Who are they?" I ran my hands through his hair as he tossed and turned next to me, making only enough room to pull me to his side as if I was his own personal teddy bear. "The people I need to sing away?"

He made a choking noise and then whispered, "People? I meant me. Make me stop..."

"Chase?" Worried, I gave him a shake. He didn't wake up. "Chase?"

He burrowed deeper against my body.

Panic pulsed through my body. Just what was he needing to stop?

I kissed the top of his head and tried to fall asleep but found myself watching the window and counting snowflakes, as if my time was limited, almost as limited as his seemed to be.

CHAPTER FIFTY-THREE

"It's hard to see past my own ambitions. But most days it's hard to see past theirs as well."
— *Ex-FBI Agent P*

Tex

I HADN'T BEEN sleeping.

What sleep I had gotten was only because my wife lulled me with sex. I wracked my brain for a way to deal with the dynasty of our families and still came up with only one solution.

A life for a life.

I knew that blood needed to be spilled when a direct order from the Capo was ignored. I just didn't want to be the one to pull the trigger, which made me weak, when I was supposed to be their leader. But my friend.

One of my best friends.

A knock sounded on my office door. I frowned. It was one in the morning, and I'd just tucked Mo in over an hour ago.

"Come in," I barked, irritated it was probably one of my men needing something that they sure as hell could get themselves if they used their brains.

So I was surprised when Nixon entered followed by Sergio, Phoenix, and Dante.

My gut churned.

Dante had whiskey in his hands.

Sergio had wine.

And Phoenix... well, fucking Phoenix had black folders.

"Shouldn't we just burn those by now?" I pointed.

Nixon's face was pale.

That couldn't be good.

Sergio started drinking straight from the bottle.

"We need to remove her from the situation immediately." Nixon tugged his hair and did a small circle. "Move her to your family, my family, anywhere but that fucking tomb he refuses to leave."

"And how do you expect to do that?" I snorted. "You're the closest to Chase, and he hates you right now."

"He hates himself," Nixon spat. "And I, or any one of us, if put in that position, wouldn't listen to shit and you know it." Fury filled his features.

I looked away.

My call to make.

Always my call.

I motioned for the wine; Sergio handed it over.

My brothers.

I would die for them.

"I don't know what the hell to do," I admitted out loud, "if he breaks the rules."

"I'll do it," Dante gulped.

All eyes fell to him.

He shook his head. "Nixon has too much baggage with Chase. I'm the newest. He's like a brother—" His voice caught. "He *is* a brother to me, but rules are rules, and Phoenix can't do it, not again—"

"I'm fine," Phoenix said in a lethal voice.

"You haven't been fine for a very long time," I said honestly.

Phoenix met my eyes and looked away.

"None of us are fucking fine!" I slammed my fist against my desk as silence blanketed around us.

"People aren't made for this kind of life. Eventually one of us will break."

"Just like Chase," Sergio said.

All of our gazes met.

"So we make a vow, like we did when we formed the Elect." I licked my lips and nodded to Nixon. "Dante gets to kill Chase if he goes AWOL. If I lose my shit—"

"I'll do it," Sergio smirked.

We all fell into laughter. He'd been trying to kill my ass for years and now… now it was a running joke between us. At least it lightened the mood.

"Nixon?"

"You shoot me. You're the one who fucked my sister." He winked.

I threw my head back and laughed. "It was so good, too. You should see the way she—"

Nixon pulled out his gun and waved it around.

"And I'll get Dante." I nodded. "Phoenix will take care of everything else."

"And why is Phoenix still alive?" Phoenix asked the room.

I stared straight at him. "Because someone has to carry on our legacy, and you're the only one who's able to cohabitate with demons."

He sucked in a harsh breath and looked away. "Fine."

It was the truth.

He knew it.

We all knew it.

Funny how, when this all started, he was the one you couldn't trust, the loose cannon.

And now we would be leaving our empires in his

very capable hands if it came down to it.

I sunk down into my chair. "Russian-fucking-roulette."

"Blood in—" Nixon swiped a blade cross his palm. "—no out."

A new pact was made in blood, above my desk, as I spoke over my men. "As burns this saint, so burns my soul."

"*Sangue en no fuori.*"

My body shuddered.

"Dante," I rasped. "If it happens, make it quick."

"He won't even know what hit him."

I nodded, just as another knock sounded at my door.

It opened.

And we all stared in shock as Andrei Petrov walked right in, sat down, turned to Phoenix, and said, "We have a problem."

CHAPTER FIFTY-FOUR

"It was always easier being bad than good."
—*Ex-FBI Agent P*

Andrei

I HATED THEM more than I hated most.

And that was saying a lot.

Italians, to me, were like the scum of the earth, lover than everyone and everything. They'd single-handedly taken down my father's empire and left my family to rot.

And I couldn't blame them.

Because I would have done the same fucking thing.

Phoenix sighed.

I leaned back.

My entrance needed work, but I was Russian. I cared nothing for the way these men flounced their expensive suits and glossy hair. I wasn't getting the results needed, which meant, we had a problem on our hands.

"What. The. Hell." Dante jumped to his feet.

"Sit down, kindergarten." I rolled my eyes and dropped my gaze to Tex, who nodded slowly at me and then to Phoenix, who slid out a black folder and slammed it onto Tex's desk.

I knew what it contained.

My secrets.

My demons.

My demands.

And my utter control of the FBI.

"Someone's been busy." Tex whistled. "Why are we just now finding out about this?"

"All black folders are need-to-know," Phoenix said in a bored tone I knew too well. "I knew, but it was too late, and the only way for Andrei to save face…"

Phoenix had saved my ass that night by killing Mil.

It was the only job the FBI had given me. Take out the rat — the snake — take down the Italian mafia, infiltrate the weakest family.

They just had no idea that the very man they trusted to do everything had been working both sides with Luca Nicolasi for years.

For the man who took a bullet meant for me, by my own father's hand.

It was too easy to fabricate my ruthlessness; Russians were known for blood.

But did people truly believe a punk kid, at eighteen, was capable of taking over an entire crime organization in that way? With that much power? Power was not earned. It was bought, fought for, and I'd had to claw for every inch.

And be taught the correct way to do it.

So I watched.

I waited.

As each of the men I loathed, yet had no choice but to trust, read my secrets out loud, exposing them to the world.

And then, one by one, swore an oath to me in blood.

CHAPTER FIFTY-FIVE

"And now we wait. Now. We. Wait."
— *Ex-FBI Agent P*

Chase

I'D WOKEN UP early.

It was the first time I'd done that in weeks.

Something about seeing the sunrise used to piss me off, maybe because she used to wake up early, too chipper for my liking, so I purposefully slept in so she'd roll in her grave.

But today felt… different.

The sun was bright against the snow. My darkness shuddered at all the light, and I cracked a smile as I started making breakfast.

The commission would be in three days.

I had three days until I knew the final decision.

Three days until I would be hunted.

Three. Days.

I cracked a few eggs and started making French toast. I wanted Luc to keep up her appetite, even though I had no clue how I was going to spend my time with her. I was rusty, and since I wouldn't touch her without her permission, I was really at a loss.

What did I even used to do during the day, other than kill people?

My fuzzy brain tried to conjure up something, but all I had was watching movies with Trace and hanging out with…

My gut churned.

Brothers. My brothers.

The ones I'd shunned.

The ones who would hunt me like I was in the wrong, when they knew damn well that the De Lange line needed to be snuffed out like a light.

Hell, even Phoenix agreed with me, and he wasn't even clinically sane!

The more I thought about it the angrier I became, until I felt a hand on my arm.

I looked up into Luc's tawny brown eyes and fresh face. Her light brown hair was pulled back into a braid, and her face was free of makeup except for a touch of gloss on her lips that immediately drew me in. "I think you've beaten the eggs hard enough."

"Yeah." I set them down. "Want to help?"

She nodded shyly then reached for the sourdough bread, but not before glancing at me, tasting the batter, making a face, and adding a bit of cinnamon.

I burst out laughing. "You make me feel as though everyone's always claimed I'm a good cook, but they were only trying to be nice."

Her eyes widened. "Sorry!"

I took the cinnamon from her hands and licked the same finger she did. "Don't be. You were right."

She exhaled, her eyes darting between my mouth and chin. What the hell. I swept in for a kiss, surprised to find her eager in my arms as she made a little moan against my tongue.

This, this is what we could do for three days straight.

Even if it was just kissing.

I would take it.

Because it made me feel desired.

Alive.

I released her before I took her on the kitchen

counter again then nodded to the stove. "Think you can handle this while I make coffee?"

She gave me a thumbs-up. "Got it."

We moved silently around each other, her humming, me listening, my ears straining to hear more of her pretty voice. It was soothing, the music she hummed.

A few times I pretended to busy myself when really I was just standing there dumbstruck while she cooked.

Normally, I would take over. I didn't trust other people in the kitchen.

But she looked so happy.

Like she belonged.

In this home.

More than I did.

And that was when I noticed it... I tilted my head and then gave it a shake. Something about her felt familiar. I squinted. Something was... the same as something else.

Her bottom lip?

Top?

She tucked a few strands of hair behind her ear and smiled down at the French toast.

Her ears. Is that what looked familiar? Or maybe it was just her entire profile?

I was losing my mind.

Probably from the high body count and lack of sleep. I poured us cups of coffee and went to sit.

Minutes later, I had a plate of French toast in front of me, but she had nothing in front of her.

"You don't like French toast?" I asked, confused.

"Oh, I love it!" she exclaimed, grabbing the maple syrup and holding it up.

I nodded, still frowning, as she made a fucking

design on my plate and then added a few sprinkles of powdered sugar around the edges.

I stared down at my plate.

Pissed.

Just pissed at the world.

Pissed at a dead wife who never really ate what I cooked her, much less shared breakfast with me.

My hands shook as I reached for my fork, only to put it back down again and cleared my throat.

Why did it always come back to my hate?

I couldn't let go.

I wanted to.

I wanted to eat the damn French toast without tasting hate on my tongue.

I thought I gripped the fork again, but somehow it clattered out of my hand and onto the ground.

And then Luciana, with her wide, fear-filled eyes, was standing in front of me, fresh fork in hand. She slowly cut a piece for me and then held it in front of my mouth.

Feeding. Me.

A gesture you make to a toddler, and I was ready to fall to my knees and sob. To confess it all and beg her to make it stop.

Make it fucking stop.

"Open." Her voice shook.

She was just as petrified as I was.

She, afraid of me.

Me, afraid of her.

I was sick with it.

The fear, the hate, the longing.

I bit down on the fork and tasted the goodness, the sweetness of her gesture and the meaning behind it.

"I hope I didn't do something…" She gulped. "… wrong."

"Sometimes," my voice rasped, "people have stronger reactions to something done right."

She licked her lips.

I pulled her into my lap. Her legs dangled on either side of me, and I didn't care. I didn't care that I was starving.

I didn't care that I told her I wouldn't touch her.

I didn't care that I was full of hate.

Anger.

I didn't care about anything but showing my appreciation.

Showing her the thank you I'd always wanted to show, but never had a chance to.

I kissed her mouth, took it in mine and savored her taste, and then pressed my head to her chest. "Thank you for making breakfast."

It sounded so stupid, saying it out loud.

"Chase?" Her voice sounded afraid.

"Yeah." I didn't move.

"Can I ask you something?"

"Maybe."

My body shook a bit as she ran her hands down my tense shoulders and then turned my face to hers. "When was the last time someone took care of you?"

I didn't answer.

Because I had none.

Because the answer was *never*.

Because the answer was pathetic.

She nodded. Like she knew my silence was all she would get, and she was okay with it. And then she reached for the fork and fed me again.

CHAPTER FIFTY-SIX

"I never thought I'd see the day that I would choose wine over vodka."
— *Ex-FBI Agent P*

Luciana

I wasn't a violent person.

I think that had already been established tenfold, but I'd never before experienced such a violent need to physically maim someone as I did right then, feeding Chase.

His eyes were glazed over like he was in a trance with each bite he took. His hands braced my hips, fingers digging into my skin like he was afraid that any second I was either going to disappear or run away.

And no matter how many times I locked eyes with him, trying to reassure him that I wasn't going away, he still looked...

Terrified.

And that was when I realized I'd been mistaking his anger. He was full of darkness, yes, but that darkness wasn't just lashing out in anger.

It was a devastating sadness.

Mistrust.

Debilitating fear.

I sucked in a breath.

"What?" He swallowed the last bite I'd given him. His head tilted to the side as if he was trying to figure me out. Piercing blue eyes raked over me like a caress;

his full lips pressed into a smile that made my chest ache. "Do I have syrup on my chin?" He wiped it.

I shook my head as I felt tears fill my eyes.

"Luc..." He pressed his hands to my face gently, as if I was precious to him, which made it even worse.

"I'm sorry," I whispered.

He frowned. "I don't understand?"

"I could kill her." I gasped after I said it out loud, and horrified, I covered my face with my hands.

He went completely still beneath me.

Great, Luciana, just when things are getting better, you tell him you want to kill the only woman he's ever really loved.

It slipped.

The anger.

And after seeing his sadness, I just... I wanted it to go away, but she'd done something unfathomable to one of the most beautiful men I'd ever met, one of the most protective, overbearing, beautiful men.

I was sick to my stomach.

I tried to pry myself away from his body, but his arms held me still on his lap.

His breathing was slow, intense; his chest rose and fell like it took effort for him to remember to inhale.

Had I finally pushed him too far?

"Look at me," he said in a harsh whisper.

Tears filled my eyes as I very slowly pulled my hands down and stared into his sharp eyes.

"I wouldn't wish that on my greatest enemy, let alone someone I consider a friend." He looked away as if he was trying to find the right thing to say then lifted me off his lap and grabbed my hand.

I tried not to shake, but it was hard.

He led me up the stairs and down the hall into two double doors.

I gasped when he opened them.

It was the most massive suite I'd ever seen in my entire life; that one suite was bigger than ten of my bedrooms growing up. It didn't have any furniture except for a mattress and a chair over in the corner, plus about three suitcases, all Louis Vuitton.

The closet was full of clothes.

Not his.

Hers.

I suddenly found it hard to breathe as he walked into the bathroom then came out with a baseball bat.

Logic told me he had a point to make.

But I'd seen what he could do.

What he did do.

And maybe I didn't trust him as much as I thought, because he was holding the bat as if he was about to do something with it, and I was the only person in that room he could aim it at.

Or so I thought.

He flipped it over and handed it to me.

I took it with shaking hands. "Why do I have a baseball bat in my hands? And why would you keep one in the bathroom?"

His lips tilted into a smile. "I'm gonna tell you a story, and every time you get pissed off, you get to hit something. Just make sure you aim for a wall. I don't want to have to explain to someone how I got my ass handed to me by someone half my size."

"I'm not half your size."

He smirked again. "Whatever you say."

I scowled and held the bat. "About downstairs, I

didn't mean—"

He held up his hand and started talking. "It was an arranged marriage."

My eyebrows shot up.

"I loved Trace," he admitted, sparking so much jealousy in my chest I had to fight to suck in air. "Or thought I did. Long story short, I don't feel that way about her now, so you can stop being jealous."

"I wasn't—"

"You were," he said with confidence.

I looked down at my bare feet; they were dwarfed by the size of his in his black boots.

"I married her to protect her. She was the first female boss and knew she would need the protection of my name, my money, my body."

I gripped the bat, hating the story already, hating that my body felt like it was on fire when I barely knew the guy.

It was a lie to myself.

That I barely knew him.

I forced myself to believe it as he kept talking.

"That day, on my wedding day, when I said my vows to Mil, I knew, no matter what she did to me, no matter what the world did to us, I would die before letting anything happen to her. I didn't love her, not yet, but it didn't matter, because I made a vow, and I took it seriously. Eventually, I fell for her. I fell so fucking hard that my head spun." He stopped the story and I tilted my head toward him. "Hit something."

I wasn't an angry person.

But I was angry now.

I slammed the bat into the side of the nearest wall, chest heaving. He came up behind me, put his hands on my shoulders, then ran them down my arms slowly.

I felt each finger, each press against my skin as he whispered in my ear, "I gave her my heart."

I trembled.

"My soul."

I hated her.

"And when I asked for the same..." His voice hitched. "...she gave me excuses."

I leaned back against him.

"She gave me all she was capable of giving," he continued. "But it wasn't enough. I was never enough."

He pulled back as I slammed the bat into the wall three more times, using everything I had. Cracks appeared, my hands grew sweaty as I gripped the bat with fury, waving it over and over again at the white wall as if it was her face, as if it would take away the anger I felt in my soul.

"She fucked me," he spat, "and betrayed me... the same day she had a miscarriage."

I could taste his anger.

"The same day she told me she was *glad* we weren't bringing a child into the world."

I gripped the bat so hard my fingers hurt. Tears filled my eyes.

"I wasn't greedy, Luc," he whispered. "Three things I wanted out of this life, only three." His mouth was near my neck, his nose nuzzled behind my ear as he whispered, "One, to love and be loved unconditionally."

I closed my eyes.

"Two..." His voice lowered. "...to have a family."

A solitary tear ran down my cheek.

"Three—" His voice caught. "—to never..." He

hesitated. "...to never outlive my wife."

The bat clattered against the wood floor.

"So, when you say you could kill her, know that it's probably one of the nicest things anyone's said to me in the past eight months."

"How so?" I finally found my voice.

"Because..." He slowly turned me in his arms. "It means someone gets my pain, my rage. It means someone didn't look at me as a man they needed to control..." He pressed a kiss to my lips. "...but someone who has every reason in the world to be unleashed."

I licked my lips and said the only thing that was left to be said, "Listen to me very carefully." I gripped him by the front of the shirt, our eyes locked, as tension pounded between us. "She didn't deserve you."

His kiss was swift, endless, as I opened my mouth to him and felt my body release every ounce of anger, letting him kiss it away, right along with his. He tasted like coffee, his mouth searing as his full lips massaged and kneaded. I tasted his sadness and pushed it away with my tongue, fought it with my body as he lifted me against him and pressed me against the wall I'd just attacked with the bat. My body slid roughly against his chest as I hooked my legs around his waist. He nipped my lips, bringing his head back before attacking my mouth again with his.

I'd never been kissed like this before.

Never felt such want from another human being that it stole my breath away and made my heart clamor in my chest like an addict.

I reached for his shirt again, needing something to hold onto, then grabbed his shoulder, pulling him closer as he spread my legs wide around his hips.

Every time we touched it was electric.

As if someone had lit a match and poured gasoline on it.

And every time, I gave in.

Because I couldn't help myself.

But also because I recognized something in his eyes, in the way he kissed, as if he was afraid it would be his last.

His kiss said, *"Love me, look at me, desire me, want me."*

His kiss was like my heartbeat, the thoughts I'd had every day growing up.

I'd always heard that souls recognized each other, and I knew in that moment, regardless of his feelings, his anger — mine recognized his.

And wanted.

Ached.

Needed.

I sighed against his mouth, ending the kiss, but he didn't stop. He kissed down my neck, alternating between biting and kissing — as if he couldn't stop; as if self-control wasn't in his vocabulary.

I slid my hand beneath his shirt.

He stilled.

Our eyes met again.

"Sorry," I whispered, mouth swollen.

"For kissing me back?" His chest heaved.

"No." Our foreheads touched. "I'm just..." Why was I trying not to cry in this guy's arms? I should be kissing him, not crying into his shirt. "I'm just so sorry."

"I thought we talked about wasting tears." He kissed my lips softly, so softly my heart ached with it.

"And I thought I told you I got to choose who I wasted them on."

His licked his lips, sucking in the bottom, making my heart race more than it already was. *"Cosi bella."*

I shivered.

Chase angry was sexy.

Chase sad… still sexy.

Chase standing… still so sexy.

Chase speaking Italian?

I might not survive.

I wasn't used to compliments, not by men like him. I closed my eyes and turned into his hand, then pressed mine against it, just keeping it there.

Something told me if I could keep holding on, he would never let go. My heart dropped at the thought of losing his touch.

"Luc."

I opened my eyes.

He shook his head back and forth like he was confused. "Another lifetime… and I would have given you everything instead of her."

"In another lifetime," I whispered sadly. "And to think, I'd take it all now."

He dropped his hand as if my truth was too much for him to handle then set me on my feet.

The doorbell rang.

Without a backward glance, he walked out of the room as I slowly sunk to the floor.

CHAPTER FIFTY-SEVEN

"He wasn't falling for it, and time was running out. Good thing I had a plan B."
— *Ex-FBI Agent P*

Chase

I TUGGED MY hair with both hands as I stomped down the hall. What was it about this woman that had me tied up in knots? That had me doubting my only task, my only purpose.

When I was kissing her, I had a thought so fleeting, a thought beyond three days from now, a thought about holidays, a house that wasn't haunted, spring. They all came in rapid succession.

Luciana smiling down at me.

And me feeling free enough to smile back without wondering if the smile was real, or if there was something else lingering behind it.

Three days, and I was already doubting myself because of a kiss? Because of sex?

Or was it just her?

I couldn't tell the difference between my attraction to her and my need for someone to just accept me.

By the time I made it to the door, the person had stopped ringing the doorbell and was knocking angrily.

I grabbed my gun, pointed, and opened.

Nixon had his out, too.

Not what I expected.

My stomach clenched as anger fueled me again. "What the hell are you doing here?"

A brief sadness flashed across his face before he

lowered his gun and tucked it in his jeans.

I kept mine trained on his face.

He leaned against the open doorframe and stared down at the ground even though I still had a loaded gun on him. "How long are you going to punish yourself?"

Again, not what I expected. Slowly I lowered the gun to my side. "Who says I'm still punishing myself?"

He snorted. "You're living in the house you built her, with her shit still in the closet."

I flinched.

"You're letting her control you even now, from the grave. I can't help but think that, even dead, she's going to destroy us all."

"Why else do you think I'm wiping them out?"

He sighed. "I want to blame you. I do." He cursed. "I can't."

"Is that why you're here?" I tried to keep the edge from my voice. "To apologize for being such a damn hypocrite?"

"Actually, no. You know how I hate admitting anything, especially to you."

Figured. I rolled my eyes and waited.

Nixon turned, his face softening. "Don't do it, Chase."

Threats, he did well.

But Nixon Abandonato never begged. And a part of me hated myself for putting him in a position where he felt like he had to.

"Please," he added, "do not do this."

I hung my head.

"Chase." He grabbed me by the shoulders. "Think it through. There is no scenario where you don't end up dead next week. None."

"You gonna do it?" I asked in a quiet voice.

He released me. "No, I get to kill Tex if he loses his shit."

"So I've lost my shit?"

He was quiet and then, "I think we all have."

"That's comforting, since we have guns and lots of money."

Nixon smirked. "You making a joke?"

"Feels foreign, a bit rusty," I admitted.

Nixon looked over my head.

I turned.

Luciana was standing at the bottom of the stairs looking very well tousled and kissed. Pride swelled in my chest. I'd put that stunned look on her face. I had sucked those lips, and damn if I wasn't going to do it over and over and over again until she begged me to stop, or until I breathed my last breath.

"Think about it," Nixon finally said pointedly.

"You never told me who pulled the short straw," I reminded him.

Pain laced his features. "Your protégé."

Something ugly twisted in my chest.

The guy I'd trained to be ruthless.

My friend.

My brother.

"He volunteered," Nixon said, driving the knife deeper into my back.

It wasn't betrayal.

It was the mafia.

And I knew... had the positions been switched, I would have done the same.

"Damn it, Dante." I shook my head and muttered

an oath. "He doesn't need that shit on his shoulders."

"A little too late, don't you think?" Nixon gave me one last pensive stare before walking back to his SUV and cranking the engine.

I slowly closed the door and then slammed my hand against it. "How much did you hear?"

When I turned around, Luc was right in front of me. I'd seen her sad, and I thought I'd seen her angry.

I thought wrong.

Her nostrils flared as she shoved me against the door with more force than I knew she was capable of. I let her. Because she'd let me talk.

So if she needed to shove me...

So be it.

"What did he mean you are going to end up dead?"

I crossed my arms. "Luc..." Damn it. "Don't worry about—"

"Stop!" she yelled. "Don't patronize me and just tell me!"

"You want to know?" I roared. "Do you really think you can take it?"

She glared.

I took a step toward her, a lethal one, one that showed power, anger. "I'm killing them all, every last member of that bloodline, with or without permission!"

"And without permission means..." She quieted.

"That you've been kissing a dead man." I tried to shove past her, but she grabbed my elbow, tugging me back.

"How many days?"

I didn't need to tell her.

Because she already knew.

Realization hit her as she dropped my arm and

stared lifelessly ahead. "That's why you don't want me working..."

"Do you blame me? For wanting to spend my last few days on this earth doing something other than hating the one woman who took my heart and stabbed it with a knife while it was still beating?"

"No." She choked out the word and then nodded her head like she was having a conversation with herself. "But don't blame me for doing everything in my power to change your mind."

"You won't."

"I will." She shoved past me and ran up the stairs.

My scowl turned into a smile as I whispered, "But I'll love seeing you try."

CHAPTER FIFTY-EIGHT

"He had to make his choice, and for the first time, I wondered if the story would end differently than I thought... differently than we'd all planned."
— *Ex-FBI Agent P*

Luciana

O{PERATION SAVE} C{HASE} was in full force.

He just didn't know it yet.

But he was about to.

I stripped off my shirt and pants, clad in only my black lacy bra and my boy-short underwear, then quickly pulled my hair back into a high ponytail so it was out of my face.

He wanted a reason to live?

I was going to give him a billion.

And if that didn't work.

I was going to do an Internet search on how to kidnap someone; I figured Nixon would even help.

I stifled a laugh behind my fingers. Was I really thinking about kidnapping a mafia member? I laughed even harder. Maybe I was getting delirious from all the shooting, the kissing, the chaos. But the thought had me actually smiling. That's how easy it was for him to corrupt me.

A week in, and I was contemplating renting a white van and parking it down by the river. Great.

I opened my door and marched down the hall.

The fridge door was open, the light on, I could see his boots from underneath it. The minute it shut, he choked on the water he was drinking and sputtered, "The hell are you doing?"

One of the security guys, the scary looking one named Vic, passed by, whistled, and kept walking.

Chase lunged.

I grabbed his hand just as Vic flipped him off and shut the door to the garage behind him.

"Next time…" Chase swore. "…I shoot him."

"Non-fatal?"

"Flesh wound." He joked like I had earlier in the week.

We shared the humor, and then his smile dropped as his half-lidded gaze filled with lust. "Is this part of your plan?" He grabbed one of the bra straps and snapped it against my skin.

The burn was such a turn-on I almost lost my nerve. I didn't have a ton of experience, and Chase tended to kiss and touch like a puppy died every second he didn't try his hardest.

"Is it working?" I put my hands on my hips.

He shrugged. "Maybe. Maybe not."

"Oh, he wants me to try harder?"

Another shrug though his eyes flashed with amusement.

I grabbed his hands and pulled them to my breasts.

He swallowed slowly, his lips parting as his eyes took on a lazy gaze.

"Dead people don't get to cop a feel."

"Don't they though? Zombies get plenty of play," he fired back.

"Oh, so you're coming back a zombie?"

"How else am I supposed to stalk you?"

I shuddered as his thumbs moved over my nipples.

Rein it in! I needed to focus.

"I've always been more a vampire girl, sorry."

He rolled his eyes. "Of course you are."

I got close enough to kiss him and then grabbed his right hand and splayed it out against my stomach.

He frowned.

I inched it lower.

His gaze dropped.

I pressed his fingertips into the top of my underwear... then stopped. "You'd be missing out on a lot of... things."

He inched his fingers forward, digging against my skin, making me want to squirm against him and beg for more. "Oh yeah? What kind of things?"

I was in over my head, definitely in over my head.

He spread his palm wide and pressed down. "You mean this?"

Yeah, this was a horrible idea. I should have just gotten naked and danced with scarves or something.

Because that was what made men not want to die. Scarves.

I jerked when a finger slid in. "Or this?"

The plan was backfiring; I was supposed to be driving *him* crazy, not the other way around.

He flipped me in his arms so my back was facing him, not moving his hand as he slowly touched me.

"Good plan." He nipped my ear. "Solid."

"I may have—" I gasped, arching against his palm. "—um, not thought—"

His fingers kept teasing.

"—not thought things—"

"Not thought things?" His breath teased my ear.

"—through. Not thought—" I bit down on my

bottom lip and sucked as my hips rocked against him. I gripped him with my free hand. "—things through." I finally got it out.

"Mmm." He was rock-hard. Hot against my ass.

I rubbed back against him.

He stumbled a bit and then bit back a curse.

I wasn't sure who was more aroused, me or him.

He moved again.

Good. Lord. Him. Him. Him all the way.

"We really should stop using the kitchen as a bedroom." He moved his hand, gripping my underwear with his fist and tugging, ripping them completely from my body. I gasped into his mouth as he pressed me against the fridge with one hand while dropping his jeans with the other.

With one smooth thrust, he was inside me.

It was the best idea I'd ever had.

Poorly executed.

But... The. Best.

I arched under his kiss as he slammed into me again. My breasts ached as they slid against the metal of the fridge. I tried reaching for something and ended up releasing a few ice cubes onto our joined bodies.

"Shit!" He jerked, tossed his head back, and laughed.

A gorgeous, *dear-God-the-man-is-too-pretty-for-words* laugh.

I never stood a chance against him.

I wondered how anyone could.

"Your laugh..." I tugged his head down and captured his lips as he pressed into me again, slower this time. "...is the sexiest thing I've ever."

He grinned down at me. "Want to know the sexiest

thing I've ever seen?"

He didn't say anything else.

Just ran his hands down my shoulders and around my ass, cupping it, angling us differently as he inched deeper, making it impossible to think. Making me lose myself in his presence, worship with his name dropping again and again from my lips.

"So damn sexy," he growled against my mouth in an almost painful kiss as I clawed at his chest in an effort to hold him closer, to keep him there forever.

Incomparable loss washed over me when he pulled out, only to have him flip me around so I was bracing myself against the counter a few feet away. The shock of being shoved from him had my fingers digging into the granite to keep me standing. I gasped for breath as he stood over me. The tip of him pressed slowly, so slowly into me. I cried out as his massive body covered me in its warmth.

"I'm going to be erect every time I make coffee because of you."

I smiled and then grabbed the edge of the counter as he moved. Painfully slow strokes hit every nerve ending I possessed. I squeezed my eyes shut as he invaded every part of me that was on fire for him, as if he knew I'd been waiting for this feeling, for him, my whole life.

"People are going to say, 'Chase it's a bagel. Nobody gets erect over a bagel.'" He shoved the bagels off the counter with his hand and filled me completely.

My body jerked in response.

"Or, 'It's just orange juice.'" He slammed into me again.

I lost my breath.

"Cereal," I whimpered as he sped up. My thighs squeezed together, closing him in.

"Luc, princess, keep doing that, and this is over."

I shook my head no, but couldn't help myself as my body naturally responded to his.

Our hands tangled together — mine pressed against the granite, his pressed against mine.

"I've always been a gentleman. I'm about to lose that track record," he rasped. "Let go."

I shook my head. "What are you doing in two weeks?"

"Next week—" He plunged forward, and the feel of him was too much — the pleasure, the situation, everything. I fell apart as he finished. "—I'll be dead."

CHAPTER FIFTY-NINE

"Sometimes we see only what we want to see. I pity the man most days, because he does not know what he has become — then again, neither do I."
— *Ex-FBI Agent P*

Chase

She was resilient.

Feisty.

Showing a side of herself that had me doing nothing but grinning all day long, as if I actually had a reason to.

There was the kitchen sex where I tasted heaven and saw a woman come completely undone because of my mouth.

Followed by more kitchen sex where she slid a bagel onto my dick and asked if she could stack more.

I was so embarrassingly aroused that I couldn't even focus when she went through the entire bag, nodded approvingly, then slowly lowered her head and started taking small bites around the holes.

The kitchen was my new favorite spot.

Followed closely by the pantry, where she trapped me and said that it was like hell — no bathroom, boxed food, and hot. She then proceeded to tell me that was my future. *Good to know she doesn't think I'm going to heaven either.*

She let me out two hours later.

And that was only day one.

At the end of every day, she asked me the same thing. "What are you doing in two weeks?"

And every day, I told her I would be dead.

On day three, Friday, the day of the commission, something changed. I'd started breakfast like I had been doing for the past few days and noticed that she hadn't come downstairs like she normally did.

It made me anxious.

Irritated at myself that I was that concerned over the fact that she was normally downstairs at the exact time every day. And that her being late messed with my head.

I stirred the eggs.

Then turned the stove off after another ten minutes and peeked around the corner.

With a curse, I bounded up the stairs and knocked on her door.

When she didn't answer, I shoved it open, only to find her lying on her bed.

"Luc?"

She didn't move.

"Luc?" I reached her side.

She was staring up at the ceiling, her eyes sad as she whispered, "That's what it feels like to wake up in the morning, ready for your day, excited to see someone, only to remember that they're no longer here, that your life is a little bit darker than it was before." Her eyes flashed to mine. "That's what I'll feel like every day you're gone, and I'm still here."

My stomach clenched as I closed my eyes and reached for her. "Luc—"

"Don't." She sighed. "I know what day it is. I just... want you to know what you'll be leaving. It's not just about this giant house or your vendetta against that family." For some reason she always had trouble mentioning their name. "It's bigger than that. Your choices affect everyone around you, me included."

"I know," I rasped.

She reached for my hand and looked away.

"It's the sex, you know," I lied. "The minute I'm out of your life, someone else is going to come barging in, and you'll forget all about the murderer you fucked and the darkness he let you touch because he couldn't say no."

She flinched and let go of my hand. "Do you really think so little of me?"

No. "It's not what I think. It is what it is."

"Another lifetime." She hung her head.

And I fought to keep myself from cracking. I would not back down. I couldn't. Not now. Not after everything. "Another lifetime," I agreed, cupping her chin.

"Hey, Chase?"

"Yeah, princess?" I pulled her into my arms as she pressed her cheek against my chest.

"What are you doing in two weeks?"

"In two weeks..." It was harder to get out this time, harder to swallow, knowing she'd be sad, knowing it would affect her. I squeezed my eyes shut and whispered, "...I'll be dead."

CHAPTER SIXTY

"Sometimes the only right choice is the wrong one. Good thing none of us have a conscience. How could we with bloodstained hands?"
— *Ex-FBI Agent P*

Chase

I DIDN'T SEE Luc the rest of the day.

I imagined she was avoiding me, and it actually stung, proving yet again, she'd somehow found the last broken piece of my heart and held it long enough to breathe more life into it.

I grabbed my gun then slammed my hand against the wall until it went numb.

She wasn't supposed to happen.

It was supposed to be just sex.

Nothing more.

And I'd done the stupid thing and let her in, only enough for her to see my darkness and run in the opposite direction.

Instead, she'd embraced it like you would a stray sick cat and had become hell-bent on saving my life.

But she didn't know.

I was way past worth saving.

And even if I had her, I wasn't good enough to keep her.

And this life — this life was one I would never choose for her.

Regardless of how much I liked kissing her, touching her, just laying my head against her. She was the peace in my war.

And the most selfish thing I could do was ask her to

pick up a gun and join the fight when her job, all along, had been to end it.

I swiped my phone from the nightstand and frowned when I saw all the new text messages.

> **Tex:** Commission moved to tomorrow night, try not to get killed before then.

I rolled my eyes.

> **Nixon:** He's too busy having sex.
>
> **Dante:** Who? Tex?

I smirked at the thread.

> **Nixon:** Keep up. He's banging the help.

I gripped the phone into my fist and then texted back.

> **Me:** I will gut you from head to toe if you say one more thing, Nixon.
>
> **Dante:** Holy shit, you're right!
>
> **Phoenix:** Good thing we don't have an HR department.

Does nobody take my threat to Nixon seriously?

> **Sergio:** So you went from threatening to shoot her to what? Threatening with your cock?
>
> **Tex:** Raise your hand if you shuddered when Sergio said cock.
>
> **Me:** Raising both hands.

Dante: Ditto.

Nixon: Didn't even know he had one it's so small.

Sergio: Cock life.

How had we gone from the commission talk to this? I wiped my face with my hands.

Tex: Family dinner at Chase's?

Me: NO!

Nixon: I'll bring wine.

Tex: I got bread.

Sergio: Salad.

The texts came so fast that by the time I typed out my response, they had already set a time.

In the next hour.

I growled and tossed my phone onto my bed just as Luc walked by. I could feel her sadness; it filled the air, making it hard to breathe.

"Family dinner," I grumbled.

"After?" She tilted her head and swallowed.

I crossed my arms. "It's been moved to tomorrow— Umph!"

She'd jumped into my arms and kissed me so hard that I saw stars, and without breaking that hot-as-fuck kiss, started pulling my shirt over my head with one hand and unbuttoning my jeans with the other.

"Is this about the dinner or the commission?" I grinned against her mouth.

"Shut up." She slid down my body and jerked my jeans to the ground. I sprung free, ready for action, ready for her, ready for… peace.

Her eyes swallowed me whole as she stood and then pulled her shirt over her head. I would die, and soon, but I would die with her name on my lips and a vision of her body in my blood-filled gaze.

I tugged her to me, needing to feel her as my anxiety skyrocketed out of control with the need to claim her, to protect her, to stay by her side.

The war in my chest fanned to life with every kiss, every touch.

She yanked me down to the bed, and when I hovered over her and took her lips in my mouth, when I licked down her body and felt the soft curve of her feet and braced her hips with my hands, it hit me.

If she was giving me everything...

What would she have left?

I grasped her chin with my hand and pressed a kiss to her lips. "No more, Luc."

I pulled away.

It was one of the hardest things I'd ever done, refusing to take those pieces with me to the grave, like Mil had taken mine.

I would never be that person.

Ever.

I stood and backed away slowly, as hurt flashed across Luc's features. "I can't."

"What?" Her face fell. "I don't understand."

I grabbed a blanket from my chair and covered her with it then kissed the top of her forehead. "I won't do it."

"Do what?" Her lower lip trembled. "What's happening?"

"I know what it's like..." I wrapped the blanket tighter around her body. "...to give yourself to someone expecting nothing in return, hoping, but not expecting, only to have that very selfish person take and take and take until you have nothing left. I've been taking. And it ends now. It's the most selfless thing I can think of doing before…" Before I died. "So I'm asking you — no, I'm begging you—" My voice cracked. "—take it all back."

Tears filled her eyes.

"Fucking take all of it!" Pain exploded through my chest at her hurt expression. "Because I won't do it!" I yelled. Why was I yelling at her? Why? "I'm not like her! I won't be like her!" I tugged at my hair and then clawed at my own chest. Everything hurt.

Everything.

"Damn it, Luciana! Promise me you'll take it all back! I can't do that to you! Don't you understand me? I WON'T DO IT!"

She stared me down, her eyes brave, her posture straight. "Too late."

I kicked the chair in front of me then slammed my hand against the nightstand, sending the lamp flying.

"Chase…" Her voice was calm. "…what are you doing in two weeks?"

I crumpled to a heap on the floor, trembling, and said, "I don't know."

CHAPTER SIXTY-ONE

"The hardest things are always the most necessary."
— *Ex-FBI Agent P*

Luciana

I SET THE table, anxious to do something after Chase's outburst. I wondered if the man had even really mourned the loss or had just lost his mind and shot anyone who spoke to him.

My throat felt like I had a golf ball stuck in it, and it refused to budge. He'd left the room, stormed out after his confession, so I'd gotten dressed and headed into the kitchen.

And nearly wept.

The counter.

The fridge.

The floor.

We'd basically had sex on every surface, near every object, and every single time I'd let go in his arms, I'd given him my soul, my heart.

No take-backs.

Had we met in another lifetime, we would have been the story people talked about on social media. Girl met boy. Girl fell for boy. Girl told boy she was going to marry him after the first date.

Boy fell for girl. Boy protected girl. Boy loved girl. Boy told girl he was going to marry her after their first introduction.

I closed my eyes against the onslaught of tears as our story continued in my imagination. I saw it all.

Us holding hands.

Laughter.

Awkward dates.

The kissing.

The sex.

Body sliding against body.

The proclamation.

A life together.

Something I'd done nothing but dream about for years, and the one guy I'd fallen for wouldn't be here to share it with me. The man didn't even realize that it doesn't matter to me if he doesn't have a heart to give.

Because I have a big enough heart for the both of us.

I finished setting the table then went about fixing a nice red sauce. Chase had so much pasta in his pantry I imagined it was the only food group acceptable to the rest of them.

I added ingredients and turned on the gas stove just as he walked in the kitchen, freshly showered. A white Henley covered his muscles, the tattoos on his right hand peeking out from the sleeves. His black ripped jeans hugged every muscle in his body making him look too good for words.

"Hey," I croaked.

He didn't respond, just took a few steps toward me and pulled me against his chest. I would miss this smell.

I wasn't sure if it was cologne or just shower mixed with lotion, but he always smelled warm and spicy.

I sighed, clinging to him, feeling his muscles

beneath his shirt.

He kissed the top of my head. "I'm sorry." His chest rumbled against my ear.

"Me too," I said.

"You weren't the one yelling."

I stood up on my tiptoes and captured his mouth in mine. It felt so natural, kissing him in the kitchen, that I lost myself.

He pressed a hand to the counter and gripped my ass with the other just as someone let out a whistle.

"Vic, I swear I will—" Chase turned and then pulled away from me as if I were diseased.

Trace looked between the two of us then winked. "He get you pregnant with that kiss?"

Chase chucked a towel in her face while I relaxed a bit and smiled at her, and then panicked as I touched my stomach.

Chase frowned at me before turning around to the stove.

Pregnant.

We'd never talked about birth control.

I was on it.

But… we'd been having sex like crazy.

I pushed the thought away and joined him by the sauce.

The others slowly filed in.

Loudly.

They didn't do quiet.

Lots of shouting, guns waving, wine bottles getting passed around.

Apparently, that was normal to them.

Chase at least looked happier than last time, until Nixon walked in the room and gave him a solemn look.

Once his back was to me, I lifted the spoon and tasted the sauce, made a face, then added a few more spices.

The room fell completely silent.

I turned to see every single individual staring at me slack-jawed.

"Did you..." Tex pointed at the stove. "...did you just... touch Chase's food?"

"She's in his workstation," Sergio said under his breath, backing away.

"Don't touch the food — that's rule umber one." Phoenix shook his head and tugged at his hair.

"Rule number two, don't touch the damn food." Dante crossed his bulky arms.

Even the women looked worried. Trace's mouth was completely ajar as if I was about to get shot.

I crossed my arms and sighed. "It needed salt."

They gasped in unison.

"It did?" Chase rounded the corner and winked.

It was like everyone in the room held their breath.

He pulled his gun.

I fought not to grin.

Then set it on the table and pulled me into his arms, kissing me softly on the mouth. "Thanks."

"What. Just. Happened?" Tex asked the silent room. "Two years ago, I touched the sauce. Chase grabbed a fucking knife and chased me until I swore I would never — and I do mean never — touch his stove again."

"She's prettier than you." Chase winked at me and then turned. "Plus, she went to culinary school for a few years. Knows her shit."

"We get two cooks now?" Tex seemed to perk up.

And then Chase had to go and ruin it by adding,

"Well, at least you'll be left with one…"

The room fell silent.

I closed my eyes.

"That wasn't awkward…" Tex nodded. "…not even a little bit. Good job, man."

"Wine?" Sergio coughed and held up a bottle.

And every single person held out a glass, and if it wasn't empty, chugged it before he made it to them.

Chase's fingers brushed against mine as he handed me a goblet.

Food was served.

But I wasn't hungry.

I was too upset over the fact that the clock was still ticking, and that Chase was letting it run.

CHAPTER SIXTY-TWO

"The thing about the taste of death — you forget what it means to breathe in the life. You forget until it is too late, until you take your last breath and realize how much you miss being alive."
— *Ex-FBI Agent P*

Chase

THE ROOM WAS tense. My family tried to keep things light, but the minute those words left my mouth, things shifted, as if they knew the future.

And that I wouldn't be present in it.

I hung my head a bit as Tex glared at me across the table.

And then Nixon slapped me on the back and poured me more wine.

I snorted and took the glass, eying Luc over the top of it as she shoved food around her plate, apparently making it look like she was eating when I knew it was complete bullshit.

Her eyes were rimmed with red.

And she looked seconds away from crying.

I jerked my head to her and eyed Nixon.

He stood and stretched. "Big day tomorrow."

Phoenix followed, and then the rest of them.

They took the hint. They knew me inside and out. All I had to do was flinch and make eye contact, and we could communicate with one another.

My gut clenched.

I would miss that.

My brotherhood.

My family.

And just as my heart stuttered to a stop, I saw blood-red as the guys all said their goodbyes to Luciana.

Dante hesitated in front of her, his eyes searching her face before he looked at me then back down at her. With a bright smile that had me clenching my hands into fists, he grabbed both of her hands and kissed the back of each before leaning down and whispering something in her ear, something that made her skin blush just enough that I wanted to kill him.

He knew the rules.

What the hell was he doing?

When he looked back at me, he winked.

I was going to strangle him to death. Pain laced through me. Why would he do that? What purpose did it serve other than to make me want to reach for my gun?

Nixon stopped next, turned to me, smirked, and kissed her on the forehead. It was a slow kiss, a lingering kiss, as his messy dark hair fell across his forehead, as he reached down and cupped her chin and brushed a thumb over her lips and then patted her on the shoulder like he had a right to touch her, a right to comfort her.

A right to fix what I continuously broke.

I jerked to my feet, my chair tumbling backward.

My chest heaved.

Don't kill him.

Do. Not. Kill. Him.

For touching what was mine, on purpose, in order to get a reaction out of me.

When he passed me, smug grin still present, he gripped me by the arm and muttered low in his throat, "You do this... you leave her unprotected."

I tried to jerk free, but his grip tightened.

"You do this, and you leave her to someone else. Her kisses, they don't belong to you in death, and neither will her body."

He might as well have just shot me.

My lungs burned, and my chest rose and fell as though I'd just been sprinting through the house, and when my cold eyes met his, I knew, I knew it in my soul. He was using her as a way to keep me alive.

And part of me hated that it was working, that for a brief moment, a life together with her had flashed before my line of vision.

Laughter.

Cooking.

Family.

Brotherhood.

"Think about it." He shoved me with his shoulder and left us alone in the kitchen, just me and the gorgeous woman that I knew wouldn't get the happily ever after she deserved.

And I only had one person to blame.

Mil.

CHAPTER SIXTY-THREE

"I hated to admit it was affecting me in a way I didn't realize it would. He said it would eat me alive. He said it didn't matter how much darkness I held within. He'd said it would break me. Maybe it already has."
— *Ex-FBI Agent P*

Luciana

My legs felt like lead as I walked down the hall to my bedroom, counting the footsteps behind me, the way he purposefully charged after me as if it was going to somehow fix things between us, between him and the demons he refused to lay to rest.

I squeezed my eyes shut when Chase grabbed me by the shoulders and flipped me around, his mouth meeting mine in a possessive frenzy that had me holding onto his ripped forearms for stability.

His tongue licked its way into my mouth as if I were a lollipop he wanted to savor, to taste, and when it swirled around my tongue, sliding against my warmth, my knees buckled. He had no right, no right to kiss me like that and leave me.

To kiss me knowing that I'd dream of that kiss for years and unfairly compare every other kiss to it.

I opened my eyes as he slammed his fists above my head without breaking the suction, and then he opened his and pulled back, chest heaving. "Who do you belong to?"

My breath hitched.

He slammed his fists against the wall again and screamed, "Who, damn it?"

"You," I breathed out. "Only you."

His eyes were crazed. I'd never seen him so out of control, so completely unhinged that I wasn't sure if he was going to hurt me, himself, or just continue to punch holes above my head.

"And you," I said bravely. "Who do you belong to?"

His stunned expression was the only answer my broken heart needed and already knew. "Luc—"

"That's what I thought." I pressed a hand to his chest. "I never asked for this, you know. I never asked to take her place. I never asked to fall for you—"

His eyes widened a fraction.

"I didn't ask to fall in love with a man hell-bent on killing himself, but I did, and you know the worst part?"

"What?" His voice trembled.

"The worst part…" I stood up on my tiptoes and brushed a kiss across his cheek. "—is he doesn't even love himself enough to give me anything but his body. His heart? The one still beating in his chest despite his protests… belongs to a woman who refuses to let it go, even in her grave. You pretend like she destroyed you." I tried to suck the tears back in. "But Chase? The only person with enough power to destroy you — is you."

I pulled away and walked numbly back to my room, shutting the door behind me then sliding down, hugging my knees as I whispered into the night air, "Good-bye."

CHAPTER SIXTY-FOUR

"He was right. Damn it. I watched her tears, watched his pain, and couldn't look away. I wanted to. I used to be able to. But then again, I'd never seen a love like this — one I was helping destroy for good because of his selfish choice, and in that moment, I'd never hated anyone more — not even myself."
— *Ex-FBI Agent P*

Chase

I𝚃 ᴀʟʟ ꜰᴇʟʟ down. Collapsed against me — my universe, my empire, my purpose — and all it had taken was one innocent woman to pick up the dark shards of my life and shove them back into my chest again. All it had taken was her. But she didn't know she was too late. She was just too damn late.

I wanted to run after her, to scream at her, to raze the entire house until it burned to the ground.

But I didn't do any of those things.

Instead, I stood there.

And stared at her door.

Then pressed my fingers to my mouth, still tasting her there, wanting more and knowing it was the most selfish thing I would ever do — try to take her with me, the way Mil had done to me.

I leaned my forehead against the wall as rage poured through me. I didn't want to feel this way, I didn't want to leave her this upset. The commission was set for tomorrow, and the last thing I wanted to do was leave this earth knowing that the final words I'd said to her were that she wasn't important.

Or that she didn't matter, when she'd been my only respite, the only good in my life these past few weeks.

The saving grace I knew I needed, but refused to want.

With wooden steps, I made my way to her door and raised my hand to knock just as it jerked open. Tears stained her face.

I'd done that.

It was becoming a nasty habit, making her cry, when all I yearned to do was hold her close and tell her it would all be okay.

But it would be a lie.

And I was done with that life.

Done lying through my smiles and easy jokes, done making this life look like it was all sunshine and rainbows when it was darkness and desperation.

"I'm sorry," I whispered hoarsely. "I didn't—"

She pressed a hand over my mouth. That would normally have pissed me off; if it had been anyone else I would have lost my shit and broken a wrist.

But this was mine.

She was mine.

So I let her.

"One more night, and I don't know what happens." She gulped. "So, I was thinking if I had one more night..." More tears filled her eyes. "...what would I do?"

I waited and tried not to get too hopeful that she was going to spend it with me instead of slamming the door in my face again.

"And..." She licked her lips. "...I want to spend it with you."

Her hand fell.

I narrowed my eyes. "You sure about that?"

She nodded and then reached for my hands.

I hadn't realized they were shaking until she held them in hers and looked down with a confused expression.

"I'm angry," I admitted. "So fucking angry."

"That makes two of us," she whispered. "You're angry at Mil, and I'm angry at you."

She'd said her name.

I was too stunned to do anything.

Hearing *her* name from Luc's lips...

Felt so dirty.

Wrong.

I closed my eyes, squeezed them tight, and tried to get my emotions under control, and then Luc did the strangest thing; she brought my hands to her mouth.

I opened my eyes. "What are you doing?"

"How many?"

"How many what?"

She didn't answer; instead, she hauled me to my bedroom and then into the connecting bathroom and turned on the shower.

Without words, she slowly undressed. My breath hitched when her bra fell to the floor, and then she started working on my jeans — button undone, zipper pulled down. She jerked them to my feet and then tugged my shirt over my head and led me into the shower.

I still had no clue what she was doing until she pushed me under the hot spray and said, "How many people? How much blood on your hands?"

My stomach clenched. "Too many to count, Luc. Enough to give you nightmares."

She nodded and then slowly lathered up the soap and began to wash me. "You know about the whole washing of feet thing, right? I'm assuming you're Catholic."

I nodded dumbly.

"So…" She ran the soap down my stomach. "…I figure since you have so much blood, it would be best to just wash your entire body."

I gripped her wrists. "I don't understand."

She refused to look at me and just kept washing. "It's like a second baptism, okay? The forgiveness of sins." Her voice caught. "Holy water washing away the sins of the damned."

Realization dawned as I stared down at her shaking hands.

"If I lose you—" Her eyes flashed up to mine. "—I want to know where your soul's going, and I refuse—" Her voice cracked. "—refuse to think I didn't do everything in my power to make sure that you were accepted into heaven, even though you deserve nothing but hell."

I always believed that Mil was the one who'd broken me, unmanned me, un-fucking-made me.

But in that moment, with this innocent girl and her shaking hands, trying to wash blood from my body, knowing that I would just spill more — that was more than I could take; it was more than I could handle.

The damn burst so hard, so fast, that I fell to the ground and shoved her away, only to have her bring her hands to my face and keep washing as my tears mixed with the water running down my cheeks.

Angry tears.

Bitter tears.

Tears that tasted like revenge when they touched my lips and burned like hell when they hit my skin.

And then she was kissing them away, kissing me, with such hopeful deep kisses that for the first time since before Mil died…

I felt loved.

I felt coveted.

I felt saved.

I gripped the sides of her face with my hands and deepened the kiss then rained kisses down her cheeks before pulling her onto my lap and thrusting into her, showing her the only way I knew how, that this — this between us — was the only good thing in my life.

The only good thing.

She cried out my name as I began to move.

"Chase, that's not what—"

"Shh…" I grit my teeth. It was not how this started, but it was how I was going to end it, inside her, loving her, claiming her. "…let me love you the way you love me."

Her eyes flashed open; they were searching, and then they were resting on my mouth as a small grin spread across her face.

I captured her lips again, felt her smile against my mouth as I pumped harder inside her, needing to be as close as possible, needing to feel the way her body clenched around me as if it needed me for survival. She started the rhythm with me as I pulled my mouth away. My head fell back against the tile as she moved. I gripped her hips holding her there. It would be over too fast, — the slick wetness of her body, the warmth of the water trickling between our bodies.

I didn't want any moment to end with her.

This one especially.

But all good things… they come to an end, don't they?

I surged forward, filling her fast and hard while she

wrapped an arm around my neck to hold on.

"So deep." She bit down on my neck.

"So perfect," I rasped and sent her over the edge in the only way I knew how, by finally giving her another piece of myself while guiltily still holding the final chess token.

Because I knew, if I gave her all, and if she took it...

When I died...

It would destroy her.

And I refused to repeat history.

"Let her go," she whispered across my neck.

My voice said, "Okay."

But my heart asked, *"How?"*

CHAPTER SIXTY-FIVE

"My mood felt as black as my soul."
— *Ex-FBI Agent P*

Luciana

I woke up with Chase's warmth, with his lips on my hips going downward, with his head between my thighs, with his taste still on my mouth.

With tears in my eyes.

No matter what he did.

It felt like death.

Everything was cold around me, even though I had blankets on top of me, even though he was doing things to my body that made me sweat with pleasure.

It didn't matter.

Because my heart knew the truth.

Today was the day.

The day he would walk out that door and possibly never come back. The day he would decide it all.

I gripped the sheets in my hands as his mouth sucked.

"Chase!" I arched on the bed. "Whatever happened to alarms?"

"Ding." His tongue swirled. "Ding." Another swirl that had my body shuddering as he sucked. "Ding."

"I'm awake. I'm awake!" I yelled, gripping his hair with both hands as he chuckled then blew against every sensitive part of me until my teeth clenched with pain.

"Almost." He slid his hands up to my breasts almost as if he was doing a child's pose over my entire body. He squeezed while he licked, driving me over the edge so fast that I almost kicked him in the face.

He lifted his head with a smug grin. "Now you're awake."

"Yeah." My chest heaved. "Ready to start the day."

I would remember this carefree smile on his face, the way it lit up his icy blue eyes, the way his tattoos swirled down his arms and chest, the way his body moved with unrestrained power and grace as he crawled up my body and pressed a kiss to my neck then whispered in my ear.

"I'll cook breakfast."

The final meal.

That was what it felt like.

I kept my smile firmly in place.

I didn't want to ruin this moment, this potential last moment of happiness, the moment I needed more than anything, so when he was gone, I'd be able to store the memories together and smile about the time we had.

The good.

I quickly dressed while he pulled on his jeans then walked around the bed and met me. I'd barely pulled on a pair of leggings and his white t-shirt when I was in his arms again, getting the crap kissed out of me.

I clung to him, gripping his shoulders with my hands so tightly that I felt them go numb.

He pressed a kiss to my forehead then and tilted my chin toward him. "It's going to be okay."

He was halfway out the door when I asked the dreaded question. "Hey, Chase?"

"Yeah?" he called. I was too chicken to turn around.

"What are you doing in two weeks?"

He was silent.

My head fell.

And then arms wrapped around my waist from behind as he whispered in my ear, "You."

Tears slid down my cheeks as I almost collapsed to the floor. He wasn't going to go through with it? At all? I was too afraid, too hopeful, to turn around.

"I'm still going to the commission, but..." He didn't need to say anything more.

I flipped around so fast, flung off my clothes in a frenzy, and mauled him like a psycho.

He lifted me into his arms and tossed me onto the bed then hovered over me with a predatory look that gave me chills up and down my body.

And then he attacked in the way he always had.

With precision.

Perfection.

Absolute dedication to every part of my body.

Chase's touch made me crazed with pleasure. He could look at me, and I was ready to orgasm on the spot. It was in his darkness, his power, his possession that I found love.

Not his light.

CHAPTER SIXTY-SIX

"Today it would end. Today it would finally end. God,
let it end."
— *Ex-FBI Agent P*

Chase

SOMETIMES A LIE is necessary in order for someone to live, in order for them to cling to hope.

As I walked out that door, got into my car and drove to the old warehouse on the lake, I knew that lie would be the best one I'd ever told to not only her, but to myself.

Because I still had a job to do.

A purpose to fulfill.

And the greatest kindness I could give Luc would be the hope that I would come back, that I wasn't driving to my death.

That my brothers weren't going to be the ones to do it to me.

I sighed as I pulled into the parking lot.

Always last to the meetings. I liked it that way; it gave me time to think, time to assume the worst, and time for Tex to fill everyone in. I shoved my hands in my pockets as gravel crunched beneath my feet.

One of the men guarding outside nodded at me and opened the heavy metal door.

The entire room was soundproofed.

Flat-screen TVs lined each of the four walls.

And five long tables were placed in the middle of the room.

Along with another five on the other side.

It was no surprise to see Nikolai on one side of the room — he was more Italian than Russian anyway. He just hated to admit that he was one of us almost as much as he hated to admit he drank more wine than vodka.

He tilted his head in acknowledgment as I joined the Abandonato table and let my eyes roam across the room.

Tex was seated in the middle of the Campisi table, his men behind him looking bored as hell.

Dante sat at the Alfero table. Frank stood behind him, most likely offering his support as the new boss. He held his head high in pride, and I couldn't blame him. Dante was making out to be a boss that people feared, and he wouldn't have it any other way.

The chair creaked as Phoenix leaned back. Nicolasis stood behind him. Most from Italy had flown in. Though he chose his home base as Chicago, Phoenix had more men in Europe than he had here, not that it mattered; he held all the power, all the secrets.

His men looked ruthless, and I knew, firsthand, that if you crossed them, you would be dead before you realized you'd even been shot.

And then there were the De Langes.

No leader.

Nobody to call boss.

Pain filled my lungs as I looked at the empty chair, the one Mil used to fill, the one she used to rule like an iron throne that she'd always wanted but never admitted she needed in order to survive.

I closed my eyes and shook my head as rage took over.

Nixon shot me a glance from the right, a silent

warning to keep my mouth shut and stop looking trigger-happy.

But I couldn't help it.

Each De Lange associate looked at me with a mixture of fear and complete hatred, and I couldn't blame them.

I wanted them dead.

All of them.

The fact that they were even here meant that they didn't think I would follow through on my promise to end their line.

The fact that Phoenix looked just as pissed as I did was the only thing keeping me from opening fire.

Five other Families from Italy were present. Their jurisdiction wasn't a part of the Cosa Nostra, but what happened between the most powerful Families in the States affected them greatly.

It was a courtesy to give them a vote.

And they knew it.

My eyes landed on the Vitela family, then the Buratti men, old enough to be grandfathers to each of us, with black eyes and dark hair slicked back with oil. One of the bosses held a cigar in his mouth.

It was every horrible mob movie come to life. Once I would have laughed, made a joke, but I wasn't that guy anymore.

I nodded to the Rossas and Di Masis, and then my gaze landed on pure treachery.

"What the fuck is he doing with the Sinacore Family?" It was out before I could stop it.

Andrei just smiled and shrugged at me while the boss looked genuinely confused and then shrugged. "He is Family."

"He is Russian," I spat.

"Half." Andrei grinned. "Surprise."

Phoenix broke eye contact with me. *Great, just great.*

"And everyone knew this?" I yelled at the entire room.

"It was kept quiet," the Sinacore boss said in a low voice, "until certain things were set in place. He sought sanctuary with us after the death of the De Lange boss. And once more information came forward…" He eyed Phoenix. "…we thought it best to do what we could to unite what was left of his family with ours."

I was too pissed to think straight.

Nixon stood and glared in my direction and then nodded to Tex. "Shall we get started?"

What? We weren't going to even talk about it?

I hated the smug grin that spread across Andrei's face. What the hell was going on?

"We are here…" Tex stood. "…to discuss the end of the De Lange line."

The De Langes didn't even flinch.

"Stay standing!" Tex barked to the men, fifty-eight of them left, fifty-eight souls I couldn't wait to wipe from this planet. Fifty. Eight. "Your crimes are as follows: drug smuggling, prostitution, sex slavery, plans to kill each of the men in this room, and dealing illegally with other crime families for information. How do you plead?"

"Guilty." One of the men stepped forward.

I clenched my fists.

"We're just as guilty as every one of you in this room. What we do with our family is our business. We follow our boss." He eyed me. "And when our boss tells us she's working with Russians, we listen. When our boss tells us we're open for business on the slave market, we do it. We are only guilty of listening to a power-hungry boss. So if loyalty makes us guilty, then kill us now."

I almost pulled my gun out.

Tex nodded. "The bosses will vote. It needs to be majority in your favor. If not, then we will allow the executions to take place."

Finally.

Tex started calling out the names of each Family.

Alfero. "Guilty."

Nicolasi. "Guilty."

Sinacore. "Not guilty."

Di Rosa. "Not guilty."

My stomach filled with dread.

Vitela. "Not guilty."

Baratta. "Not guilty."

I clenched my teeth.

Abandonato. Nixon looked at me straight in the eyes as he said loudly, "Not guilty."

My best friend.

My brother.

My betrayer.

Campisi. "Guilty."

I closed my eyes.

Tex sighed. "It seems that you're free to live another day." He eyed the De Lange family. "Who will take over as boss?"

A man stepped forward.

How was this happening?

How?

I reached for my gun.

"Wait," Nixon hissed next to me.

I was shaking so hard I felt like my body was making noise as one of the De Lange men stepped forward. "I nominate myself."

The rest of the men rolled their eyes.

A few laughed.

And then a fight broke out between two of them while the rest of us watched.

"Sometimes," Nixon whispered, "it's best to let someone destroy themselves from within. Then again, you already know that, don't you?"

I shoved him. "It's weird that you think your vote counts, when technically I'm the boss to this family, right? Blood bond to lead."

"Careful," Nixon snarled through his gritted teeth. "You stepped down."

"And if I challenge you again? If I kill you?"

His eyes fell. "Then you not only lose your brother. You lose the last part of your pathetic soul holding on, for what, Chase?" He shook me by the shirt just as a gunshot rang out.

The De Langes shot at each other; one of the bullets ricocheted toward us.

I shoved Nixon behind me, pulled out my gun.

And fired ten rounds.

Direct hits.

In the chest.

And as each body fell.

I felt nothing but rage.

Chaos erupted between the bosses as I was jerked back from the group by a pair of hands.

"Go," the gruff, familiar voice said.

I turned to yell and wondered in that moment if I was dead. I spread my hands over my chest and shook my head. "What the fuck?"

"Go." His hair was longer.

His face older.

His posture more relaxed.

"Luca?" I felt myself cave then, felt myself want to reach for him, to make sure he was real.

"Go," he said it again, blocking me with his body before I ran out of the building and into my car.

CHAPTER SIXTY-SEVEN

"And it comes full circle — my secrets, his, our demons, the life set before us before we had a chance to even agree to the war put in place. Everything will always come down to choices. He made mine for me and died for it, but does anyone ever really stay dead?"
— *Ex-FBI Agent P*

Phoenix

I HAD KNOWN it was coming.

I had the folder to prove it.

The folder that had come to me last week when my wife was sleeping, and as I held my son and read over the contents, I hadn't been sure if I was happy or pissed.

The folder had a burn notice in it.

Burn at all costs.

For your eyes only.

It held more than secrets; it held the whole damn plan, from beginning to end, how things were supposed to go, and where it had all fallen apart.

I hung my head then stood as the room suddenly fell very quiet. As Luca Nicolasi rose from the very dead and walked, head high, into the middle of the room and eyed me.

"You've done well, son."

"Thank you," I croaked, my body felt heavy, my soul light. "Are you ready?"

He nodded.

I stood on stiff legs and then walked around the table and knelt in front of him as he placed his hands over my head.

Blood pooled around us == the blood of my enemies, the blood of my blood, the blood that I refused to hold in my body, in my soul.

Two people performed this ceremony.

Tex was ready.

I told him there was no need.

My world faded to darkness as Luca slit his palm with a knife and then trickled his blood over my head.

I lifted my right hand as he sliced through my palm then pressed them together. He pulled out his Saint; it was on a broken piece of paper, crumpled and used.

I pulled mine out.

He ripped it in half.

Then pulled out a lighter and whispered, "As burns this Saint, so burns my soul. Blood in, no out."

The rest of the room repeated the mantra.

He held up his Saint then pressed it against his palm and grabbed my hand; our fingers joined, his blood, mine, his marker, no longer his own.

His Saint...

Now mine.

"Let it be recorded," he rasped, "that Phoenix De Lange is no more. He is now Phoenix Nicolasi, blood of my blood, adopted son into my family. Let nobody rip apart what God has ordained."

"Amen." Everyone made the cross motion in front of them and kissed their fingers as I stood and pulled him in for a hug.

And then the painful part.

"To live," he whispered against my neck, "is to die."

The gunshot rang out, going right through the right side of my body. I felt the bullet go out my back and almost collapsed against Luca as I nodded and limped back to my chair.

Bleeding.

Alive, but bleeding.

I'd never felt better.

Reborn.

He'd saved my life.

Given me purpose.

And then his name.

I owed him everything.

But it was time for the secrets — his secrets — to be laid to rest.

He hung his head and then smiled over at Dante. "You look just like me."

Dante was pale. He stood and leaned over the table as if he was going to be sick.

"I've never been prouder." He eyed Dante and then Frank behind him. "Never prouder of all of you." His gaze roamed across every man in that room, as he finally said the words I knew would either end his life again or welcome him back into the fold. "The FBI refused to let go of the Families, regardless of our threats, regardless of what we did, so I made a deal."

Nixon cursed.

Frank closed his eyes.

"I was to leave a successor and an informant. If I staged my own death and did these two things, they would leave the Families alone for good." He sighed. "So I did what was best to protect those whom I loved. I retired, I died, and then, things went south..." He eyed Andrei. "Didn't they?"

Andrei nodded, his eyes compassionate. "I tried."

"I know, son." Luca held out his hand. "I was never supposed to come back to you. This was not part of the plan, and if the FBI ever finds out, the ramifications will be worse for all of you. I'm here—" He cleared his throat. "—I'm here as a courtesy to the man I mentored, and to my bloodline." He nodded to Andrei.

And then all hell broke loose.

CHAPTER SIXTY-EIGHT

"That. Didn't go… well."
— *Ex-FBI Agent P*

Luciana

I watched the clock like a hawk.

One hour.

Two hours.

He'd said it could last all day.

I wasn't sure if that was a good thing or a bad thing. I tried to busy myself with things in the house, but a person can only bake so much before going a bit stir-crazy.

I decided to get the mail and organize the office. Chase didn't want me working, but I figured since he decided not to go through with everything that he wouldn't mind if I got a few things done.

The trip to the mailbox was quick.

I stopped in my tracks when I noticed one of the packages bore my name. It was from my parents.

I quickly tore it open and pored over all the notes; then, with shaking hands, almost dropped it onto the pavement.

"No—" I shook my head. "—no, that's…" I read the next page, my birth certificate from Washington State, the name — the stupid name — over and over again. It was spelled the exact same way, which I knew. I thought it was a figment of my imagination, that it would be spelled differently, that I was losing my mind and it wasn't the same name.

Italian's adopted me.

My name... from an Italian family.

The notes from the hospital stated that I had been dropped off.

That was it.

Just dropped off with a letter that said what my name was.

Did that mean anything?

With trembling fingers, I darted into the house, dropped the rest of the mail in the kitchen, and ran up the stairs to look over Chase's records.

There had to be something.

Something on all the crime families, right?

Two hours later, I still hadn't found anything useful. No family trees.

Nothing.

My head pounded.

I yawned and went in search of some Advil.

Chase kept most of his medicine in the pantry.

I was just grabbing a bottle when I heard the door slam and someone run up the stairs.

Elated, I quickly shut the pantry door, took my Advil, and ran up the stairs after him. "Chase? Chase? Is that you? Is everything okay?"

His back was to me.

He stood frozen on the stairway.

I reached for him. He turned, gripped my hands, and wordlessly pulled me down the hall

He didn't speak.

Didn't do anything except drink from my mouth, press his body against mine, and strip my clothes until they made a pile on the floor.

"Never again," he whispered between kisses.

I gripped his head. "What do you mean?"

"I won't survive it." He pressed his face to my neck. "Falling in love... I promised myself never again."

"And?"

I hesitated, waiting, while he pressed a kiss to my chin and admitted, "And then I fell..."

I was so overjoyed I forgot about the papers, my birth certificate. I forgot about everything and enjoyed the moment when the man I had been fighting for finally surrendered in my arms, and when he entered me, when he watched our bodies join, I gasped in awe as he gave me his soul.

Without holding back.

We were in the room for hours. Finally, Chase stood and then bent over and kissed my cheek. "Want anything to eat?"

"No." I cuddled back into the mattress. "Why? Where are you going?"

"Kitchen." He grinned. "I'll make coffee then fill you in. Things are... tense."

"Tense, as in..."

He just shook his head. "If someone comes at me with a gun, know that it's only partially my fault if I pull the trigger first."

"Reassuring," I said with dryness in my throat.

His lips twisted up into a smirk. "I thought so too."

He kissed me again like he couldn't get enough of me and disappeared from the room.

I fell back asleep and woke up later to sunlight streaming in his window, kissing my bare legs and warming my face.

It felt like a new day.

A bright day.

A fresh start.

I stretched my arms over my head and looked at the empty spot next to me on the bed where he'd been. My blood chilled.

Because sitting on his pillow... was a white horse.

"Run." I remembered Andrei's words.

Run. Run. Run.

Panicked, I looked around the room.

Not a sound.

The house was silent.

He wasn't throwing things and raging. Maybe it was a test? A mistake? Panicked, I threw on my clothes and ran down the stairs to the kitchen.

And on the table were the scattered papers from my parents.

Footsteps sounded. "I did warn you."

"Chase—"

"Don't. Speak."

I turned around and whispered, "I'm not her."

"STOP!"

"I'm. NOT. HER!" I screamed. "I had no idea! And do you really think I would be stupid enough to tell you my real name when you hate anyone and anything that sounds like her? I'm adopted! You know this! I've worked for Nikolai for—"

He paled further. "Nikolai knew? FUCK! HE KNEW!"

I felt myself flinch.

"It doesn't matter." He pointed the gun again. "This family no longer exists. They're dead to me. She's dead to me. You're dead to me. I can't trust you. Don't you get it? If I can't trust you, I can't—"

"No..." Tears streamed down my face. "...no, Chase, you don't understand! It's a misunderstanding! Seriously, just, please, just listen." My voice rose with the fear pounding through my chest. He wouldn't, would he? And then every time he'd threatened to kill me rolled through my brain.

His hate.

His hatred for that name.

His dead wife.

All aimed at me with one betraying point of his gun.

He shook the barrel in front of my face, taunting me with his madness. "A fucking misunderstanding? What? Did they plant you? Just to see if I would be that stupid a second time? Fall for another De Lange? What sort of sick joke is this?" he roared.

The weapon was pointed directly at my chest, driving into my skin. I'd never been so terrified in my entire life as his eyes crazed.

"Tell me, before I shoot you, so I know who to kill next."

"Chase..." My voice shook so hard I wasn't even sure if he understood it was his name that kept falling from my lips like a prayer, like I was begging him to listen and see reason. "...I swear to you I had no idea until today."

"No idea that your last name was De Lange?" His head tilted in that predatory way animals did before they struck.

I felt my face pale as my body almost gave way. "I knew, but, I thought it was just a common name, like Smith or something. A lot of people have the same last name."

"Try again." He ground his teeth, his finger on the trigger.

I knew that look.

There was no rational.

No logic.

He would kill me.

And it would be my own fault.

My body went numb as blood pumped through my legs, warning me to turn and run, but I wouldn't make it far, and I figured my chances were better facing it head on, seeing his face, locking onto his eyes.

My mind wasn't working as fast as I needed it to. I didn't know how to prove my loyalty, my love.

He pressed the gun to my chest.

Our eyes met.

Torment filled their depths as his body shook.

He didn't want this.

He wanted to believe me.

I had to believe that, even if it was a lie.

Without thinking, I gripped the gun.

"What are you doing?"

I shoved it to my shoulder. "I would never hurt you or betray you. But if you think I could, if I would, shoot me."

It was a gamble.

One I wasn't sure I would win.

"Shoot me!" I cried.

His head shook as his eyes darted back and forth between my eyes and my mouth as if he wasn't sure if I was lying or just buying more time.

I pulled the gun against my shoulder; felt his finger press against the trigger.

I closed my eyes and whispered, "I love you, and you are enough, Chase."

"What?" he yelled right back.

"You. Are. Enough. Even though you gave me a sliver of your heart, what's left of your soul, your body... it was enough. It will always be enough." I closed my eyes and pulled the trigger. A sound rang out as I stumbled backward and fell against the wall just as Vic ran into the room yelling.

I blinked up at Chase. "I love you... always love you."

CHAPTER SIXTY-NINE

"The secrets I kept. The lies I told. Worth it. At least that's what I told myself at night when blood dripped from my hands, when I lied and lied and lied again."
— *Ex-FBI Agent Petrov*

Nixon

We'd send the rest of the Families away; this was not their business, not any longer. All it took was a few bottles of wine to get them to stop grumbling about our lack of... discipline. Well, that and promises that we would all continue doing business with them.

The De Lange men started to stand.

"Sit. Down." Tex grit through his teeth. "*Your business is not finished yet.*"

I exhaled slowly, partly in relief that I wasn't picking up my best friend's dead body, partly in fear that I couldn't undo what had already been done. Someone had fired toward us.

And his retaliation had been killing ten people in cold blood. Even those who didn't raise a gun in our direction.

By saving me...

He'd damned himself.

I knew it. The rest of the guys knew it. One body, the one guilty, that was justifiable, but shooting another nine in cold blood? During a commission?

Blood must be spilled. A life for a life. It was our motto.

"Luca..." I pinched the bridge of my nose. "...help me understand this."

Sergio stepped forward instead and held up his

hand. "I was the informant. When I stepped down—"

"Threatened the higher-ups," Andrei snorted.

Sergio gave him a glare. "When I pointed my gun, when they took my badge away, they lost their foothold. I can only imagine they desperately wanted that back and were willing to do anything to get it."

Luca sighed. "I gave them what they wanted the only way I knew how. I left my family in the best hands. I left every inch of information I had on every single person close to the Families, and when I met an eighteen-year-old misfit who hated his father almost as much as everyone else did, I made a choice. I knew his parentage, knew his father had not sired him, knew that he would be our last hope if the Petrovs were taken down..."

I wasn't sure I liked where this was going.

"We needed control of the Russians, so I made a trade." Luca shrugged. "I offered Andrei our safety, our protection, and in return, he sold me his loyalty, I hand-fed him everything he needed to know and brought him to the FBI on a silver platter." He chuckled. "You should have seen their faces. Not only had I given them another informant, but I'd done the impossible. I'd delivered the next boss to the Petrov empire."

"But..." I ran my hands through my hair. "...last year—"

"You know why I did what I did," Andrei spoke up. "I had no choice. Everything had to look real. The FBI wanted a presence with the Italians, and they figured the only place you had lost a foothold was the University. I brought in a few of my oblivious men and did what needed to be done. I brought fear back into the school — power, prestige — and you nearly ruined it all by sending him." He pointed to Dante.

Dante flipped him off.

Which only made Andrei laugh harder.

"I gave them the reins, but I still controlled the horse." Luca nodded. "Because I controlled Andrei, until he stepped down after Mil was shot. The FBI wanted nothing to do with our little war… so they let him go after he told them everything he knew, which was a bunch of BS, mind you."

Andrei saluted us with his middle finger.

Stunned, I could only stare at Luca. "So what happens next, old man?"

He sighed. His grin seemed almost foreign on him. I'd never seen him so relaxed, so free. I fought the jealousy I felt at that expression, wondering if I would ever experience it, at least in this lifetime. "Golf."

"Golf?" Frank finally spoke up with a frown. "You don't golf."

"I do now."

"Golf?" Frank repeated, as if he couldn't believe it.

Luca smirked. "I'm dead, remember? I can do whatever I want."

He eyed Phoenix one last time. "Another favor."

Phoenix only shook his head slowly and stood. "Just add it to your debt."

Luca laughed at that, hard.

Phoenix's lips twitched as Luca said, "Andrei needs a mentor, someone alive preferably."

"Let me guess. I've been nominated?" Phoenix said in a bored tone.

"So smart. I chose well." He nodded, his eyes falling to Dante. "I chose very well, indeed."

Dante looked uncomfortable as he finally found his

voice and spoke, low and threatening. "Why is it that I feel like killing you right now?"

"Misplaced hurt, anger, betrayal." Luca shrugged. "But I'll be around, son. I've been watching you this whole time, and I've never been prouder to see my blood—" His voice caught while Dante looked ready to pull the man in for a hug. "—to see that our blood, Joyce's and mine..."

Frank nodded as if it was okay.

"...produced such a strong young man, worthy of the names Alfero and Nicolasi."

The silence was palpable.

Each of us lost in our own thoughts.

The De Langes sat there in stunned silence.

I eyed Tex. It was time, time to give them their sentence, their last chance at freedom before we wiped them from the face of this earth.

The door to the room burst open as Vic dropped a bleeding Luciana onto the table. "He shot her. Chase shot her."

I ran to her side. "Is it deep?"

"In and out the shoulder." Vic wiped his forehead. "Sorry, boss. I had no other choice but to bring her here."

"And Chase?"

He gulped and looked around the room. "In the kitchen, staring at his bloodied hands... still screaming her name."

CHAPTER SEVENTY

"Blood betrays us, blood saves us, blood may be the
only way to bring life back — maybe even his."
— *Ex-FBI Agent Petrov*

Chase

I STARED DOWN at my hands.

The blood.

Her blood.

Mil.

Luciana.

Lines blurred as my vision went black.

No, no, no! Why? Why would she pull the trigger? Why would she do that?

I was screaming her name.

"Luciana!"

I hadn't even realized the noise was coming from my mouth until I had to suck in air to breathe — until I almost passed out.

And by the time I came back to myself, to reality, there was only blood where she'd once been.

I leaned against the counter then ran over to the sink and puked the contents of my stomach everywhere. I grabbed some water and washed out my mouth, eyeing my gun, the one that had put a bullet in her perfect skin.

Did history have no choice but to repeat itself?

I grabbed my cell and called Nixon. "Where is she?"

"You'll have to be more specific," he said in a clipped tone.

I gripped my phone and sneered. "Luciana, where

the fuck is she? I won't hesitate to kill you. I won't."

"I know." He sighed. "And she's safe, for now."

"What the hell is that supposed to mean?"

"You've been absolved of all crimes. The five Families have decided to wipe your slate clean. You're welcome."

I almost dropped my phone. "I-I don't understand. Why would you do that? Why wouldn't you hunt me down? I don't..." I shook my head back and forth. "What's going on?"

"A life for a life. Blood. The De Langes demanded blood, yours or whatever is most important to you," Nixon said in a cold, detached voice.

"Nixon..." My voice cracked. "...what are you saying?"

Please don't let it be what I think it is.

Please, God, listen to me at least once in my miserable life!

I fell to my knees, as he said clear as day, "Luciana has decided to take your place. We agreed. Stay home, Chase. Think about your actions and remember... every choice has consequences. She's made hers... and you made yours."

"Nixon, NO!" I roared. "DON'T DO THIS!"

"It's already done." His voice held no emotion.

I wanted to kill him, strangle him with my bare hands. "NIXON!"

"Her last request was that you'd know she was innocent. She says in her death she hopes she can prove her loyalty has always, unequivocally, been yours."

The phone line went dead.

And I stayed on my knees.

Wrecked.

And full of shame.
The hatred was gone.
And in its place.
Utter loss and despair.

CHAPTER SEVENTY-ONE

"Blood changes things. It changes us. But without it, we are nothing."
— *Ex-FBI Agent Petrov*

Luciana

I KEPT MY head high as I made my requests.

As Nixon wrapped my hands behind my back and then to the metal chair in the middle of the soundproofed room.

All of the men stood in a circle around me; nobody moved. Phoenix looked to Sergio, then Sergio to Tex. Tex looked to Nixon, who looked down at my body. Frank was the first to say something as he took a step forward. "We aren't sure this will work."

"It will," I said with a shaking voice. "It's the only way to save him, right?"

Andrei made a noise in the back of his throat as Nikolai made purposeful steps toward me then leaned down until we were eye-level. "Is this really what you want? To be tortured until you beg for death? To get your fingernails ripped one by one from your hands, all in order to take the place of a man who shot you?"

"He loves me," I said, voice clear. "And it's the only way to prove my love for him." I looked down as a single tear ran down my cheek. "What greater love than taking the sins of those you care for and putting them on your own shoulders?"

I'd never seen Nikolai look more pained as he

slowly rolled up his sleeves. Tattoos marked his arms.

I gasped as the sickle design on his forearm glared at me.

I'd seen that tattoo before.

I glanced to the side as Andrei rolled his sleeves up as well.

Both of them.

Both Russian.

The rumors were true then.

I shook my head and laughed. Maybe it was my mind going crazy, but it was funny, all the talk around the breakroom about who Nikolai was.

True.

"You're a killer," I stated.

"Nikolai's art form is torture," Nixon said, his voice catching. "Killing… is too easy to us. What's the suffering in a bullet through your head?"

My mouth went dry as Nikolai opened up a black case and pulled on latex gloves. Seconds later, he grabbed a syringe and sucked the clear liquid from the vial.

He wrapped a rubber tourniquet around my arm, tight, and then pressed the needle into my vein.

I hissed out a breath as a cold sensation ran up my arm.

He pulled the needle out and stood. My vision went blurry.

"I'll keep the adrenaline shots close by in case her heart stops," he said to the room.

My heart could stop?

I tried not to shake.

But it was impossible.

I was going to be tortured.

And if I survived it — *if* — then all would be forgiven.

That was a big *if*.

"Who goes first?" Tex called.

Nobody moved.

It was as if they were afraid to start the process, afraid of what it would do to me, and maybe even a bit afraid of what it would do to them.

Nobody volunteered.

And then the door cracked open, revealing what little light came in from the hall, and slowly, one by one, the wives filed in.

Mo approached me first. Without warning, she grabbed a knife and stabbed it into my thigh. "My turn."

I cried out.

She left it there.

Trace was next. She held a gun to my temple then very slowly lowered it and shot through the other shoulder.

Bee was next. I'd always thought she was so friendly... and then she pulled out a band and wrapped it around my neck and pulled tight until I almost passed out, and when my legs kicked, when I felt my vision slipping, something sharp went directly into my arm.

She left it.

Val approached. She was the one I hadn't spoken to that much. I recognized her striking features and saw a rounded belly. Pregnant.

I licked my lips as she very slowly brought a knife to my right wrist and tugged it across my veins.

I was dripping blood everywhere, in so much pain,

delirious from whatever Nikolai had given me.

My head fell forward as Trace spoke. "You said blood must be spilled. You never said now much."

You could have heard a pin drop.

And then Nixon barked out a laugh. "Clever."

I tried to focus on him as he pulled her into his arms, but I was losing blood fast, losing the last shred of consciousness.

Someone walked behind me and grabbed one of my bound hands and very slowly brought the knife to my palm and sliced. Then came a whispered, "Don't die."

CHAPTER SEVENTY-TWO

"He would come. I hoped he would come."
— *Ex-FBI Agent Petrov*

Chase

It took me five minutes to stop mourning the life that hadn't been taken from me yet, and another four minutes to grab as much ammo as I could and strap it to my chest.

I made it out the door only to come face-to-face with Vic.

I could shoot him.

I could attack.

Or I could let him attack first.

He shook his head and then tossed me the keys to the SUV he'd just pulled up. "For once in your life, think about your actions."

"I have."

He snorted. "Two weeks in, and I already hate this job."

I frowned. "It's not a job, Vic. It's life." I eyed the SUV. "Where is she?"

"Where else do you guys like to torture and maim?"

My stomach clenched. "They wouldn't."

His eyes were sad as he whispered, "They already have."

CHAPTER SEVENTY-THREE

"And now, we wait."
— *Ex-FBI Agent Petrov*

Tex

I STARED AT the blood dripping down her arm and winced when she cried out his name again.

Over and over again, she said his name.

And I wondered... would Mil have done this?

Would she have sacrificed her body? Her very soul? For the man she loved?

And I had to admit to myself, even though I hated it, Mil would have fought. That was what she did.

Mil, however, would never have surrendered.

Not the way Luciana had.

It was the ultimate sacrifice.

The ultimate test of loyalty.

So no, I couldn't bring myself to break her fingers one by one.

I couldn't even bring myself to watch the beauty of her sacrifice, of the life that left her body, and of the way his name fell from her lips.

I hated myself.

For making an innocent woman believe she had no other choice when it came to saving the damned.

"Tex," Nixon said through gritted teeth. "You have to."

"It's enough," I said in a strange voice.

Nixon closed his eyes briefly as if to say, *"Please don't make me do this."* Then he stomped over to Luciana, stood behind her back, and very slowly leaned down and broke two fingers.

I heard the crunch.

I felt her pain like it was my own.

Darkness surrounded us as Nixon stood, his body trembling. "No crime goes unpunished."

"No crime goes unpunished," we all said in unison as the red warning light flashed on in the corner of the room.

Intruders.

Or intruder.

Just Chase.

He had keys.

He knew where we were.

"Let the games begin." Nikolai actually looked excited, sick Russian. He grabbed his gun while the wives, Mo included, exited through the back of the room, behind the secret door and up into the living room.

We filed out, one by one, as the sound of footsteps neared.

Chase held his hands up in surrender.

No gunfire.

Only peace.

His eyes were crazed.

Like an animal needing to be put down.

I left the door open on purpose as Luciana screamed out his name again.

He started to run toward her.

I closed my eyes and pulled the trigger.

Chase fell to the ground and got up again, running toward her without any sort of armor, without his gun, with nothing but his fucking heart in his hands and wild eyes full of desperation. I'd never seen him look that way before.

I'd never seen a man so broken.

So livid.

He held his hand to his arm as he sprinted toward the room. Nixon looked at me, then at him, and turned his head and pulled the trigger as well.

Chase fell to his knees.

Andrei was without his gun. Instead, he walked up to Chase and knocked him out with one swift movement. Then he grinned up at us. "That felt good."

God, I wanted to kill that guy.

Nixon grabbed Chase's body, pulled him into the room, and dropped him next to Luciana. I helped him strap Chase to the chair and tied his hands behind his back as his head lolled forward.

"What now?" Nixon crossed his arms.

"Now…" Frank pulled his sleeves back down. "We wait for him to wake up."

CHAPTER SEVENTY-FOUR

"I could almost respect him, almost… maybe."
— *Ex-FBI Agent Petrov*

Chase

Blood. Blood. Blood.

It covered my hands.

It surged through my heart.

It dripped from my fingertips onto the concrete floor.

Trapped.

Broken.

Finished.

Hungry.

I wasn't tied well. It was as if the person who tied me forgot to knot the ropes properly. I jerked my hands free and stumbled to my feet, then reached down and pulled out the gun strapped to my calf.

Insanity scratched its way into my psyche as I eyed the door and waited, one heartbeat, two heartbeats, three.

It opened.

I fired two rounds, and acrid smoke filled the air. Not caring who I hit, what I hit, just needing to save her, to touch her, to rescue.

I'd thought I known what love was. I had been a fucking idiot. Every single bone in my body shuddered with rage, with the need to rip something apart, someone, anyone — all of them. My friends. My brothers. I'd brought the war to our house, and they would finish me because of it.

I'd thought I'd loved *her*.

Our love had been a lie.

Her betrayal was my only truth.

And now?

Now, I finally knew what love was. I'd seen it, smelled it, tasted it.

And lost it.

I'd fucking lost it.

They would pay. They would all pay.

For taking her.

For turning her against me.

For making me believe that blood was everything, only after mine had been spilled.

"I'm not worth dying for," she'd whispered that last night when she hadn't thought I was still awake. *"But you, Chase Abandonato... you're worth living for, breathing for, existing for. The only way to break — is from being already broken."*

"I am broken." I'd whispered as if I was in a dream.

"But..." She'd placed a hand on my chest, and my heart had surged to life. *"You don't have to be..."*

Two more steps, three, I kicked the door open and fired as bullets whizzed by my ear, and when one struck true against my leg, and I collapsed to the ground, I swore up at the barrel of the gun.

I'd live.

For her.

I'd choose life.

I wanted life.

Not this.

They surrounded me.

I wasn't afraid.

I'd cheat death.

With a bloody smile, I crawled to my knees and yelled as I fired rounds into the ceiling, as my screams of pain filled the room.

As the broken...

By finally shattering...

Became whole.

"You've made your choice," he whispered, closing his eyes and turning his gun to my head. "And this was it."

"I don't choose me." Blood trickled down my chin. "I choose her."

Nixon pulled the gun away, leaned down and whispered, "Right. Fucking. Answer."

"What?" I hissed in pain. "What the hell are you talking about?"

My eyes fell to Luciana. She was bleeding, badly, but she was alive, with a fucking knife sticking out of her thigh.

They hadn't finished her.

I knew what that meant.

Mercy.

But why?

Anyone taking my sins deserved death.

Pain choked my throat, threatening to close it up completely.

Her eyes met mine; they were unfocused, full of pain. "Am I dead?"

"No..." My voice cracked. "...no. You're not dead."

"But how are you here?" She looked down at her thigh. "Why is a knife sticking out of my leg?"

"Why isn't she yelling anymore?" I asked to no one in particular.

"Morphine," Nikolai answered. "It has a delayed release. She felt it all, and then she felt nothing. It's my own concoction, my own brand of mercy to those who truly deserve it. You feel it all, and then you lose all feeling, as you watch yourself slowly bleed to death."

How that guy was still sane was beyond my understanding.

I moved to my feet and stumbled toward her then jerked the knife out of her thigh and pulled off my shirt, putting pressure on the wound. "Why, Luciana? Why?"

"Because..." Her head fell forward. "...they were going to kill you — they said so — because you didn't trust me, because this is the only way..."

"From here on out," Tex said in a loud voice, "this will be the only way for a woman outside the Family to infiltrate."

Each and every one of the men slit their hands and waited as I slowly rose to my feet, grabbed the same knife that had spilled her blood.

And did the same.

A blood oath.

To protect those we loved.

To protect ourselves.

A De Lange had started this.

And somehow, a De Lange had ended it.

CHAPTER SEVENTY-FIVE

"I had never known joy — but now I know what it looks like."
— *Ex-FBI Agent Petrov*

Luciana

I JOLTED AWAKE, so hot I thought someone had thrown me into an oven. I tried to get up, but something heavy was draped across me.

An arm.

I frowned as my blurry mind and memories tried to conjure up what could possibly have led me to lying in a bed with gauze all over me, an IV drip in one arm.

"Take me," I'd told Nixon in a strong voice, even though my arm was killing me. "I'll take his place."

His eyes had widened. "You know what this means."

"It means he lives."

Nixon was quiet. "And you?"

"It means I die for the most important thing I can think of."

Nixon had gulped and looked down at the ground before whispering, "Okay."

I looked at the golden arm, the one filled with familiar tattoos, and traced my fingers up the arm until it hit more white gauze wrapped around the shoulder. My wrists were wrapped; my other hand had a mitten-like wrap around it.

I gasped when he opened his eyes.

When his icy blue expression met mine.

He leaned in and brushed a kiss across my lips. "I don't even deserve to ask for your forgiveness—"

"Ask anyway." My voice was scratchy.

"Please..." His eyes filled with tears. "...please, forgive me."

"Already have," I answered back, using my good hand to run my fingers through his hair and down his chin. "You look you've been shot a bit."

He snorted out a laugh and winced. "Flesh wound." His voice was garbled, as if he was still in a lot of pain; either that, or on a lot of pain killers.

I tried to laugh with him.

But all that came out was a strangled cry as he kissed me on the forehead and brushed my hair away from my face. "Thank you."

"For what?"

"Being the most selfless, giving person I've ever known, and for loving me when I don't deserve anything but hate." He kissed my cheek, kissed the tear that ran down it. "For being you..."

"Even if I'm really a De Lange?" I had to ask.

Pain filled his eyes as he whispered out a harsh, "Yes, even then."

It wasn't perfect.

It wasn't said without hesitation, without regret, and possibly with a bit of hate.

But it was still said.

And it was enough.

He was still healing.

And I couldn't blame him.

I loved him where he was at.

Not where I wanted him to be.

And I knew one day, one day, he'd hear that name

and not want to murder the person who belonged to it.

I pulled him closer and hugged his massive body as tight as my wounds would let me.

"Chase?"

"Yeah?"

"Did Nixon really break my fingers?"

He stilled. "Yes."

"And the whole stabbing and shooting, that all happened?"

"Yes."

"Huh." I frowned.

He pulled away slightly. "It's how we do things. It's—"

I shrugged. "It's the mafia, got it."

"Loyalty above all else."

"And me? What happens to me?"

"You never leave my side," he said quickly, "ever."

"What if I have to use the bathroom?"

"Very funny."

"Or I need to take a nap?"

His mouth spread into a grin. "You'll just have to be comfortable with me being around twenty-four-seven."

My body warmed. "I think I'd like that."

"Yeah." His lips caressed mine. "Me, too."

CHAPTER SEVENTY-SIX

"The fact that I had a new mentor — one that looked at me with such disdain I dreamed about his murder every night — ruined my year."
— *Ex-FBI Agent Petrov*

Chase

WE STAYED IN bed healing for five days while Nikolai tended to our wounds and basically used what was the worst bedside manner I've ever seen in another human, poking and prodding me until most of my wounds bled all over again.

I would have been insulted if he'd treated me any differently.

As if he was still trying to get a rise out of me while he basically spoon-fed Luciana and told her how strong and brave she was.

Hell, give her a sucker and a sticker already.

"Teachers pet," I snorted when he left on day five, the day we were given permission to walk around Nixon's house.

I hadn't seen any of the guys.

They hadn't visited.

It had only been Nikolai.

So when, hand in hand, Luciana and I made our way down the hall and into the kitchen I'd spent countless hours in, I nearly swallowed my tongue when Luca sat there with Nixon's kid on his knee, fucking bouncing her like he wasn't the ghost of Christmas past.

"What the hell?" I blurted.

Luca looked up. "Chase, you look well."

"Am I hallucinating again?" I asked the room.

"He's still here? That was real?"

Nikolai just snickered.

I jabbed a finger in his direction. "What? You can't kill me anymore, so now you're drugging me?"

"Oh…" He crossed his arms. "…I could easily kill you. I just choose not to."

I nodded. "Great, thanks, very reassuring for my further care under Dr. Death."

Nixon laughed.

I met his gaze.

He tilted his head as if I owed him an apology.

And I glared back, as if he was the one in debt.

"Can you guys just hug already?" Tex asked. "So he broke her fingers! How else was he supposed to get the point across? He was the only one brave enough to face your wrath over it, alright? We needed you to hear her scream… the morphine was kicking in, and she was starting to fade."

I didn't like it.

I wanted to end his life for touching her.

He smirked.

God, I hated that guy as much as I loved him.

It was a problem.

The fact that he'd told me he'd purposely numbed her with a special blend of opiates that delayed until the body was under extreme duress was the only reason he was living right now.

Through clenched teeth, I sneered, "I'm. Sorry."

Tex slapped Nixon's back. "That's probably as good as you're gonna get, bro. Now, your turn."

Nixon looked heavenward and then said, "I'm sorry, too."

"Now hug it out." Tex grinned while we both gave

him the finger.

"It seems some things never change," Luca said as he kissed the top of the baby's head. But seriously, what the hell?

"Care to fill me in?" I pointed at Luca.

He smiled right back. "I think I'll go take this little one into the family room and play a game of Hide-and-Seek."

"Oh, good, the killer's back from the dead and wants to play Hide-and-Seek with your daughter, and everyone's just okay with this?"

"I think I'll join him." Frank got up from the table, leaving me with all the guys and Luciana, who clung to my side like it was a lifeline.

"We've got her," Trace said, entering the room. "And for the record, I only did what I did so the guys wouldn't actually hurt you more. It bought us more time."

"More time?" Luciana asked.

"For Chase to come to his senses." Trace shrugged. "I knew he'd come after you. I'm also painfully aware how long it takes for these guys to break someone, and my plans would've been completely ruined if you were dead."

"Plans?" Luc said in a confused voice.

Trace just grinned and looped her arm through Luc's. "Plans for your future happiness..." Her eyes locked on mine. "...and his."

I mouthed a silent, *"Thank you,"* as Trace pulled Luciana from the room. I wanted to run after her, but I also knew Trace would protect her with her life, and we were at Nixon's. The man had more security than most diplomats.

CHAPTER SEVENTY-SEVEN

"It is not the end... though I wish it was."
— *Ex-FBI Agent Petrov*

Chase

"So." I CLENCHED my teeth as I pulled a chair out and sat. The rest of the guys, fucking Andrei included, stared at me as if I was going to go on a shooting spree. I didn't have the energy to even blink, let alone pull the trigger. All of it had been spent with the anxiety I had over Luciana healing properly and staying alive; even though I knew she was okay, I had to actually see it.

I'd woken up countless times to check her breathing.

To press my hand against her chest to make sure she had a heartbeat.

Because I knew, if anyone deserved it, I did.

For God to take her. I imagined that would be the worst punishment He could give me and the most just for my sins.

Instead, every time I'd touched her, I'd felt warmth.

And a boundless amount of guilt.

I choked down a swallow of the glass of water in front of me then crossed my arms. "So, Luca's alive now?"

"Not really," Phoenix spoke first. "As far as we're concerned, he's dead and stays dead. As far as the US government is concerned, he was killed, a few gunshot wounds to the chest and all…"

I scowled. "Has he been playing puppet-master this whole time?"

445

"No." Phoenix actually smiled a bit, which surprised me more than the fact that he was even speaking to me after the things I'd said to him. "I wasn't even made aware until last week and nearly had a heart attack. The secrets this man holds weigh on a human's soul so heavy it's hard to breathe sometimes." His eyes flickered toward the table then back up at me.

The rest of the guys looked to me, too.

I hung my head and said the words that would make them hate me forever. "I can't say I'm sorry that I went after the De Langes. I can't say I'm thrilled they're living to see another day. If that's what you want, then I'll leave, but I still don't think they deserve to be a part of what we have…"

"And what's that?" Nixon asked out loud. "What do we have?"

"Loyalty," I said with conviction. "A brotherhood. A fucking family. They will never have what we have because they're too obsessed with money to see what's right in front of them — each other."

Tex snorted out a laugh. "You going soft on us?"

"You wish," I snapped right back.

"Good answer," Tex said, running a hand through his hair. "The commission, after the De Langes decided to open fire on Nixon and the rest of us, have given us permission to deal with them accordingly."

I grinned up at him. "Oh?"

"Yeah," Nixon chimed in. "Naturally, we nominated someone to take care of them…"

They were handing the family over, and for once I didn't feel rage at the thought of holding them at gunpoint; I just felt justice.

And misery.

"Dante is going to help clean up," Nixon continued, locking eyes with me. "No torturing, just quick, clean deaths of those who oppose our leadership. As of today…" His voice deepened. "…the De Lange family is burned. Any and all monies associated with their name as of tomorrow will be frozen by the FBI. Anyone still loyal to our Families is welcome into the fold and now…"

I frowned at him. "Now what? Nixon, you do realize if we take on any of them, we have no way to test their loyalty."

"I know." Nixon grinned. "That's where you come in."

I wasn't sure I liked the way this was going.

"You've always been like a brother, Chase." Nixon stood. "Now I make you my partner."

"What?" My reaction was slow, cautious. "What do you mean?"

"The Abandonato Family is the largest in the Cosa Nostra. I need help. I need you. Be my second?"

"It's like he just proposed," Tex whispered.

I gave him the finger behind my back. "You sure you want to do that?"

"You held the position as long as I have. Why not make it official, huh, underboss?"

"Underboss," I repeated.

"And," Nixon added, "in charge of any new men that may come into the fold. Besides, you're happier when you're torturing new captains, and look how well Dante turned out!"

Dante scowled at all of us and reached for the wine.

"I don't know what to say," I said hoarsely, unable to even look him in the eye. The guy I'd threatened to kill, more than once these past few months, the only one other than Phoenix who probably still saw good in me. "I'm not… exactly stable."

"Understatement," Tex coughed.

Phoenix sighed. "And you think I am?"

"That's true." Dante nodded thoughtfully. "Am I the only normal one left?"

"Blood, on your right cheek," Nikolai pointed out then handed him a handkerchief from his pocket.

Dante jerked it away while Sergio chuckled into his wine glass.

I sighed. "We're all a bit fucked up, aren't we?"

Everyone nodded in agreement as I stood and took Nixon's right hand and slammed my hand over it. "Wouldn't have it any other way, would you?"

"Not at all," Nixon said seriously. "Heal up. We have shit to do."

"Ha." I nodded. "Yeah, I'll get right on that."

Luciana walked in with Trace.

The room fell silent.

She was still bruised and had bandages around her fingers.

Nixon didn't apologize.

I thought she probably would have be insulted if he had anyway.

I know I would.

She rounded the corner and reached for my hand. "Everything okay?"

"Yeah…" I frowned down at her. "…it really is."

What was this feeling growing in my chest?

This expansion of my skin as my body filled with goose bumps.

I opened my mouth to say something, but she

pressed a finger to my lips and shook her head. "Don't ruin it."

"What do you mean?"

"That feeling of contentment you have, you'll ruin it by being a jackass. Just... no speaking for a while. You're a bit out of practice, remember?"

"What the hell?" Tex wondered aloud. "She a lion-tamer, or what?"

"Something like that." I grinned down at her and then pulled her into my arms and kissed her soundly across the lips, my body instantly relaxing against hers. Yeah, it was something.

CHAPTER SEVENTY-EIGHT

"Future looked bleak. Real. Bleak."
— *Ex-FBI Agent Petrov*

Luciana

Dante and Val were sitting next to Luca while he held his niece in his arms and told them why he had to leave, the setup with the FBI, and Andrei's part in everything.

I still couldn't wrap my mind around the details.

It seemed so horrific, sacrificing everything you know just to save a few families, but that was what Luca had done. That was what he was doing. He no longer existed, and somehow he looked younger than the pictures I'd seen him in around the house.

Free.

And I wondered if this life would do the same to me and Chase.

If it would burn us from within, especially now that he was second-in-command to the biggest crime family in the US.

Ha, yeah, my parents could never know that was who I'd decided to fall in love with. Then again, part of me had to wonder if they'd known all along.

Nikolai made his way toward me, looking sleek in black jeans and a blue V-neck that hung low enough for me to see the swirl of one single tattoo in the middle of his chest.

"You look more Italian today," I said over my wine glass. It was weird to see him like this, a ruthless assassin, feared doctor for the Russian mafia, in jeans, drinking whiskey straight.

He just shrugged. "Italians are like a weed. They grow on you until you suffocate and just give in."

Tex flipped him off from across the room.

"Oh good, make the Godfather pissed," I grumbled under my breath.

"He's not pissed. Trust me, you don't want to see him pissed," Nikolai said in a warning tone. "How are the fingers? Any pain?"

I flexed my hand and shrugged. "The pain is pretty numb now. Thanks, though."

"Good." He took another sip.

"So, double life, huh?"

He choked a bit and then grinned. "The government is well aware of what I offer the Russian mafia and pays me handsomely to keep criminals off the streets. They are good at looking the other way when needed."

"Huh." I guess that made sense. "And my parents? Did they know? I mean my last name?"

He shifted on his feet. "I would not ask questions you don't want the answers to. Not yet."

"But I need to know. I want to know."

Nikolai paled a bit then looked away. "There were several prostitution rings under the De Lange family, and many of the male members took great pride in breaking girls in before they were purchased."

My stomach clenched. "And?"

"And your mother was one of them," he said in a low voice. "She was taken by a De Lange family member and raped several times, escaped, and gave her baby away. We tried to locate all of the offspring. With Sergio's help, we were able to locate you and hire you right out of college."

My jaw nearly dropped to the floor. "So that's how I got my job?"

"Well that, and you're damn good at it." He winked.

"And my father? Is he still alive?"

He shook his head and then lowered his voice. "Your father is dead."

I nodded. It was what I'd expected.

"You're half-brother, however... lives."

I jerked my head up so fast I nearly knocked it against his chin. "Who?"

I followed Nikolai's gaze all the way to Phoenix and nearly puked.

It was just one more chasm that would separate me and Chase.

For him to know.

I clutched my stomach.

He would hate me.

He wouldn't handle this well.

Run. I needed to finally run. Take everyone's advice and run. I slowly backed out of the room and with wooden legs, went to the bedroom and started gathering my things.

"Going somewhere?" Chase's sexy voice said from the door.

"Uh..." I couldn't get my shaking under control. "...no, I um..."

"No lies." He wrapped his arms around me from behind. "Truths, only truths."

I hung my head. "And if the truth means I lose you forever?"

"Not possible," he said quickly. "Since you're the one who found me in the first place."

I sighed a bit in relief but still didn't want to say anything.

"Out with it," he murmured against my neck.

Oh, God, I would miss this.

Miss his touch.

His kiss.

How was I supposed to live without him after being with him?

"Nikolai said something about… my real parents."

Chase froze.

His heart thudded heavily against my back.

"And… um, he said that I was a daughter of one of the prostitutes from the drug ring, and that he and Sergio—"

"Went looking for all of them to make sure they were safe and had food to eat and shelter. Yes, I know. I was with them in Seattle when everything went down."

"Right." I shuddered. "But it seems that the mafia guy who took my birth mother… was… Phoenix's father."

Chase slowly turned me in his arms. "I would kill him again, but then I wouldn't have you."

"Wait, what? Why aren't you angry?"

"I'm so fucking tired of being angry, Luc. So tired." A muscle worked in his jaw as he ground his teeth. "What do you want me to do? Kill them all for you? Because I will. Want me to torture a few and gain some apologies? Name your price, and I'll give you the world. Just ask for it."

Tears filled my eyes. "I don't need the world. I just

want you."

"Then have me," he growled against my mouth, picking me up in one smooth motion and dumping me on the bed as he tugged my shirt over my head and started devouring my mouth. "Have. Me." He gripped my hips, pulling them in the air as he jerked off my sweats and underwear. "Take me."

"Yes." I nodded. "Yes." Tears slid down my cheeks. "Now."

He slid inside me as my eyes squeezed shut, and then he was cupping my face with both hands. "I only see you."

I opened my eyes and met his gaze. With a nod, I gripped his wrists as his hips rolled. "I only see you, too."

"Then that's all that matters." He reached behind me and grabbed my butt and pulled me into his lap, gripping the headboard with one hand and holding me with the other. "You." My walls tightened around him. "And me." Our foreheads touched as we moved in sync.

"You and me..." I breathed as I sank so deep on him I saw stars.

"Just us."

I was so full I cried out his name.

And when I looked into his eyes, I believed him.

I believed in us.

EPILOGUE

Luca

My heart was heavy.

It wasn't lost on me that I was a different man than the one who'd died for the sake of my family.

I gripped the umbrella in one hand and used my other to brace myself against her marble stone.

Here lies a woman loved.

Raindrops slid off the black umbrella in front of my face as Frank let out a slow exhale, his breath puffing out in a cloud in front of his mouth.

I'd loved her more than anything.

So had he.

"Your children — our children," I said gruffly to the flat, lifeless stone, "are beautiful. Dante gets his good looks from my side…"

Frank snorted.

"…and Valentina, well, she looks just like you did, same cherry red lips, same posture, she even has—" My voice cracked. "—she has your laugh."

Frank closed his eyes briefly as I tried to regain my composure, while the wind howling around me played tricks with my old mind, bringing back memories of her scent, and the way it would wrap around a man until he was consumed with obsessive thoughts of her.

"You are... missed," I finished, while Frank nodded numbly next to me.

"I'm getting too old for this," Frank whispered in a hoarse voice. "Now that Dante is head of the Alfero family—"

"The way it's supposed to be," I added in.

He nodded. "I think I could learn to like golf."

I smiled. "It does pass the time."

"I think I would miss my guns, though," Frank confessed.

The corners of my mouth turned up in a rueful smile. "Just because you retire doesn't mean your guns retire, brother. It just means your trigger finger isn't what it used to be."

"Speak for yourself. I have perfect aim," Frank joked.

I wrapped an arm around him, and we each held our umbrellas high to keep the rain from our faces as we walked to the waiting black limo.

Our driver opened the door.

We gave him our umbrellas and sat across plush leather. A cigar was waiting next to a crystal decanter of whiskey and a few bottles of wine.

Frank straightened his tie. "How long are you staying?"

I sighed. "As long as I can without being seen. I'm a ghost, remember?"

"No fingerprints?" he asked.

I waved my fingers at him. I'd done my best to wipe traces of my print the only way I knew how — with a knife. "Not if I can help it."

The car drove smoothly over the hill, taking us back

to Nixon's fortress, and I had to smile to myself. Of all the roads I assumed the Cosa Nostra would take, these men, these new young bosses, always took the most difficult, the most painful, the one paved with the most blood.

I'd thought that by leaving instructions like you would spoon-feed a child, they would obey and all would be well.

Instead, I'd come back to betrayal.

Death.

So much death that they were wrapped in it.

When I'd left this earth, I'd left boys.

Upon my return, I'd found men.

And as proud as I was, a part of my heart was sad for them, mourned the loss of innocence as they filled our shoes better than we could have, and kept the Families stronger.

It was with sadness that I looked upon my own son and saw darkness reflected in his eyes, anger, the need to punish. And it tore at me. As a boss, I was proud; as a father, I was devastated that this is what it had come to.

The car pulled up to Nixon's. I followed Frank out.

Dante was waiting at the door, arms crossed. Damn, if Joyce could see him now. He was too good looking to be mine. Even I, in all my vanity, could admit that. He was all the perfect parts of Joyce and the best parts of me wrapped up into one angry package.

"You're going to leave again," he said it as if it were truth.

I nodded. "To keep you safe, I can't linger, no."

"So you're just going to abandon your own fucking kids again?"

Damn, I liked his spirit.

"Looks like it, doesn't it?" I tilted my head. "But you know the truth now that you are boss. You know the sacrifices you make. You know their screams at night, the faces of people you've taken, souls you've damned. You know if there was any way I could have kept you from this life, I would have done it. Any way to keep you safe, and I would have taken it. I did take it. The last twenty-one years of my life have been spent creating a dynasty you would be proud of and making sure that every hair on your head is accounted for. Did I do it the right way? No. Were people killed for my secrets? Yes. Would I take it all back? Never."

Dante's arms fell to his side as he took a step towards me. "I want to hate you."

"I would welcome your hate," I admitted. "Hate is a strong emotion. I can work with hate."

He lifted his hand. "But I'm just so damn happy you're not dead that I can't even find it in myself to raise my gun to your temple, even though a part of you knows you deserve it."

My pride grew and grew, until my smile reflected it. "Unfortunate."

His lips twitched. "Frank's probably already drunk a full bottle of wine. We should go in. You know how Chase gets when he cooks."

The conversation was over.

The threats said.

The *"I love yous,"* unnecessary because he didn't raise his gun, and I did not raise mine. It was enough.

Chase

Three months later

THE NIGHTMARES WERE still there, the blood caking my fingertips, and with every De Lange I took, the less human I felt, and then I would come home to dinner.

An actual, honest-to-God dinner.

In my new home.

In Nixon's neighborhood.

That I shared with one person.

The most important person.

"Chase!" Luc wiped her hands on her apron and then tugged at her pearls. "You're home early! I was baking bread."

I gave my head a shake.

God sure had a sense of humor.

There I was, blood literally dripping from my hands, another ten De Lange men in body bags who refused to abide by Abandonato rules, and I come home and it was like the fifties had thrown up all over the kitchen.

My woman.

Her belly swollen with our first child.

In an apron with fucking flowers on it.

Wearing pearls and red lipstick.

It wasn't what I'd had in mind.

It was everything the universe knew I would die for, fight for, continue to kill for, and it was mine. All. Mine.

"You shouldn't be on your feet," I scolded.

She was used to my gruff attitude, especially after a rough day trying to keep more men in line under a new boss, a new Family.

"My feet are fine." She grinned. "And you'll feel so much better once you eat."

That was her plan: feed me until I was too stuffed to move, then ply me with wine, sex.

She was pregnant, and yet I felt like she took care of me.

From cutting fresh flowers every week and putting life around the house so I'd reflect on the good... to cooking... to just being my best friend.

She was everything.

I gave my head a shake. "What would I do without you?"

She just shrugged. "You'd be really bored. Horny. Probably dead. Alone, still in that giant mansion feeling sorry for yourself with your blood-stained bat and—"

I covered her mouth with my hand. "That's enough."

She just grinned and whispered, "Hey Chase?"

"Yeah, princess?"

"What are you doing in two weeks?"

I just laughed, eyed her up and down, and whispered what I always whispered, "You."

ABOUT THE AUTHOR

Rachel Van Dyken is a *New York Times, Wall Street Journal*, and *USA Today* bestselling author. When she's not writing about hot hunks for her Regency romance or New Adult fiction books, Rachel is dreaming up *new* hunks. (The more hunks, the merrier!) While Rachel writes a lot, she also makes sure she enjoys the finer things in life—like *The Bachelor* and strong coffee.

Rachel lives in Idaho with her husband, son, and two boxers. Fans can follow her writing journey at www.RachelVanDykenAuthor.com and www. facebook.com/rachelvandyken.

ALSO BY
RACHEL VAN DYKEN

Eagle Elite
Elite
Elect
Entice
Elicit
Bang Bang
Enchant
Enforce
Ember
Elude
Empire
Enrage
Eulogy

The Bet Series
The Bet
The Wager
The Dare

Seaside Series
Tear
Pull
Shatter
Forever
Fall
Strung

Eternal

Seaside Pictures
Capture
Keep
Steal

Waltzing With The Wallflower
Waltzing with the Wallflower
Beguiling Bridget
Taming Wilde

London Fairy Tales
Upon a Midnight Dream
Whispered Music
The Wolf's Pursuit
When Ash Falls

Renwick House
The Ugly Duckling Debutante
The Seduction of Sebastian St. James
The Redemption of Lord Rawlings
An Unlikely Alliance
The Devil Duke Takes a Bride

Ruin Series
Ruin
Toxic
Fearless
Shame

The Consequence Series
The Consequence of Loving Colton
The Consequence of Revenge
The Consequence of Seduction

RACHEL VAN DYKEN BOOKS

87078138R00285

Made in the USA
Lexington, KY
20 April 2018